Praise for JL Merrow's
Pressure Head

"You just can't expect anything formulaic in [JL Merrow's] books...but do expect very unique characters that jump right off the pages."

~ *Fiction Vixen*

"The characters were cheeky yet believable and well written. The murder mystery combined with the ever evolving relationship between Tom and Phil kept me engrossed...a joy to read!"

~ *Guilty Pleasures Book Reviews*

"The author does a wonderful job wrapping up *Pressure Head*, leaving the reader with a story that they will be sure to read time and again."

~ *Top 2 Bottom Reviews*

"I would be thrilled to see Merrow turn this into a series with Tom and Phil solving mysteries. I just loved them together! Merrow gives us a great combination of mystery and romance."

~ *Joyfully Jay*

"Overall, I highly recommend this book to those who like mysteries, or who are just looking for a fantastic story with great characterization."

~ *Reviews by Jessewave*

Look for these titles by
JL Merrow

Now Available:

Pricks and Pragmatism

Camwolf

Muscling Through

Wight Mischief

Midnight in Berlin

Hard Tail

Pressure Head

JL Merrow

SAMHAIN
PUBLISHING

Samhain Publishing, Ltd.
11821 Mason Montgomery Road, 4B
Cincinnati, OH 45249
www.samhainpublishing.com

Pressure Head
Copyright © 2013 by JL Merrow
Print ISBN: 978-1-61921-362-3
Digital ISBN: 978-1-61921-258-9

Editing by Linda Ingmanson
Cover by Kanaxa

First Samhain Publishing, Ltd. electronic publication: September 2012
First Samhain Publishing, Ltd. print publication: August 2013

Dedication

To the members of Verulam Writers' Circle, for all their constructive criticism, good-natured ribbing and general encouragement over a drink or two—cheers!

And, as always, with thanks to my wonderful friends Jo and Pen. You know I couldn't do it without you.

Chapter One

Whatever it was I was following, it was dead ahead. Calling to me, tugging at my mind. I fought my way through prickly hawthorn and incongruously festive holly, a minor annoyance as it clutched at my padded jacket. When I reached a clearing I broke into a run. Melanie's face was seared in my mind, and I thought, please, God, let it not be her. Let it be some drunk's alcohol stash...

I already knew it wasn't. There was the stench of guilt about this one, turning my stomach even as it dragged me nearer. Guilt and violence—and death.

I reached a thicket, dropped to my hands and knees and crawled in. Twigs scratched my face, caught in my hair. Damp soaked through the knees of my jeans, the chill reaching to my bones, numbing my core. There was barely any light to see by, but I didn't need any, my questing fingers meeting cold, waxy flesh. I fumbled to be certain and found I was holding her hand.

For a moment, I was six years old again, with the little girl in the park.

But when you're twenty-nine and you find a body, you don't get to go blubbing for your mother.

It started with a phone call, as these things usually do. I haven't exactly got an office, more like a stack of files in a cardboard box that I hand over to my accountant once a quarter, and the answer phone's on the blink, so if anyone wants to get in touch with me, they have to call my mobile.

I was out in one of the villages when he rang. There are a lot of villages around St Albans, most of them filled up with people who commute into London to work and keep the house prices sky-high. In between, you get the green belt made up of pony farms and golf courses, plus the odd actual working farm tucked in, with small herds of placid cows looking like refugees from the nineteenth century as they chomp on the grass and idly wonder what happened to the neighbourhood.

I was fitting some new kitchen taps for Mrs. B., who made great coffee and liked to chat. I always had to be careful I didn't go over time there. It wasn't easy when I knew the next call was to Mrs. L., a sour-faced old biddy who always watched me like a hawk in case I made off with the teaspoons or did something unspeakable to her pet poodle.

I put down my spanner and dug my mobile out of my pocket. "Paretski Plumbing," I answered in my jaunty "trade" voice, flashing Mrs. B. an apologetic smile. She dimpled.

"Tom? Dave Southgate. Got a little job for you."

"Oh, yeah? Blocked toilet down at the station? Must be all those doughnuts you lot eat." I wasn't talking about the place you catch a train from. Dave Southgate is one of our boys in blue—or he would be, if he still wore a uniform. And when he rang, the job was never all that little, though I lived in hope.

"I wish. No—young lady by the name of Melanie Porter. Last seen going off to meet person or persons unknown three days ago—*if* you believe her useless yob of a hoodie boyfriend, who I personally wouldn't trust as far as I could throw his drugs stash. We've received information suggesting we have a look for the young lady in the woods up by Brock's Hollow."

"I do have a proper job to do, you know." Even I could hear the resignation in my voice.

"Cheers, Tom, I owe you. We're up on Nomansland Common. Up past Devil's Dyke—you know the area? Combing through the woodland, the usual drill. How soon can you get up here?"

I looked at my watch. "About ten minutes—I'm only down the road, as it happens. Just need to finish up." And I'd have to ring Mrs. L. and apologise for the no-show, but that'd be more a pleasure than a duty.

I shoved my phone back in my pocket and finished tightening up the taps. Opened the supply pipes and turned the taps on and off to prove they worked. "There you go," I said, wiping my hands on an old rag. "All sorted."

"That's lovely. Sure you wouldn't like to stay for another coffee?" She gave me a winning smile, and the dimples deepened. "I've got some Belgian chocolate biccies."

"Sorry, Mrs. B.," I said regretfully. "Duty calls."

I first met Dave Southgate around three years ago. A kiddie went missing in Verulamium Park, and they put out an appeal on local radio for help finding the little lad. He was only three. I tracked him down under a bush right next to the main road, crying his little heart out and clutching a half-eaten loaf of bread he'd taken to feed the ducks.

Obviously, me being a single gay man who'd managed to find a missing toddler, it wasn't just as simple as handing the kid over and receiving the effusive thanks of a grateful police force. There were a lot of searching questions about just how I'd known where to look. Eventually, I managed to convince Sergeant Southgate, as he then was, I just had this knack of

11

finding stuff. Or people, as it might be. Since then, he's called me in a few times to look for things—burglars' loot, hidden drugs—and bodies.

It's a bit hard to explain, but I can't just find any old thing. I'm not some bloody database on the location of everything in the world. It's only certain types of things. And usually, there has to be some strong emotion involved. So lost things are almost always impossible, because if you'd been feeling that strongly about the thing at the time, chances are you wouldn't have lost it, would you? Hidden things, on the other hand, call out to me. All the guilt and shame and sneakiness involved in the hiding acts as a kind of beacon. And I can often tell from the feeling just what sort of thing it is that's hidden.

I mean, say you buried a suitcase in your garden. I'd have a pretty good idea before I dug it up whether it'd contain your collection of hard-core porn, letters from a lover, or the body of your dead baby.

Bodies, actually, are the classic one. I have to be close enough physically—although there's tricks I can do to help, I'll get on to those later—but once I'm there, it's like they're howling at me.

The first one I found, I thought she really was howling.

It was back when we lived in London. She wasn't anyone I knew. I think Mum knew her mum a bit, but that was all. She was too young to have played with me, and certainly too young to have played with my sister. She was only four, you see, when it happened. Just wandered off in the park, I guess, met a man who seemed really friendly...do I have to spell it out for you? He'd hidden her under some bushes, right in a patch of nettles. Must have been wearing gloves, I suppose. I had shorts on when I found her, and I got covered in stings.

But she was crying, at least I thought she was, and I knew I couldn't leave her there. So I crept in after her, calling out, "Don't cry—it's all right."

Of course, it wasn't all right. Not for her, and not for her poor mum and dad. For them, I expect it was never all right again. She stopped crying as soon as I found her, so maybe she found some peace. I don't know. I thought she was asleep, but she was so cold. I tried to drag her out, but I was worried I'd hurt her, so in the end, I left her there and ran and got my mum.

And then things got very grown up, very fast.

Anyway. Hidden things. Lost things, sometimes. And water, funnily enough. I've never really understood that one.

I rubbed my hip as I walked over the rough grassland of the Common to the edge of a scrubby patch of woodland, where I could see Dave and a couple of police dogs with their handlers. I broke my pelvis badly when I was seventeen—got hit by a car and spent months recovering—and it aches whenever the weather turns cold and damp. Which, this being Britain, it does quite a lot, especially in November. Maybe I'd move to Florida when I retired.

Maybe a passing porker would be able to fly me there.

"All right, Dave?" I called out when I got to where they were standing, grim-faced.

Dave's face broke into a relieved almost-smile, although the men with the dogs cast me sceptical glances. Dave was a big bloke, by which I mean a bit too fond of beer and takeaways. He was tall compared to my five foot eight, but probably only average compared to everyone else. I don't mind. In fact, it's pretty handy for a plumber, being small—especially when you're working in one of those new, shoebox-sized houses they throw up everywhere these days, with the sort of bathrooms where you step out of the bath to find you've got one foot in the toilet.

"Tom. Good to see you." Dave took a deep breath. "Right. Melanie Porter. She's a twenty-three-year-old estate agent, works down in the village. Boyfriend, as I said, a bit on the dodgy side. He's got previous for drugs, petty crime—that sort of thing. Supposed to have settled down since he met the young lady—at least, he's stayed out of trouble for nearly a year now. His story is she got a call Saturday night and told him she had to go out. They had a blazing row about it—we've got the neighbour's corroboration for that—and she left, and he hasn't seen her since. Or, depending which theory you subscribe to, he bludgeoned her to death and disposed of the body sometime in the early hours of Sunday morning."

"So why do you think she's here?" I nodded over at the trees.

"Anonymous tip-off. Said if we want to find Melanie, we're to look around here." He scratched his nose. Somebody really ought to buy him some nose-hair clippers for Christmas, I thought, distracted for a moment by the bushy growths that sprouted unchecked from his nostrils. "Be pretty convenient for him, if he did do it. They lived just over there, in a council flat." Dave inclined his head towards the Dyke Hill estate, an unlovely but functional collection of houses and flats for the less-well-off of the village.

"Right, let's get started, then," I suggested. The longer I stayed out here, the worse my hip would ache. And I still had Mrs. L.'s blocked drain hanging over me, metaphorically speaking. "Have you got anything for me?"

It doesn't always work, but sometimes a picture of the person I'm looking for will help. Dave handed me a snapshot, taken on a sunny day down by the river. Melanie Porter was a pretty girl, although she'd never make the cover of *Vogue*, or even *Nuts*. She had a roundish face, chestnut hair and large, blue eyes. Her smile was a little crooked, which gave her a sympathetic air.

Suddenly I didn't want to find her. She looked like the sort of girl you hoped your brother would marry.

"There's this too." Dave handed me a carrier bag with a cardigan in it. "She was wearing it at work, the day she disappeared."

"I'm not a bloody sniffer dog." I took it anyway, in case it had some vibes for me. I pointedly didn't sniff it. I didn't feel any vibes, either. It was just a plain, slightly bobbly cardie.

"Oh, bloody hell—how did he find out about this?" I looked up from the photo to see Dave glaring at a tall, blond figure striding our way across the common. The new guy was big in a totally different way to Dave—his shoulders were broad, his legs were long and lean, and the bulk of his chest wasn't all due to the bodywarmer he was wearing over a thick sweater. Well, it was a bit nippy up here, as I was finding to my cost. I gave my hip another rub.

There was something vaguely familiar about the bloke. "Who is he?"

"Private bloody investigator. Hired by our girl's mum and dad. Private bloody pain in the bum, if you ask me. Ex-copper, couldn't hack it, so left to go private." He gave me a speculative look. "Course, you might get on all right with him. He's one of your lot, not that you'd know it to look at him."

"What, a plumber?" I asked innocently.

"Piss off. And he's not a bloody psychic either. He's queer, all right? And if I catch you two canoodling on police time, I'm taking pictures and bunging them on the Internet."

"I'll try and control my raging homo desires," I said as dryly as I could. "I've managed to keep my hands off you all these years, haven't I?" I added to wind him up.

Dave shuddered. I wasn't offended. I was too busy fighting off a shudder myself. Dave's a great bloke, and I love him dearly, but not like that. Dear God, *never* like that.

I had to admit I wouldn't mind a bit of canoodling where the PI was concerned. Dave's comment about his sexuality had piqued my interest, no doubt about it. As he approached, the sense of familiarity deepened, and I wondered if I'd seen him around somewhere. I was fairly sure we'd never hooked up or anything embarrassing like that. This guy was way out of my league—with a body like that, and a square-jawed, classically handsome face above it, he could take his pick, and he looked like he knew it too.

He nodded at Dave as he got up to where we were standing. "Southgate."

Dave didn't so much nod as curl his lip. "Morrison."

And it hit me where I knew him from. It was all I could do not to stagger back, winded from the blow.

Morrison. Phil Morrison.

The last time I'd seen him, we'd still been at school. It wasn't a time I looked back on with a nostalgic, rosy glow. My last name's Paretski, a legacy of my great-grandma's Polish stepdad, so naturally enough I was known for most of my school life as Parrotski. With the occasional Parrot-face or Polly thrown in for variety. I didn't exactly like it, but I couldn't say it really bothered me either. Although I did feel a bit envious of my older brother for having managed to get away with plain old Ski as a nickname.

Then Phil Morrison caught me looking at him in the changing room after PE—well, who wouldn't look? He was the fittest lad in the school—tall, blond, athletic—and he came up with the bright idea of calling me Poofski.

It caught on instantly. Soon, hardly a day went by without a joke at my expense. Games lessons were the worst. "Don't let Poofski follow you into the shower!" was a gag that never seemed to get old. My maths teacher, Mr. Collymore, even called me it once. I mean, I'm sure it was a genuine slip of the tongue, and he apologised afterwards, but they were laughing about that one in the classroom for days afterwards.

For all I know, they laughed about it in the staff room too.

And now he was here. Against all laws of probability or even human decency, apparently queer. And I was supposed to get used to it?

Morrison must have noticed my reaction, as he looked at me with his eyes narrowed. Suddenly, his face cleared, and a half smile flickered across his lips. "Parrotski," he said with grim satisfaction.

Well, it could have been worse. And I was long over being intimidated by him. "That's *Paretski*, if you don't mind," I snapped.

"You've changed a bit," he said cryptically.

"So have you." I tried to inject as much meaning as I could into those three words. I wanted him to know I knew his little secret. I wanted him to feel like the bloody hypocrite he was.

Zero reaction. Either it didn't work, or more likely, he just didn't give a monkey's what I thought about him.

Dave huffed impatiently. "*If* you don't mind me interrupting this touching reunion, we do have a body to look for. And Morrison? Unless you're here to hand deliver a map drawn by the murderer, your services are not required. This is an official police investigation, not a bloody free-for-all."

Morrison raised an eyebrow. "Oh? When did you join the force, Parrot—Paretski? Good thing for you they dropped the height restrictions."

My jaw tensed. "I'm just here as a consultant."

"Know a lot about hiding bodies, do you?" God, I'd forgotten just how much his snide tone got up my nose.

"Used to think about it all the time back in school," I said pointedly.

"Girls!" Dave broke in with an exasperated shout.

We both whirled to look at him, probably with identical hangdog expressions. "Sorry, Dave," I said, to establish myself firmly as the reasonable one. "Time to get started?"

"Too bloody right. Come on. And Morrison? If I find you trampling on the evidence, you'll be cooling your heels in jail, understood? As soon as we find anything—*if* we find anything— the family will be informed." Dave grabbed my elbow and more or less hustled me into the trees. We stopped once we were out of sight of the grassland. "Right—do your stuff."

I sighed. "What, after all that?"

"Oh, come off it, Tom. Don't play the prima donna with me, now. What was all that with you and Morrison, anyway? The short version, please. Young love gone bad?"

"Don't let him hear you say that," I warned. "Not unless you fancy pulling him in on a charge of assaulting an officer. We went to school together, that's all. We weren't exactly friends."

I jumped as a hand like a bag full of sausages clapped me briefly on the shoulder. "School bully, was he? I know his type. All bluster and no bloody bollocks."

Phil Morrison had bollocks, all right. I remembered that from the school showers. You might say I'd made something of a study of the subject. Didn't think Dave would appreciate me mentioning it, though. I took a deep breath, and tried to clear my mind.

Phil Morrison's bollocks kept creeping back in there, though. Sod it. "You want to give me that picture again?" I asked.

Thirty seconds staring at Melanie's pretty, kind face soon got my mind out of the gutter. "Right. Okay." I handed it back again and closed my eyes. Could I hear something? Feel it tugging at me? I turned around slowly, trying to judge where the pull was coming from. There. I stepped forward, remembering in time to open my eyes before I walked into a tree.

Dave didn't say anything, and neither did I. We just followed the line I'd sensed. My work boots soon picked up a thick coating of mulched-up leaves, stuck on with mud. On a crisp, frosty morning, this might be a pleasant place for a walk, but right now it was just soggy and dirty. It even smelled damp. Every now and then a twig that had somehow managed to escape getting soaked through would snap loudly under my foot, but more often I'd put my boot in a muddy patch and have to pull it free with a squelch. Brambles snagged my jeans and clutched at my hair.

As the pull got stronger, I sped up. Dave started puffing a bit and occasionally cursing, probably at the mess the mud was making of his shoes. I forced myself to slow down, but it was nagging at me, and I found my pace quickening again.

It wasn't Melanie's voice. I don't see ghosts—at least, I don't think I do. The girl in the park when I was a kid had seemed like a spirit, but I think it was just the way my child's brain interpreted things. These days, I just feel a pull, a sense of something *hidden*, of something *not-right*. It's like... I've never taken drugs—too much weird stuff going on in my head as it

19

is—but I imagine it's like the pull a hopeless addict feels towards the next fix. Only without the high when I finally give in to it.

Fortunately, I usually only feel it when I'm actively listening—I know you can't listen for a feeling, but language really isn't accurate for this sort of thing—or I'd probably go stark raving mad. After all, when you think about it, the average household has six to a dozen things hidden in it. The wife's saving-up-to-leave-him secret piggy bank; the teenage son's porn. His dad's porn. These days, quite often, his mum's porn. And don't get me started on the subject of sex toys...

I'd veered off course, I realised. Feeling guilty, I wrenched my mind back to the matter in hand. Where had she gone...? Dave started to say something, so I held up a hand to shush him.

There. I stepped forward.

When you're twenty-nine and you find a body, as I said earlier, you don't get to go blubbing for your mother. You get Dave clapping you on the shoulder and heaving a resigned sigh, while the other police officers throw you suspicious looks. Nobody shields you from the sight as they shine their torches into the bushes and light up the mess some bastard made of a young woman's skull. Your mind's well able to interpret the blood, the misshapen dent where the bone pushed into the brain, and your imagination fills in the pain and the terror she must have felt.

And when you walk out of the forest and leave them to it, you find Phil Morrison waiting for you.

It was twilight by now, but he wasn't exactly easy to overlook. He loomed out of the shadow of the trees like Herne the Hunter on steroids.

"Have they found her, then?" he demanded.

I nodded curtly and went to walk past him. He grabbed my arm.

To say I wasn't happy was an understatement. I don't like people grabbing me. Never have. "Oi! Get your bloody hands off me!"

"Don't get your knickers in a twist. I just want to talk to you, that's all." He didn't let go.

"Why don't you go and talk to the police? They're the ones doing all the detecting. I just found her for them." His eyes narrowed, and I realised I'd given away more than I should have.

"How did you know where she was? Did you see her being dumped here?"

"I didn't see anything, okay?" I tried to shake off his grip, getting more and more annoyed as he refused to let go. "I just find stuff."

"Stuff? Like dead people?"

"Yes, okay? Look, for fuck's sake, I've had a hard day and it ended with me cuddling up to a corpse. Will you let go of me or do I have to call one of the coppers over? I'm sure Dave Southgate will be only too happy to pull you in on the trumped-up charge of my choosing."

He released me, and I rubbed my arm. "So what's the deal?" he asked. "You know people in low places, they tell you stuff, you tell the police?"

"No. I'm just good at finding stuff, that's all. It's a talent. Like dowsing."

"What, that water-divining crap? Bollocks!"

"Whatever." I strode off towards my car, pissed off beyond belief to find him walking by my side, his long legs easily keeping up even with my most annoyed pace.

"Come on, what's the real deal? Look, I'm working for her parents, here. They're going to be devastated when they find out she's dead. The least anyone can do is get them some justice."

Great. Now I felt pissed off *and* guilty. I rubbed my hip, realised what I was doing and jammed my hand in my jacket pocket where it couldn't betray me.

When I glanced at Phil, I could tell he'd seen.

"Look, I'm sorry about that," he said, with an awkward grimace.

"About what?" I asked nastily.

"Well, you know. About the leg."

"Oh. I see. So making my last year at school a living hell, you'd do all that again, would you?" Bastard.

"Oh, for—" Phil's hand made some kind of abortive gesture, and he looked up and away from me. "We were kids. That was just joking around."

"Too bad I never went through with the suicide attempt, then. That'd have made a great punch line."

"Like you'd have ever killed yourself."

Right then, I could definitely have killed him. I'd just ripped the bandages off my soul, and all he'd done was sneer and rub salt in the wound. "Oh, and you know me that well, do you? I suppose you've been on one of those profiling courses, and now you think you know everything about everyone."

"No, but I know you. We were at school together, remember?"

We'd reached the car park by now. I fumbled in my pocket for my keys. "Like I could ever forget—"

"Yeah, and I remember you too. You were always so bloody..." He threw his hands up, as if clutching for a word. "Self-contained," he finished.

"Self-contained? What the bloody hell does that mean?"

"Oh, you know. Don't try and pretend you don't. Like you didn't need anyone else. Like we were all just a little bit thick compared to you."

What? I stared at him, speechless.

"You know," he continued, "you wouldn't have got so much stick from everyone if you hadn't been so bloody standoffish."

"Standoffish? *I* was bloody *standoffish?*" My voice rose so high on the last bit it cracked.

"Yeah. Always looking down your nose at people like me just because we came from the council estate."

"I—*what*? Bloody hell, Morrison, have you even noticed you're a foot taller than I am? If I wanted to look down my nose at you, I'd need a sodding stepladder! I can't believe you're even saying that. *I* was the one nobody liked. Poofski, remember? Because I haven't bloody well forgotten what it was like, being the butt of your oh-so-funny jokes every...bloody...day." The keys in my hand jangled as I punctuated the last few words with jabs of my finger at his overdeveloped chest.

Then I got in my van, slammed the door and drove home, seething.

I've got a little house in Fleetville, which is part of St Albans but has its own shops and pubs, so it feels like a separate community. It's way less pretentious than most of the villages around here. It's pretty ethnically diverse, so the shops are more interesting than in a lot of places—there's a halal food shop and more takeaways than you could get tired of in a month of not cooking. You see a lot of ladies in saris or headscarves, and blokes in ethnic gear too. Brightens the place up, I always think. I live just off the main road, handy for the shops and the pub. Parking can be a pain—well, it's St Albans, isn't it?—but I can fit the van on the drive, and there's usually room to park my little Fiesta in front.

At least the cats were pleased to see me, I thought with a smile as I walked in my front door. Merlin wove his slender, black body in and out of my legs ecstatically, and even Arthur deigned to get off his fat, furry arse and pad into the hall to welcome me.

They're both toms, although most people assume slim, sleek Merlin is a she. Personally, I think he's gay. He's always rubbing up against Arthur as if he'd like them to be more than just good friends. Fortunately Arthur's too thick to notice. He's a big ginger bruiser who'd probably flatten Merlin if he realised he fancied him. Not very metrosexual, old Arthur.

I fed them the dish of the day (lamb with rabbit, yum, yum) and set about rustling myself up some comfort food. A mug of Heinz tomato soup the size of your average bathtub, and hunks of baker's bread with tangy cheddar cheese melted into it. Lovely. For dessert, I took a couple of ibuprofen. I don't like popping pills all the time, but my hip was really killing me, and every twinge was a reminder of Phil bloody Morrison. And the accident.

I'd been seventeen when it happened. I'd made the mistake of heading out to the shops on my own. Just as I turned a corner, I ran straight into Phil Morrison and his gang. Literally.

He hadn't been pleased to see me. "Oi, watch where you're going—bloody hell, it's Poofski!"

"He was touching you up, Phil!" That was Wayne Hills, a nasty little shit who did an awful lot of arse-kissing for a rabid homophobe.

"Get him!"

After a greeting like that, there was only one thing to do. Run. When it came to verbal sparring, I liked to think I gave as good as I got, but there were four of them threatening to get very physical, very fast, and they were all bigger than me.

So I ran.

Unfortunately, my talent for knowing where things are didn't extend to the oncoming car that hit me square on, shattering my pelvis and breaking my leg. With hindsight, it would have been a lot less painful to stand my ground and take the beating they'd threatened. As violent thugs went, Phil and his gang were strictly minor league. The car, on the other hand, was a four-by-four. With bull bars on the front.

So I ended up missing my A levels, and I never did go back and take them. My parents were disappointed, but with my older brother a consultant oncologist and my sister a barrister, I suppose they thought on average, they'd done all right by their kids. Either that or they were worn out with the whole thing by then. My sister's ten years older than me, my brother, twelve— I'm fairly sure my parents thought I was the menopause. I've never quite dared ask if they were pleased or not to find out the truth.

The plumbing thing came about more or less by chance, although once I'd thought of it, it seemed like the obvious choice. We'd had a pipe burst under the floor, and after ten minutes idly watching the plumber effing and blinding as he tried to work out where the leak was, I realised I could tell him to the inch. His comment of *"Are you trying to do me out of a job, son?"* got me thinking.

Anyway, as my dad always says, it's useful having a plumber in the family. Usually, he says this right before he asks me if I'll take a look at the drip in the shower.

(At which point I generally say, *"Oh, I didn't realise my brother was visiting, and won't he mind me staring at him?"* Family rituals—you've got to love them.)

I put down my mug and scratched Arthur's chin. He leaned into me and purred—he may look like a bruiser, he may even swagger like one, but he's just a big softy at heart. Talking of swaggering bruisers... Phil Morrison, a poof. Who'd have thought it?

Of course, it occurred to me, just because Dave had heard Phil was queer didn't mean he actually was. I smiled to myself. Maybe he'd been the *other* sort of bent copper, and Dave had got the wrong end of the stick. Now that I could believe.

Chapter Two

I was eating my breakfast next morning when the doorbell rang, so I went to answer it with my hair uncombed, my face unshaven and a slice of toast and marmalade in my hand. I don't know anyone who manages to look presentable before eight o'clock in the morning. It's just not natural.

I wasn't pleased to find myself facing an immaculate Phil Morrison. His broad shoulders filled my doorway, and a hand rested casually in the pocket of his designer jeans. "How did you find out where I live?" I asked, just about managing not to spit crumbs all over his sweater. It looked expensively soft, maybe even cashmere, not that I'd be able to tell for sure without reading the label. Knowing him, if he had to get it dry-cleaned, he'd probably send me the bill.

He smirked. "Private investigator, remember?"

"What do you want?" I was uncomfortably aware I'd been wearing this shirt yesterday. I had a clean T-shirt on underneath—I'm not a slob—but he still made me feel like something the cats had dragged in and then played with for a bit before losing interest and batting it under the sofa.

"Can I come in?" Phil asked, sounding annoyingly reasonable.

My first instinct was to slam the door in his face, but I was brought up proper, so I muttered, "If you must," and stood aside for him to enter. He walked in, casting a professional, and no doubt unimpressed, eye all over my little semidetached house, which I liked to think of as cosy and unpretentious. Morrison probably saw it as poky and scruffy.

"Nice place," he said in a tone so completely devoid of sarcasm I reckoned he had to be taking the piss.

"Yeah, and the weather's lovely for the time of year. Now are you going to get to the point? I've got a blocked drain that was put off yesterday, *and* all the jobs booked in for today." I shoved the rest of my toast in my mouth impatiently, still standing in the hall. I wasn't going to invite him to park his arse on my sofa and get comfortable. That was the last thing I wanted.

Morrison watched me chew for a moment. "Melanie Porter's family want to meet you."

"What? Why?" This time I did spit out a few crumbs.

"You found their daughter, remember?" His gaze was open and bland, and I didn't trust it as far as I could throw its owner. "Maybe they think you'll be able to tell them something about how she died."

"I won't." I pushed past him and stalked off to the kitchen, where I'd left my morning cuppa. Merlin and Arthur were busy demolishing their breakfast, furry bums in the air. I envied them. Life was so much bloody simpler for a cat.

Morrison followed me in, and I briefly wished I'd gone for a couple of Dobermans. "Come off it, Paretski—you must have had some grounds for knowing where to find her."

I took a long, steadying swallow of PG Tips. "I didn't. I told you yesterday, I'm just good at finding things, that's all. Now, if you don't mind, I've got work to do." I shoved my plate into the dishwasher, gulped down the rest of my tea and rinsed out my mug.

"You've changed, Paretski," he said, and this time the tone was clearly disapproving. His impressive bulk loomed even larger in the narrow confines of my kitchen, and it didn't help that I was only in my socks. One of which had a hole in the toe, I noticed. "I'd never have thought you'd leave an old mate in the lurch like this."

I whirled, droplets of water flying onto his tan leather jacket from the mug still in my hand. I hastily put it in the sink before I could ruin his entire wardrobe. "An old mate? For fuck's sake, Morrison, we hated each other's guts!"

There was an odd look on his face. "Not me. Graham Carter."

For a moment, I couldn't place the name. It'd been so long since I'd heard it. Then it hit me.

We'd been friends at school, of a sort, me and Graham. He'd distanced himself from me after the *Poofski* thing broke, but I hadn't blamed him really. The poor sod had had a hard enough time already, without being tarred with the same brush as me. He was a kids' home boy, shy, nerdy and crap at games. He really didn't need to hand the bullies any more ammunition.

Now I thought about it, I couldn't actually remember Morrison being a git to Graham. He'd saved that for me, the bastard.

"What the hell has Graham Carter go to do with all this?"

"Melanie Porter was his girlfriend. They lived together, up on Dyke Hill. He was the one who gave the Porters my number, back when Melanie first went missing."

"You and Graham are friends?" I couldn't keep the scepticism out of my voice. It was like hearing Tweety Pie and Sylvester had suddenly become BFFs. "How the hell did that happen?"

"That's not important. What *is* important is that he's being set up for this."

I folded my arms and leant against the draining board. "I thought you were working for Melanie's parents, not for Graham."

"I am. They don't believe he did it—and they want to find the bastard who did."

It didn't seem to add up to the picture I'd formed in my head. "Dave Southgate said Melanie's boyfriend was a junkie."

"He was. Past tense." Morrison sighed. "Look, he went through a bad patch after leaving school. A lot of us did," he added, but went on before I could ask him about it. Not that he'd have told me anything, I thought sourly. "He was living on the streets for a while, doing smack, petty crime, that sort of thing—but he'd started to sort his life out even before he met Melanie."

"So at which point did you and he become friends? The junkie bit, or after?" I persisted.

Morrison folded his arms, mirroring my posture. I couldn't help noticing he had a lot more trouble than I had getting his beefy forearms in position. "I help out at Crisis, all right? Saw Graham there and got talking to him."

"Crisis?" My flabber was well and truly gasted.

"The homelessness charity," he supplied impatiently.

"I know what it is, all right? I just wouldn't have imagined you playing the good Samaritan to a bunch of tramps." Then again, I'd never have imagined anyone telling me Phil Morrison was queer either.

"There's a lot about me you don't know, Paretski."

Not as much as you think. I found myself giving him an appraising look and wondering what kind of bloke he liked, and if he was seeing someone at the moment. Then I gave myself a mental shake. Still perving over Phil Morrison after all these years, for God's sake?

Trouble was, he was just the sort of bloke I go for. Always had been. He'd filled out a bit since his school days, but then so had my image of the perfect man. Physically, obviously, because personality-wise, I still couldn't stand the git.

At least, that was what I'd thought. In the light of all these revelations, I wondered if I ought to revise my opinion.

He heaved a heavy sigh, his arms rising and falling with his chest. "Look, can we focus on what's important here? Graham's in trouble. Are you going to help, or not?"

"I...." I had to look away. "It's not that I won't help. I just don't see how I can, that's all."

"Fine." His jaw set, Morrison unfolded his arms and marched towards the door.

"Oh, for—hang on a minute, okay?" I found myself chasing after him and grabbing hold of one granite forearm, only to drop it like a ton of, well, granite when he turned and glared at me. "I didn't say I wouldn't go and see them. I just don't see how it can help. I don't know anything. I just find stuff."

He drew in a breath as if about to say something, then stopped and shook his head. "Okay, then. I'll pick you up here at seven o'clock tonight, all right?"

"Okay," I said, regretting it already. What would it do except raise hopes I couldn't fulfil?

I felt in dire need of someone to talk to after that, but work came first, seeing as mortgage companies tend to get a bit nasty if you don't cough up each month. But I called my mate Gary and asked him to meet me for lunch up the Dyke between jobs.

The Devil's Dyke pub in Brock's Hollow is actually named after the Iron Age earthworks still visible nearby, but you could be forgiven for thinking the place took its name from its landlady. Henrietta "Harry" Shire is over six feet tall and built like the proverbial outhouse. She may have hung up her boxing gloves, following not inconsiderable success on the amateur ladies' circuit, but it'd still be a brave man who dared cause trouble in her pub. The place is staffed by a gaggle of pretty young girls who all seem to live in and never, ever have boyfriends. They're referred to locally as Harry's harem, but only when the speaker is one hundred and ten per cent certain the Devil's Dyke herself isn't listening.

Anyway, they do decent pub grub up there. It's down a quiet country lane, and there's a large garden on one side of it, so summer weekends it gets pretty busy with kiddies playing football while their parents enjoy a pint. On a Wednesday lunchtime in November, there was still a respectable crowd, although we were all over school age and we stayed in the public bar and kept warm by the fire. The Devil's Dyke is an old-fashioned country pub and still has two bars: the public bar and the lounge bar, only the latter of which they let the kiddies into. As is usual in these places, it's the nicest one that's adults only. It's a shame, really, as Harry's border collie Flossie makes her home in the public bar, whereas all the lounge bar has to recommend it is a secret passageway in the walk-in fireplace which is, in any case, locked and marked "Private".

Flossie likes to lie down on top of the covered-up well. What a pub wants with an in-house well is beyond me—personally, I'd have thought they'd want to discourage the drinking of water—but maybe they had their reasons back in Ye Olde Times. Anyway, all that's left now is a circular plinth about two feet high, with a glass cover you can look down to see that yes, it really does go all the way down. It keeps Flossie's tail safe from being trodden on and gives her a vantage point from which to fix a beady eye on anyone daring to eat meat in the place. I generally go for fish when I have a meal there.

There are plenty of low beams, none of which I have to duck for, and the walls are tobacco-coloured, maybe to compensate for the fact you're not allowed to smoke inside any longer. Pride of place on the walls is given to Harry's collection of exotic beer bottles, with a few horse brasses tucked in apologetically here and there.

Gary was currently ruffling Julian's neck fur as we waited for the food to arrive. "Who's Daddy's sweetie, then?" he cooed.

"That's a good question," I said, leaning back in my chair. "What happened to that bloke you met in London?"

Gary made a face. He's one of those blokes who are not exactly fat but still soft all over, like an overstuffed teddy bear, although in his case it conceals a quite respectably muscled upper body. He works from his house in Brock's Hollow, doing something in IT—or as the website has it, "implementing software solutions for the forward-looking business". He's got a big St Bernard called Julian that's as soft as he is, and he treats it like a furry baby.

"Turned out to be a total *cow*. We shall not speak of him. No we *won't.*" The last bit was to the dog. "And how's your love life, darling?" That was to me, Julian's love life having long been consigned to the vet's dustbin.

"Dead as a dodo," I admitted sadly. "Just don't seem to meet any decent blokes these days."

"Well, that's a disappointment. I thought you'd dragged me up here to tell me all about your latest conquest."

No one pouts like Gary, and I had to smile. "If only. Although I did have breakfast with a tall, well-built blond this morning..."

"Tom! I am *agog*!" He was too. His eyes were practically popping out on stalks. Even Julian was looking up at me, his tongue hanging out like a slice of Spam as he panted out bone-breath. "Tell me more. At once."

I laughed. "Not nearly as good as it sounds. Sorry. He turned up on my doorstep before eight."

"Now that's just rude. Nobody's got their face on at that hour." Gary sat back in his seat, looking horrified on my behalf. Made me wonder just how much of a beauty routine he went through every morning.

"Yeah, well, that's him all over. Bloke I knew at school. Phil Morrison." I half wondered if Gary might have heard something about him. I don't often meet a gay bloke from around here who Gary doesn't know.

"Unlike yours truly, it doesn't ring a bell." Gary's a campanologist. He likes to tell people he took up bell-ringing because he's always up for anything with "camp" in the name. Some people even think he's joking. "Old boyfriend?"

I made a face. "Old school bully."

"And he's knocking you up in the early hours of the morning *because*?"

I sighed and lowered my voice. "I found a body yesterday."

Gary's eyes widened to the size of the dinner plates the waitress chose that moment to put in front of us. "The girl from the estate agent's—that was you?"

"Thanks, love," I said, smiling mechanically at the waitress. She just gave me a funny look, probably because she'd heard what Gary had said. *Thanks, Gary.* "Well, I found her, yeah." I stared at my steak-and-kidney pie, suddenly not feeling half as hungry as I had when I'd ordered it. "I didn't put her there."

"Well, go on." Gary leaned forward over his lasagne. "Tell Uncle Gary all about it. Was she"—he lowered his voice— "*naked?*"

Gary's a good bloke, really he is. It's just—nobody ever really gets it. You tell anyone you've found a body, and it's just not real to them. They think it's like being an extra on *Midsomer Murders.* "No. I probably shouldn't be talking about it, and to be honest, I really don't want to. It wasn't exactly the highlight of my week."

"Sorry, sweetie. Poor you." Gary laid a hand briefly on my arm, then chomped thoughtfully on his salad for a minute. "To coin a phrase, if I had a gift like yours, I'd return it."

I shrugged and picked at my chips. "At least she's been found now. That's got to be better for her family than not knowing." I reached for the ketchup bottle, then thought better of it, visions of poor Melanie dancing in my head and threatening to take away my appetite. "Trouble is, the old school bully is a private investigator now, and he doesn't believe in my so-called gift. Thinks I must know something about her death I'm not telling."

"But the police don't think that, do they?" Gary leaned over to put a hand on my right knee, and Julian showed his concern by slobbering on the other.

Knowing from experience just how unpleasant it would be when the drool soaked through the denim, I pushed his ton-weight head off gently—the dog's that is, not Gary's. "No—but I ended up agreeing to talk to the girl's parents this evening. What the hell am I going to say?"

"The truth, the whole truth, and nothing but the truth, so help you God?" Gary declaimed, one hand on his heart and the other thrust skywards. Heads turned, as they often do when Gary's around.

"It's not going to be what they want to hear. Don't s'pose you fancy meeting up for a drink afterwards, drown my sorrows and all that?"

"Can't, sweetie—Wednesday is practice night, remember?"

I remembered. I hunched up one shoulder and did a passable imitation of Quasimodo lisping, "The bells! The bells!" Gary just smiled and gave me a V sign.

Chapter Three

Morrison knocked on my door on the dot of seven that evening, which meant that as a job had overrun, I was still shovelling pasta into my gob at the time. I answered the door, plate in hand, and gazed up at his bulky figure, still chewing. He'd dressed up to go and see the Porters, even put a jacket and tie on. He looked good—but it made him seem more remote, more dangerous, without his hard lines softened by cashmere. I jerked my head to indicate he should come in. It's rude to talk with your mouth full.

"Do you ever stop eating?" he asked, once again following me into the kitchen like he owned the place.

I was stung and swallowed my mouthful a bit more quickly than I really wanted to. "Do you ever stop to consider it might be someone's mealtime before you start beating down their door?"

He went to fold his arms, then obviously remembered it'd crumple his expensive jacket, and put his hands on his hips instead. The gesture could have looked camp but somehow, on him, it really didn't. "First, do you think you could stop being so sodding touchy about everything? And second, we had an appointment."

"Oh, excuse me. I suppose I should have left the lady with water dripping through her ceiling and told her I'd come back tomorrow, because sorry, I've got an *appointment.*" I rolled my eyes, shoving the plate back on the kitchen counter. I'd had enough anyway.

Morrison sort of huffed. "Does everything have to be such a bloody production with you?"

"Comes of being queer, I expect. Wouldn't you say?" I put a bit of emphasis on the *you*, narked he was making me out to be such a drama queen. Anyway, it was about time we got it all out in the open.

He stilled. "Who told you?"

I wasn't about to drop Dave in it, even though he probably couldn't give a monkey's if Morrison was pissed off with him. "Maybe I read your mind," I joked weakly. "Maybe there's no end to my psychic powers."

For a split second, he actually looked worried. Then his expression relaxed. "Stop trying to mess with my head, Poof—shit." He looked away and didn't say anything more.

I took a couple of deep breaths. I was about to say, *look, let's just leave it, okay*—but he beat me to it. "Sorry," he said, like it caused him physical pain to say it. "That wasn't—I didn't mean anything by it."

There was a short silence. I didn't know what to say, so I just nodded curtly. Acknowledging his apology, although not necessarily accepting it.

Morrison spoke again. "I checked up on you today. Apparently you've got previous, on the finding-things front. Doesn't mean I believe in all this mumbo-jumbo."

Bloody fantastic. He'd checked up on me—so now he knew which porn I watched and had read all the rubbish I'd posted on Facebook after a few beers too many. "If you're not going to believe what I say," I said slowly, to make sure he was really listening, "then what's the point of asking me questions?"

"Are you going to come with me to the Porters' or not?" he asked, sidestepping the issue.

I sighed. "Let's get this over with."

This being late November, it was dark and beginning to get a bit nippy as we drove off in Morrison's silver VW Golf. The car wasn't new, but the interior was impersonal, devoid of any touches of personality like the "ironic" retro furry dice I had swinging from the rearview mirror of my Ford Fiesta like a couple of cubist bollocks. As we passed under a street lamp, something glinted, and I noticed for the first time that Morrison was wearing a wedding ring.

"You're married?" I blurted out, just managing to stop myself carrying on with, *To a man?*

Morrison's gaze flickered over at me. For a moment, I thought there was something like hurt in his eyes, but it was gone before I could tell for sure, and he turned his attention back to the road. "No."

"But you wear a ring."

There was a pause before he answered. "People are more ready to trust a married man."

God, and here I'd been thinking... I don't know what I'd been thinking. But not this. "So it's just a prop? For fuck's sake, that's so bloody cynical." Disappointment sharpened my tone. "I suppose you'd do anything, say anything to get what you want."

"And you've never told a customer work needs doing when it doesn't, or got them to pay for fancy copper pipes when plastic would do?"

"No, actually, I haven't. And I fucking well resent you even suggesting it." I folded my arms and glared out of the window. I could see this being a very long evening. Why the hell hadn't I brought my own car?

"Look," Morrison said after a painful silence. "If I'm going to do my job—the job my clients pay me to do—sometimes I need to get people to trust me. So maybe some of it's an act—but don't go telling me you don't do the same thing in your line of work."

"What, lie to people? No, I don't."

"And I suppose you've never flirted with a housewife? Just so she won't argue about the bill, or to make sure it'll be you she calls in next time some work needs doing?"

"That's different, and you know it."

"Is it? Didn't notice any rainbow stickers on your van."

"Yeah, well, for some reason, I thought it might be safer not to advertise I'm queer. Can't imagine where I got that impression, can you?"

"For fuck's sake, I never laid a finger on you! It was that prick in the Chelsea tractor who did the damage, not me." He was breathing hard, and his knuckles were white on the steering wheel. I was starting to wonder just how safe I was in his car when he spoke again. "What the hell do you expect me to do? I tried to apologise, but—fuck it." Morrison clammed up, his jaw tense.

I wasn't sure if I felt more angry at him—or guilty. Was my moral high ground really the boggy ditch he was making it out to be? Then again, did he think an apology was some kind of emotional Band-Aid? Stick it on, give the kid a kiss better, and all the pain goes away? "You can't just turn up after a dozen years, say *oh, sorry,* and expect us to be best mates all of a sudden," I said, softening my tone a bit. "It doesn't work like that." I wished I knew how it bloody well did work.

"Want me to go down on my knees, do you?" Phil asked wearily, and all of a sudden I got a picture of just that. Him in his posh suit and all. My throat closed up with desire, and

40

things below the belt got a bit uncomfortable. I stared straight ahead at the pitch-black road lined with trees that loomed ominously over us, dark shadows against the cloudy sky. Out of the corner of my eye, I caught Phil—Morrison—flashing me a strange look. Did he know? I wondered—could he tell he still got to me?

I cleared my throat. "So where's this house, then?"

The Porters' house, like Morrison's suit, was big and posh, out in the well-kept rural wilds towards Kimpton. I wondered what they'd thought about their daughter moving in with an ex-junkie on a council estate. Morrison had said they believed Graham was innocent, but just because they didn't think he was a murderer didn't mean they necessarily thought he was a good prospect for a son-in-law.

I supposed I'd find out soon enough. Morrison rang the doorbell, which even sounded classy—old-fashioned and mellow, like something Gary might approve of, not a tinny little buzzer like the one that'd come with my house. The door was opened by a lady who looked to be in her sixties. She tried to raise a smile for us, but her mouth settled back into its haggard lines before the effort really got off the ground. Melanie's mother, I guessed.

"Come in, please," she said.

Morrison's voice was gentler than I'd ever heard it as he introduced us. "Mrs. Porter, this is Tom Paretski."

She nodded and held out a cold, dry hand for me to shake. "Please come in," she said again, and led us to a largish sitting room. A man who must be Melanie's father was sitting in an armchair, staring at the curtains. His gaze flickered to us briefly, then returned to the pale pink damask.

I really, really didn't want to be here.

"Howard, this is Tom Paretski," Mrs. Porter said. "He's the one who…who found Melanie."

The man didn't react. "Please sit down," she told us, and we perched gingerly on the sofa while she sat in an uncomfortable-looking upright chair. "Would you like a cup of tea?"

I wished she'd offered something stronger. "No, I'm fine, thank you," I said firmly. I wanted to get this over with as quickly as possible. What was the point of me even being here, intruding on their grief? "I'm really sorry about your daughter," I said, the inadequacy of it a bitter taste in my mouth.

Morrison shook his head in his turn, and Mrs. Porter reached over to put her cold hand on mine. I tried not to shiver reflexively. "Thank you for finding her. I don't like to think of her, all alone…" She sat back and blinked rapidly a few times, her face turned away from me.

"Tom," Morrison said, my Christian name sounding strange in his voice. "If there's anything you can tell us—anything at all that might help…"

I stood up convulsively and walked over to the fireplace. "I wish there was," I said, looking at a photograph of Graham and Melanie on the mantelpiece. He'd hardly changed since I'd known him—still the same skinny, serious face and unruly dark hair. They both looked well and very happy together. "I really wish there was. I'm so sorry. I just—I just have this knack of finding things, that's all. Or people," I added, realising what I'd said.

"Philip told us you were a friend of Graham's," Mrs. Porter said. It sounded like she'd got up and followed me over here. "We know Graham could never have done this."

How could she be so certain?

"He loved her too much. He worshipped her," she went on, answering my unspoken question.

You always hurt the one you love, I thought.

I steeled myself and turned round. As I'd suspected, she was standing right by me. "I'm sorry, Mrs. Porter," I said. "If there was anything I could do to make sure the killer of your daughter is brought to justice, I would. But there's nothing I can tell you. I'm sorry."

We drove off in silence. After a while, Morrison spoke. "I believe you don't know anything."

"That's nice of you." It might have come out sounding a bit sarcastic. I certainly meant it to.

He sighed. "Look, put yourself in my position. The girl you've been hired to find turns up dead, and now her fiancé—a friend of yours—faces getting stitched up for murder. Wouldn't you do anything you could think of to get a witness to open up?"

"They were engaged?" I flashed back to when I'd held her hand. God, yes, there had been a ring. I shivered. "Look, for God's sake, I don't want Graham going to jail for something he didn't do any more than you do, but—"

"I told you, I believe you." He cut me off impatiently.

"Have you seen him?"

"Earlier today. He's a mess—no surprise there. It doesn't help, the police pulling him in for questioning every five minutes."

"Maybe he should stay with the Porters," I mused.

Morrison gave a derisive snort. "*She* may believe in him, but the husband's not so sure. Didn't you notice he didn't say word one this evening?"

I'd taken his silence for simple grief—but yeah, thinking about it, there could have been hostility in there too. God, what a mess.

When we got back to my house, it wasn't yet nine o'clock, but I felt like I'd been up for a week. "Can I come in?" Morrison asked.

"Why?"

"To talk."

"Fine. But that's all you're getting," I quipped without a lot of humour.

The cats had come back in from wherever they spent their days and sent suspicious glares Morrison's way before greeting me effusively. Probably because I hadn't had time to put their food out earlier. I rectified this whilst waiting for the kettle to boil, then made a cafetière of coffee while they scarfed down their Fisherman's Choice. It occurred to me I hadn't asked Morrison if coffee was what he wanted, but then it further occurred to me that actually, if he was going to be fussy, he could make his own drinks. I was too bloody knackered. I sloshed in some milk and handed him the mug.

"Thanks," he said.

"So talk," I told him.

"Can't we take this somewhere more comfortable?"

Grudgingly, I made my way into the living room and slumped into an armchair. Morrison parked his arse on the sofa without waiting for an invitation, leaning back and resting his ankle on the opposite knee. Making himself at home, and incidentally providing me with a view of his crotch I tried very hard not to stare at. Even if he did improve the looks of my battered old sofa by several hundred percent.

"What did Southgate tell you about me?" he asked, his tone and expression neutral. I bet he practised that sort of thing in front of the mirror.

"All he said was that you're an ex-copper and you're queer. Oh, and a pain in the bum. But I knew that already." I reached down to fondle Arthur, and he jumped up onto my lap and kneaded it into submission before graciously deigning to curl up and purr. Merlin, the little traitor, went over and rubbed his chin all over Morrison's trousers. "So, this being a poof. How's that working out for you?"

"Could be better," he said frankly. "Look, Tom—all right if I call you Tom?"

"You did earlier. Phil," I added pointedly.

"Right. Look, school wasn't an easy time for any of us."

"Yeah, being the leader of a gang of thugs can't have been easy for a sensitive little flower like you."

"Like we ever laid a finger on you. All right, maybe there was a bit of pushing and shoving—"

"It's not all about the physical stuff!" I'd have stood up, but Arthur was restraining me. As it was, he opened one sleepy eye to reproach me for disturbing his rest. I lowered my voice. "Have you got any idea what it was like for me, everyone calling me names, laughing at me—to my face?"

"Water off a duck's back," he said, but he wasn't sounding as certain as a moment ago.

"Oh, so now you're the mind reader, are you? Let me tell you, you big bloody hypocrite—" I broke off as he stood and crossed the room to loom over me. His expression was unreadable, and I wondered if I'd pushed him too far. My heart was racing, and to my shame, my cock stirred, which, when you've got a cat on your lap, feels beyond wrong.

Morrison—Phil—bent down and reached out to cup my face with a hand. "Always did know how to wind me up, didn't you, Tom?"

What? It was the other way round, wasn't it?

Wasn't it?

Phil straightened and walked out without so much as a good-night kiss.

Chapter Four

Despite the dowsing, I'm not psychic in any other way, shape or form. So I had absolutely no grounds for trusting my gut feeling it wasn't the last I'd be hearing from Phil Morrison. When the phone rang on the way to a new customer for a bathroom leak, I answered with "Paretski Plumbing," because it could have been anyone—Phil hadn't given me his number, obviously being a *don't call us, we'll call you* sort of guy.

"Tom? It's Phil. Are you busy right now?"

"Just on my way to a job. Over in Harpenden. Why?"

The line crackled. "I want you to come and talk to Graham."

I didn't have a clue why he'd want me to do that, but I'd have to admit I was curious to see Graham again. Leaving aside the fact that it'd mean seeing Phil again. "Can't come right away. Would, say, an hour and a half's time do? Give or take. You're up at his place, right?"

"No. St Albans. I just got a call from his lawyer. I'll meet you at yours, all right?"

"Fine. Although if you're charging the Porters by the hour, I hope you'll be bringing some work to do while you wait."

I hung up and drove on to sort out Mrs. M. She was a yummy mummy in skinny jeans, presumably to showcase the figure she'd sweated blood to get back after popping out the kids. "You're my last hope," she told me. "I've had three plumbers round this week and *none* of them could find where the water was coming from."

Nice to know where I stood on her preferred plumbers list. I checked out the ceiling, noted the water stains, then headed up to the bathroom, which was about the size of my living room. If there's one thing I can do, it's locate a leaking pipe. All part of the weird and wonderful stuff that goes on in my head. I stood on the rustic floorboards next to the bath, making sure I didn't wipe my clod-hopping feet on the fluffy white bath mat, and let my spidey-senses loose.

Nothing. I knelt down and put my hands on the fittings, because sometimes touch helps—but still nothing. All those connections were sealed up tighter than a puritan's arse.

There was no leak. But how the hell was I going to persuade Mrs. M. of that? Some blokes I know would have just banged around in there for half an hour doing nothing, then told her it was fixed and charged her a hundred quid. But I'm not like that. Plus, it was bugging me now. What had really been causing the water to come through the ceiling? As I stood there, frowning, a round little face with big blue eyes like mummy's peeked around the bathroom door.

I smiled. "Hello, poppet. Come to watch me work?"

She nodded, but didn't smile back.

"Well, come on in, then—I don't bite."

She edged her way into the room and scurried to hide behind one of the gleaming white bath towels. Just before she disappeared, I noticed she was carrying something.

Light began to dawn. I crouched down to toddler level. "What have you got there, sweetie? Is it a Barbie?"

Shyly, she held out the toy. It was Barbie all right. Mermaid Barbie.

"She's pretty, isn't she? I bet she likes going swimming."

There was another vigorous nod of her head—and then the door swung open. *"There* you are, Jocasta. You mustn't bother the man while he's working."

"No problem—I love kids," I said from my crouched-down position. I usually add, *"Couldn't eat a whole one, though,"* but I didn't think Mrs. M. would see the funny side.

I straightened. "Your pipes are fine. There's your leak," I said, nodding to the kid.

"I beg your pardon?" Mrs. M. looked horrified.

"Just ask her to show you how Barbie goes swimming."

Ten minutes and about a gallon of spilt water later, I was walking out of the house while Mrs. M. wrung her hands in embarrassment. "I'm so sorry," she kept saying. "Dragging you out all this way for nothing."

"Don't worry about it," I told her, and made sure I gave her a cheeky grin with my business card so at least I might get some work from her in the future.

She smiled back. "You know, your English is awfully good. How long have you lived in this country?"

I didn't let the grin waver. "Oh, a few years."

When you've got a Polish name and you're a plumber, it's no use trying to tell people you grew up here. They'll only be disappointed.

When I swung the van back into my road, I found Phil sitting in his Golf outside my house, scribbling in a notebook. Damn. I hadn't expected him to be here already—thought I'd have time for a cup of tea, at least. Mrs. M. hadn't bothered offering any.

Phil spotted me coming and leaned over to open the car door. "That was quick," he commented. "Right, get in, and I'll drive you."

I shrugged and slid into the Golf's passenger seat. "False alarm. I didn't have to do any actual work."

Phil laughed, and I tried not to do an obvious double-take. I hadn't known he could do that. He was dressed a lot more casually than the last time I'd seen him. I liked the more relaxed look. The bodywarmer was getting another outing, this time over a thick padded shirt that looked like something I might have worn, only a lot more expensive. "Easy money, then."

"Nah, I waived the call-out fee. I'm not going to charge seventy-five quid when I didn't even do anything."

"Too soft for your own good, you are. You were in Harpenden, right? They're loaded, people who live there. Seventy-five quid's small change to that lot. Wouldn't even cover the weekly wine bill at Waitrose."

"Listen, you live by your moral code, I'll live by mine."

"Nice to know you believe I've got one," Phil said, his tone wry.

I gave him a sidelong look, treating myself to the view of his square-jawed profile. "Well... I believe in giving people the benefit of the doubt, at any rate."

My house is on the east side of St Albans, and Graham's flat was at the south end of Brock's Hollow, so it was only about ten minutes or so before we pulled up outside. We cut across the communal front lawn to the main door, and Phil rang the bell. "Graham? It's Phil."

There was no answer, but the door buzzed open. We clattered up the stairs, our steps echoing from the concrete walls of the stairwell. It was fairly grim, but at least it smelled clean. Phil rapped on the door of 14c.

It turned out that when he'd said Graham was a mess, it'd been like saying the Ice Age was a wee bit nippy. Graham looked wrecked. No two ways about it. Granted, I hadn't seen him for over a decade, but I was pretty sure it wasn't just the passage of time that had done this to him. His face looked like a skull, with sunken eyes peering out from under his greasy fringe. He opened the door warily, as if worried there might be a lynch mob on his doorstep, and let us in without a word. Phil stepped straight up to give him a hug, while I looked on in amazement with maybe an undertone of jealousy. I hadn't known Phil could do that either.

We trooped into the tiny, cluttered living room, where Graham perched uneasily on the sofa he'd shared with Melanie. Poor sod. The flat smelled stale and unsavoury, like unwashed laundry and over-filled bins. Phil sat next to him, and I shifted a stack of papers so I could make use of an armchair.

"I didn't do it," Graham said, looking directly at me, as if he thought me believing him would have any influence whatsoever on whether he went down for the murder.

"Course you didn't, mate," I said, my voice cringingly hearty. As if I was trying to jolly him out of his bereavement. "I'm really sorry about Melanie," I added in a more sympathetic tone. It felt weird, talking to him as if it hadn't been twelve years since the last time—but then, asking him how he'd been and what he'd been up to would have been completely ludicrous. And I couldn't blame him for having more on his mind than what had happened in my boring little life since last we'd met.

"How...how did she look, when you found her?"

Oh God. Dead. She'd looked dead, and when the police shone their torches on her, I could see the back of her head was a broken, bloody mess... "Peaceful," I said and had to clear my throat. "Like she was asleep."

"Thank you," he said and reached out a hand to grip mine. It was cold and clammy. It felt exactly like Melanie's hand had felt. My stomach clenched, but I managed not to wrest my hand from his grip.

Phil's voice rumbled from beside him. "Tell us again what happened that night. The last time you saw her."

Graham's grip lessened on me, thank God, and I was able to pull my hand away without it seeming unnatural. He looked at Phil and swallowed.

"I'll make a cup of tea," I suggested, my voice sounding way too loud.

Phil made an impatient noise, but I ignored him and strode on into the kitchen. The decor was outdated, but it looked basically clean and cheerful, just a stack of takeaway containers by the bin giving a clue that things weren't exactly normal around here. I wondered how many meals Graham had bothered to cook since Melanie's disappearance. The tea bags were in a vintage-style caddy next to the kettle, and the milk in the fridge was still just in date. I made three mugs, added two sugars to Graham's on general principles, and carried them back through.

Phil accepted his tea with a nod. Graham clung on to his as if it was the only thing holding him back from the abyss. One knee had started jiggling, but he didn't seem to have noticed. Despite the clutter, despite the smallness of the room, it felt empty and cold.

"Right," Phil said with an annoyed glance my way. "Tell us what happened."

Graham took a gulp of his tea. He didn't complain about the sugar, so I reckoned either he usually drank it sweet, or he just didn't have the energy to complain about it. "We were going to watch a DVD. She'd been working late a lot in the last few months, so we hadn't had an evening together for ages. That was why..." He trailed off and stared into space.

"That was why you had the argument," Phil prompted.

He drank another mouthful of tea and nodded. "I didn't want her to go. I said it wasn't reasonable, she should tell him she couldn't make it. But she said it'd only take half an hour."

"Did she say what it was about?"

Graham frowned. "You asked me this. Before. I told you—"

"This is for Tom's benefit, Graham," Phil interrupted, a lot more patiently than he'd have done if it'd been me, I was sure. And anyway, why did Phil want me to hear all this from Graham? Couldn't he just have told me himself and saved Graham a bit of grief?

"All right." He drank some more of his tea and stared out the window. "All she said was, 'I'm sorry, I've got to go out for a bit. It's the boss.' She said we could start the film when she got back. Like she wasn't going to be gone for long, you know?"

"Did she take anything with her?"

"Her handbag. Her iPad was in it."

"Did she put it in specially?"

"I don't know. I didn't see her. She always carried it around, anyway. She used to read books on it."

"Did she seem worried? Annoyed? Furtive?"

Graham's knuckles were white on the handle of his mug. I hoped he wasn't about to snap it off. "She was...annoyed with me for making such a big deal about it. The last time I ever saw her, and she was annoyed with me."

"But before that?" Phil's voice was soft and coaxing, a tone I didn't associate with him at all.

"She was...puzzled, I think?" Graham frowned. "Yes. But it was almost like she was pleased too. Like she wanted to go. More than she wanted an evening in with me."

I didn't need to look at his face to see how much that hurt him. The pain in his voice was already almost more than I could bear.

"Well?" Phil demanded as he strode away from Graham's flat.

There was a cold wind blowing old newspapers and discarded carrier bags through the estate, and my hip ached as I hurried to keep up. It didn't improve my mood. "Well what?"

The breeze ruffled Phil's blond hair, but he looked snug and warm in his posh bodywarmer, the git. "Was he hiding anything?"

I stared at him. "How the hell should I know? I'm not a bloody lie detector."

Phil frowned. "I thought you could tell if things were hidden."

"Yes—*things*. Actual stuff. Not if someone's telling porkies. And it doesn't just happen, either. I have to, you know, think about it. So if you want me to find something, next time just ask me, okay?"

"How does that work, then?" His tone was curious. "I mean, how did you first find out you could do it?"

I shrugged. "Don't remember. I mean, I was a kid when it started. Far as I know, I've always been able to do it. Even when I was a toddler."

"Have you got brothers and sisters? Because I bet they just loved you."

I had to unclench my teeth to answer. "I've got one of each. Both older than me. If I'm lucky, they send me a Christmas card, but apart from that, we don't see each other."

"Christ, what did you find? Hard-core porn? Pregnancy tests?"

"Amongst other things. Why the bloody hell do you think I kept so quiet about it at school?"

Phil laughed, the unsympathetic bastard. "Are you having me on?"

I was going to get toothache at this rate. "What about your family? All right with you turning out bent, are they?"

He didn't answer, which had the predictable effect of making me feel about three feet tall. "Look, I'm sorry—"

He cut me off. "Forget it." We got back into his car and headed off to St Albans in silence.

I hadn't planned on being the one to break it, but as we neared Fleetville, a thought that'd been nagging at me earlier resurfaced. "Anyway, I thought you were on Graham's side. Why do you think he's hiding something?"

"Because everyone does." He didn't even sound bitter about it. Just matter-of-fact, like this was something everybody knew.

"Well, maybe—but it doesn't have to be anything *bad*. Not if they're innocent."

"Bollocks. Still believe in the Tooth Fairy as well, do you?"

"Does it make you happy, believing the worst of everyone? Because I'd rather give people the benefit of the doubt."

"You'll learn." He parked in front of my house, pulling on the handbrake so viciously I wouldn't have been surprised if it'd come off in his hand. I didn't bother to argue anymore; my headache was bad enough already. "And no, it doesn't," he said as I got out of the car.

I leaned back down despite myself. "What?"

His eyes were haunted. "It doesn't make me happy, all right?"

Then he revved the engine and put the car back in gear, so I had no choice but to close the door and let him go.

Chapter Five

I wasn't expecting to hear from Phil again. Morrison, I mean. I thought he'd have decided my peculiar talent was of no further use—and it wasn't like we'd been getting on all that well.

He called me next day. I was in the van, just coming down King Harry Lane, so I pulled into the lay-by next to the park to take the call.

Not that I thought it might be him or anything.

He didn't bother with *hello*. "Can you come round to Graham's?"

Again? What the hell had happened? "What, now?"

"Yes."

"Why?"

"The police have taken him in for questioning again."

"And?" It was like pulling teeth.

"I want to have a look around his place while he's not there."

I drew in a sharp breath. "That's illegal. And hang on, I thought you and him were mates?"

"We won't be breaking in. Melanie's mum gave me a key. Are you coming?"

I sighed. It was a good thing I hadn't given the customer a definite time I'd be there. "Fine. I'll be around fifteen minutes, okay?"

The gods of the traffic lights smiled on me, and I got there in ten. Phil was sitting in his car outside the flat. Probably tapping his fingers impatiently on the steering wheel, but if so, I didn't manage to catch him at it. As I parked my van behind him, he got out of the Golf and stood waiting for me on the path, arms folded.

"Ready for the crime spree?" I asked, tongue in cheek.

He almost smiled. "All in a day's work."

We set off across the grass to Graham's front door. "What do you reckon we'll find?"

Phil shrugged. "Maybe nothing. That's the best-case scenario."

"And the worst-case scenario?"

"Oh, blood-stained clothes, murder weapon and a video recording of the whole thing so he can sit down and watch it on cold winter evenings when there's nothing on the box?"

It was a bit sick, but we both laughed. Phil's laugh was a low, quiet rumble of genuine amusement that took me right back to when we'd been at school, reminding me I'd noticed more about him than his physique back then. You get a bunch of teenage lads together, often it's like they're competing to see who can laugh the loudest, but he'd never been the sort to fake it like that.

Funny, the stuff I'd forgotten about him. I shook my head. "Seriously, I can't see Graham as the killer. I mean, come on, this has practically wiped him out."

"Guilt can do that to a bloke." He looked away from me.

"Got a few skeletons in your own closet, have you?" I couldn't resist needling him. "Still, at least you're not sharing it with them anymore. Must have been bloody uncomfortable, that—all those bony elbows."

He gave me a look as we jogged up the stairs to the flat. "Yeah, well, I'm surprised you ever came out of yours."

"Why?" I asked, suspicious.

He smirked. "Wouldn't have been short of headroom, would you?"

"Are you making fun of my height? Don't answer that. Where do you want me to start, then?"

Phil shrugged. "I don't know. Just do your stuff. Get out your divining rod, or whatever it is you do."

"I'll get mine out if you show me yours," I said with a leer. He pointedly turned away to start searching a bookshelf.

I sighed and started looking. It wasn't easy to concentrate with Phil in the room, so I decamped to the bathroom—you wouldn't believe the kinds of stuff I've found in toilet cisterns over the years. Red faces all round, and a husband who'd be getting an ear-bashing when he got home from work.

I had to do it the old-fashioned way, using my eyes—all that water messes with the vibes—but all I found in Graham's bathroom was a flourishing crop of mildew. And it looked like the loo would need a new siphon pretty soon.

I moved on to the bedroom. It was small—barely bigger than the admittedly king-size bed. There were built-in wardrobes with not an inch of door clearance to spare, and a small chest of drawers that obviously served—had served—as Melanie's dressing table. It was covered in sad, abandoned little trinkets of costume jewellery, and various skin and hair products, all cheap brands. Maybe the iPad had been a present from her parents—Melanie's salary must have gone to support

59

her and Graham, which made me wonder what he was doing for money these days. A photo stood in the centre, showing Melanie's parents looking around twenty years younger than they had when I'd met them.

There was definitely something there—the mental tinnitus started up immediately. Trouble was, it was coming from all directions, making it hard to isolate what was where. Most people hide stuff in the bedroom. Not just what you'd think, either. Besides all the porn and the marital aids, there's usually jewellery, old love letters, all kinds of stuff. I tried to get a bead on the nastiest trail. There was a greasy, dirty, *shameful* sort of feel to one of the tracks. It yanked at my mind, and I took a step towards the bed—

"Find anything?" Phil's voice grated in my ear, making me jump a mile and totally lose concentration.

"Chance'd be a fine thing with you yelling in my ear the minute I get close," I snapped.

He backed off, holding up his hands. "Sorry, sorry. Didn't mean to smudge your aura or scare away the spirit guides, whatever. But we don't know how long they're going to keep him in, so we can't afford to hang around."

"I know, all right?" I sighed. I turned back away from him and tried to regain my scattered focus.

Phil, for once, was quiet. Didn't mean he wasn't distracting me, though. I could just imagine those hefty forearms sliding around my waist from behind, that hard body pressing up against my back...

Damn it. "I need you to leave the room, okay?"

"What? You're telling me you can't do it while I'm watching? How old are you?"

"It's just—you make me nervous, standing behind me like that. Happy now?"

He didn't answer, just walked slowly out from behind me and around the bed, until he was standing pressed against the wall to one side of it. In my field of vision, but not right in my face. "Better?"

It was, actually. I tried to relax. My vision unfocused, and the tugging started up in my brain again—in several different directions, just like it had before. My eyes dropped half-closed, and then I had it. Clearly fate liked a laugh as much as the next girl, because the strongest vibes were coming from right next to Phil. I strode up to him, thought, *what the hell*, and dropped to my knees.

His expression was priceless. Managing not to laugh, I felt all around the corner of the pine bed frame—and found a packet taped to it. It felt plasticky but soft—like, say, a packet of some kind of powder.

Shit. "I think I've found Graham's drugs stash," I said, looking up. Phil seemed around fifty feet tall from this angle, a big unfriendly giant. Getting down even lower, I managed to peel away the tape holding the packet to the wood, and I passed it up to him. It was a sturdy plastic Ziploc bag holding half a dozen little baggies, and the powder in the smaller bags was light brown in colour—for some reason I'd been expecting white, but maybe that was just coke. Like I said, I don't do drugs and I never have.

Phil echoed my thoughts. "Shit."

"Yeah. Can you tell what it is?"

His scowl deepened. "It'll be heroin. The stupid prick. I'm going to kill him."

I felt all around the bed frame again, but there was nothing else. Awkwardly, because Phil was still taking up way too much space, I stood, my hip giving a sharp twinge to remind me it didn't hold with crawling around on floors.

As I hissed in a breath, I felt Phil's hand under my elbow. Supporting me. Sending electric tingles up my arm from the point of contact. Suddenly this whole situation seemed way too intimate. I muttered something I hoped he'd interpret as thanks and stepped back, hurriedly, to a distance where I couldn't feel the warmth of him anymore.

"Are you going to tell the police?" I asked, hoping my heartbeat would slow down now.

Come to that, Phil seemed a bit short of breath himself. "What the hell do you think? If they find out about the drugs, they'll stop looking for anyone else. Christ, what a wanker. I'm going to put the fear of God into that stupid little tosser. What the bloody hell was he thinking?" Phil paced up and down the narrow bit of space in the bedroom so fast I expected to see sparks flying from the cheap carpet.

Maybe he saw it as a personal failure or something. "Don't a lot of ex-addicts slip up in times of stress? I mean, this hasn't exactly been a picnic for him."

"So handing the police a motive on a silver platter is going to help his case? You know what they'll think: he started using again; she came home from work and found him high as a kite; they had a massive row, and he bashed her head in."

I winced as his words brought back images of Melanie, lying dead up on Nomansland Common. "Look, I hate to say it—but maybe that's how it was?" I held up a hand to ward him off as he advanced on me like a pissed-off pit bull. "People change when they're on drugs. Do stuff they wouldn't dream of, normally."

Phil's glare deepened to an extent that started to get a bit worrying—then he sighed and sat down heavily on the bed, his face in his hands. "I just don't want to believe it. We got, well, close, back when he was picking himself up from the streets.

And no, not like that, all right? It kind of... Helping him got me through a difficult time."

I wondered what that had been, but I didn't think he'd appreciate me asking about it. I sat down next to him, and put a hand awkwardly on his shoulder. "I'm sorry. What were you hoping I'd find? Really?"

"Graham told me, before, she'd been a bit distant in the last week or so. Like she'd had something on her mind." He lifted his head, and immediately that weird, unsettling intimacy was back, so I let my hand fall from his shoulder. A tiny frown creased his forehead, just for a moment. "I can think of a couple of possibilities. She could have been having an affair—in which case, there's another bloke running around who's a prime suspect for the murder. Or, maybe there was something funny going on where she worked. That call from the boss—sounds dodgy to me. Particularly as I happen to know he's denied meeting her that night."

"So...you weren't looking for dirt on Graham at all?" I frowned. I wasn't too keen on the way he'd been holding out on me.

"Oh, for—" He stood suddenly and flung his arms out, so wide I ducked instinctively. "I'm looking for whatever there is to find, all right? I don't know who killed her. *I don't know.* I'm hoping it wasn't Graham—but if there's evidence he did it, I'm not going to cover it up."

"Apart from the drugs," I reminded him, nettled.

"That's just evidence he's a prat!"

I stood, not much liking the added height difference with him standing and me not. "It doesn't mean he's a prat; it just means he was desperate. Have you ever tried to give up something you were desperate for?"

It was a rhetorical question, so I was surprised when he answered it. "What the hell's that got to do with you?"

"You were on drugs?"

"*What?* No, I wasn't." His fists clenched, and I tensed, wondering what the hell this was all about. Phil turned away from me, and I heard him take a couple of deep breaths. "Was there anything else? Hidden in here, I mean."

"Yeah." I frowned, not that he could see me. It was probably just as well. "You'll need to get the drugs out of here, though, if you want me to find it."

"Why? We've found them—they're not hidden anymore." He turned but made no move to do as I'd asked, the annoying git.

"I don't know why! They're still giving off vibes, all right?" Actually, they were already shouting at me a lot less brightly— oh, you know what I mean—but I was damned if I was going to backtrack now.

He stared at me, eyes narrowed. I stared stubbornly back.

"Fine." Phil stomped out, plastic baggies of heroin stashed in his pocket.

Feeling smug, I set to work. Trouble was, as I said before, everyone hides stuff in the bedroom. I found several items neither Graham nor Melanie's parents would thank me for mentioning, plus a little suede case where she kept her decent jewellery.

Nothing that'd explain her death, though. I made sure I put everything back exactly as I'd found it. Not so much because I was worried Graham would realise I'd been in here, but because, well, I like to have a bit of respect for people's stuff. Most of my work is in other people's homes, so I get to see a lot of things even their best mates never see. Doesn't mean I have to trample all over it in hob-nailed boots, does it?

"Drawn a blank," I said, returning to the living room.

Phil stepped back from the bookshelf he'd been rifling through and rubbed the bridge of his nose. "How about in here?"

I listened. "Nope. Are we done here, then?"

Phil sighed. Then he nodded. "Have you had lunch yet?"

"No," I said cautiously. Was he about to ask me out?

Apparently he was. "Come for a pub lunch, and I'll fill you in about Melanie's boss."

I didn't get why he wanted to talk to me about the bloke— but sod it, I was hungry, and having a good-looking bloke sitting across the table from me has never been known to harm my appetite. Plus, I reckoned he owed me, after all that. "All right. Where did you have in mind?" We left the flat, Phil locking the door behind us, and clattered downstairs. Either all of Graham's neighbours were out, or none of them were curious enough to poke their heads out of their front doors to see what we were up to.

Phil shrugged. "There must be places in the village."

"Don't you know?" I frowned. "Are you still living around here?" I'd have thought we'd have bumped into each other *somewhere* before now, if he was. Up at the Dyke, if nowhere else.

"Just moved back to St Albans. I was in London before that."

"Oh? I'd have thought that'd be better for business, in your line of work. How come you moved back out to the sticks?"

His face went stonier than a brick wall. "Personal reasons." His tone said loud and clear, *Ask me at your peril.*

I managed not to roll my eyes like a teenager. "All right, keep your hair on. I'm not the one who makes a living poking his nose into other peoples' business. How about we try the Duck and Grouse? The Four Candles is all right, but the Duck and Grouse is more relaxed. And the food's cheaper."

"Fine. Your car or mine?"

"Why don't we both drive?"

"Got it in for the environment, have you?"

"Fine. Yours, then. I'll save my petrol as well as the planet."

It took all of two minutes to drive there and park in the little car park at the back of the pub. It was just down from the village primary school, and I could hear the shrieks of the kiddies in the playground as we got out of the car. Phil's head turned towards the sound, and I could have sworn he got a wistful look in his eye.

I thought about asking him if he was planning on having kids one day, but something told me it'd just piss him off. "Coming?" I said instead and led the way into the pub.

The Duck and Grouse in Brock's Hollow is a cosy sort of place. It dates from around Shakespeare's time, but bits have been added on or taken off in the centuries since then, so it looks more grown than built. Inside, there are ancient timbers and fireplaces, and the sort of red patterned carpet you only ever see in old pubs or your Gran's hallway. And they've got a pool table and Sky Sports, a definite improvement on Ye Goode Olde Days. It's a bloke's pub, I suppose. Even the girls who go regularly tend to be a bit laddish, although not in the Devil's Dyke sort of way. More in the getting pissed and showing your knickers sort of way.

And the food's decent, although if I kept on having pub lunches at this rate, I'd end up as soft as Gary, I thought ruefully as I ordered my fish and chips.

"Garden peas or mushy?" the girl asked in a perky voice.

"Mushy, please, love." I gave her a smile, which she returned, a pink tinge on her cheeks. I could practically hear Phil rolling his eyes behind me. I noticed she didn't smile as he ordered his steak-and-kidney pie.

We got our drinks—pint for Phil; Diet Coke for me—and pulled up a couple of stools around a wobbly table in the corner. Bloody awful sight lines for the telly, which meant we had a bit of privacy. "If that's what you're like with bar staff, I'd hate to see you with the bored housewives," Phil murmured, sounding amused.

"Oh, for—I only smiled at her." I folded up a beer mat and slipped it under a table leg. Perfect.

Phil paused for a moment, as if he wasn't sure whether to say it or not. "I think you underestimate the power of that smile."

"Yeah, well, maybe you should try it some time. Smiling, I mean," I added, in case he thought I was suggesting he tried my smile, not that I was actually sure what that would have meant in any case. Mostly because ninety percent of my brain was a bit preoccupied with the thought that Phil liked my smile. I coughed. "So come on, what was it you were going to tell me about?"

Phil reached into his jacket and drew out a small sheaf of papers. One of them was a photo, which he slid across the table to me. "That's him. Robin East. Manager of Village Properties."

The photo showed a man in his forties or so, his face turned away from the camera to give an excellent view of a classically handsome profile. "Nice," I said without thinking. I wasn't sure, but I think Phil might have tutted. "So this is the bloke Melanie went to meet that night?"

"Yeah. Except according to him, she didn't. He claims he didn't even call her."

"Can't the police check phone records and find out who called?"

Phil nodded. "They can. I can't." He looked down at his pint for a minute. "How good a mate of yours is Dave Southgate?"

Great. Bloody brilliant. "No."

"No, what?"

"No, I'm not going to do your sodding job for you. Dave's a mate. I'd like him to stay one. And hang on, didn't you used to be on the force anyhow? You must have friends there yourself." His jaw tightened, and I wondered if it was a sore point.

"I can get the information. But it'll take time—and it'll mean calling in favours. Would it kill you just to ask the bloke? For Graham, if not for me?"

I heaved a sigh and looked pointedly over at the bar. The sooner they served our food and I could eat it and get out, the better. "Fine. I'll try. But I'm not making any promises."

Phil nodded slowly. "Seeing anyone at the moment?"

I nearly spilled my Coke all down myself. "Jesus! Where the hell did that come from?"

He laughed, the bastard. "Just passing the time of day."

"I'll give you passing the time of day, you smug—" I didn't finish the insult, because our food arrived. "Cheers, love," I said instead. "That looks smashing. Got any ketchup?"

The waitress smiled and fetched a bottle of Heinz from the side. "Here you go. Enjoy your meal."

"I will, don't you worry." I watched her walk back to the bar with a spring in her step.

"Are you sure you're even gay?" Phil muttered, poking at his pie like he thought there might be a body hidden in it.

"There are other reasons to be nice to people than just because you want to get your leg over." I gave the ketchup bottle a hefty whack on the bum, and tried not to think about other sorts of red stuff.

Phil made a derisive sort of noise. "So, are you, anyway?"

I frowned. "What? Nice? Or hoping to get my leg over?"

"No, you— Are you seeing anyone?"

"Why do you care?" Did he care? Did I want him to? "No, as it happens."

He paused, a forkful of pie halfway to his mouth. "Not the relationship type?"

"Yeah, that's me. Shag a different bloke every night. And you know those porn clichés about the plumber turning up to give your pipes a good seeing to? They're all true, every one." I managed not to roll my eyes at him and jammed a forkful of fish in my gob.

"Still a touchy little sod, aren't you?" He sounded amused.

"Less of the little, if you don't mind." I raised an eyebrow deliberately. I wasn't sure Phil spoke innuendo.

His smile spread, so maybe he did understand me. "Why? It's true. You should put it on your business cards—*Tom Paretski, the pocket-sized plumber. No job too small.*"

"And again with the height jokes. What do you have on yours? *Phil Morrison, the muscle-bound moron?*"

"Now, come on—that's a poor effort. How about *Private Dick—the biggest in the business?*"

I grinned. "So is it, then?"

His turn to say, "What?"

"The biggest. Come to that, is it private, or can anyone apply?" I took another forkful of plaice.

Phil stared at me a bit too intently for comfort, his eyes dark and unreadable. For all the fish was melt-in-the-mouth tender, suddenly my throat was too dry to swallow it. I reached blindly for my drink, unable to break eye contact.

"They can apply," he said at last. "Doesn't mean they'll get the job." Then he bent his head to his pie and started chowing down like a champion.

Obviously we'd finished with the flirting part of the meal. I followed his example and chomped in silence. Well, it'd be a shame to let it get cold—the fish really was good.

"Why did you leave the force?" I asked after a while, when I'd begun to feel full but didn't quite want to stop eating yet. "Did the institutionalised homophobia get too much for you?" Although I couldn't imagine Phil taking any crap about his sexuality from anyone.

"Not exactly." He paused; decided it was safe to let me into the secret. "I'd always planned to go private. Just joined the force for the training."

"Sneaky."

"Sensible."

"That's my taxes paid for your training, though."

"You got six years out of me. I reckon it's a fair trade." He speared a carrot. "And how much tax do you ever pay, anyway? I'd have thought half your work was cash in hand."

"Doesn't mean I don't pay tax on it."

"I thought fiddling the tax man was one of the perks of the trade."

"Spoken like a true upholder of law and order. Although I suppose now you've gone private, you can afford to be a bit more flexible about that, can't you?"

"I've got my ethical standards, same as everyone. Are you done there?"

"Why, in a hurry, are you?" I looked at my plate. It still had some chips on it, but at least I'd eaten all my greens, Mum. "Yeah, I'm done." I supposed this was good-bye. Maybe I'd see him at Graham's sometime—I was definitely going to have to keep in touch with the poor sod. Someone needed to make sure he was eating right, that sort of thing. If they hadn't already locked him up and thrown away the key, that was.

"Good," Phil said, pushing back his chair and standing. "Come on, then—the estate agent's just down the road."

I did a double-take. "Hang on a minute—when did I become your unpaid assistant?" I had to hurry after him, the long-legged git. "What do you want me along for, anyhow?"

About to push the door open, Phil turned back to me. "Your van's up at Graham's. You're not seriously expecting me to take you back there and then come back down here, when the place is only yards down the road?"

Had he set this up? I sent him a suspicious look, but seeing as it only reached the back of his head as he set off down the hill without waiting for an answer, I might as well have saved myself the bother. Still, I wasn't exactly averse to spending a little more time in his company. If he could only keep his mouth shut, he'd be perfect. I smiled as I got a vivid image of Phil Morrison in my bed. Gagged.

"Something funny?" Bugger. He'd turned at just the wrong moment.

"Trust me, you don't want to know. This it, then?" We'd stopped outside the offices of Village Properties, which was next door to the Women's Institute shop. I could see hand-knitted dollies peeping coyly out from behind patchwork cushions and strange, vegetable-shaped ornaments in their window.

Phil, of course, didn't spare a glance for the ladies' handiwork, and pushed open the estate agent's door. I followed him in—and nearly tripped over the doormat when I saw the bloke at the desk. Bloody hell, that photo had done him no justice at all. He wasn't just *nice*; he was gorgeous.

Chapter Six

For a moment, I thought George Clooney must have decided to turn his back on the acting profession in favour of flogging houses to the middle classes. And while he was at it, turned the clock back fifteen or twenty years.

"Good afternoon," he greeted us in ringing, mellow tones.

"Hi," I said, giving a daft little wave like I was a geeky teenager with a crush. I think I even blushed. Phil stared at me for a moment, which helped to bring me back to earth.

"What can I help you with?" Cloney Clooney asked, rising from his seat and extending a hand. "I'm Robin East, delighted to meet you." He glanced shrewdly between me and Phil. "First house together, is it?"

If Phil had looked any stonier, Cock Robin would probably have taken his details and sold him to a family of four as a desirable property in need of some modernisation. "Mr. East, I was hoping I could ask you a few questions," he ground out while I stifled a laugh.

Gorgeous brown eyes narrowed, looking no less sexy for all that. George Clooney playing some kind of legal eagle; he could cross-examine me any time he wanted. "Press?"

"No. Private investigator." Phil handed him a card. "I'm looking into Melanie Porter's death."

Robin slumped back in his chair, looking genuinely troubled. "God, what a nightmare. Such a sweet girl—I can't believe anyone could do such a thing." Now he was back in the ER role, and a patient had just died despite all his efforts... I had to stop doing this, I told myself firmly. The bloke might be sex on legs, but he was probably straight and definitely a suspect.

"You saw her the night she died, didn't you?" The expressionless way Phil asked it sent shivers down my spine.

Robin's eyes widened. "No! No, as I told the police, that wasn't me. The phone call, that is. I was working late, yes, but I didn't call Melanie."

"So you were here alone?"

Was it my imagination, or did Robin's cheeks start doing a faint impression of his namesake's breast? "Yes, I'm afraid so. Quite alone."

"Make any phone calls at all?"

"Ah, no. Catching up on paperwork, I'm afraid." Robin fiddled distractingly with a pen on his desk. It was a Montblanc, which didn't surprise me; I'd seen the prices in the window on the way in.

Phil nodded; I wasn't sure what he was agreeing with. Maybe he just liked to nod at people he was interviewing, so they'd think he was on their side. "Did Melanie mention she was going out that night?"

"Not to me." He put the pen down very deliberately—sensible; you don't want to risk breaking a posh pen like that—but then his fingers started drumming on his stack of papers. I read the top one: *Exceptional living space and stunning views make this superb barn conversion...* I stopped reading before I could get to the price and have a heart attack.

"So who might she have talked to?"

Robin didn't look like he wanted to tell us, which seemed weird as he'd presumably gone through exactly the same thing with the police already. "Well...there's my secretary, of course."

"Then maybe we should talk to her?"

His lips thinned. "Of course. Pip?"

I started as a colourless shape I'd been vaguely aware of at the corner of my field of view unfolded itself from a desk in the corner and walked towards us.

"This is Pip Cox, my secretary. Pip, this is Mr. Morrison, a private investigator, and..?" He looked at me expectantly.

"Tom Paretski. Plumber." I thought, what the hell, and handed her a card. "Call me any time. No job too small," I added, mainly for Phil's benefit. I smiled, but she didn't return it—just ducked her head, hiding beneath a fringe of hair. Pip Cox? Anyone less like an apple it was hard to imagine. She was tall to the point of awkwardness—she had a good eight inches on me, and she wasn't wearing heels—and bone-thin, with worried brown eyes and shoulder-length, unflatteringly cut mouse-brown hair. She wore a flared skirt, blouse and cardigan that looked like they belonged to her gran and did nothing for her face or her figure.

"Miss Cox?" Phil said politely. "Is there anything you can tell us about that day?

Her thin fingers played with a spot on the edge of her cardi she'd half worried into a hole already. "Not really," she said in a voice I had to strain to hear, her eyes fixed on the carpet. "Melanie just said she'd be having a night in. With Graham."

"She specifically mentioned that to you?"

Pip nodded.

"Did she sound like she was looking forward to it?"

Another nod.

"Graham mentioned she'd been working late a lot recently," Phil said, obviously trying to coax her out of her shell a bit.

"Well, of course," Robin butted in. "We've been extremely busy. There's a mini-boom going on at the moment, and with the new school being built—well, it's a seller's market." Not to mention, an estate agent's one, I thought. He must have been doing very nicely indeed on the commission.

Phil glared at him briefly. When he turned back to Pip, he softened his expression with what looked like a painful effort. "Have you had to work late as well, then?"

She seemed a bit flustered by his sympathetic tone. "I— well, no, not really—I mean, I don't—my husband doesn't like it if I—" She was married? I glanced at her hands, and sure enough, there was a ring. I couldn't believe I'd missed it. I imagined some IT nerd with a beard and glasses, and wondered if they ever had sex or if they just played Minecraft and Skyrim together.

"Pip doesn't show properties," Robin interrupted. "So she works mainly nine to five."

She sent him a grateful smile, and just for a second, her face was transformed. She looked almost pretty, and suddenly it wasn't such a stretch to imagine her married.

"It must have been pretty rough on you," I said. "Losing a friend like that. Was Melanie the only other girl in the office?"

Pip darted a glance my way and nodded.

"Did you see a lot of her outside work?" I continued, seeing as Phil seemed content to let me do the talking for a bit.

This time she shook her head. "Not really. She was always busy."

"With Graham?"

"And the church stuff, of course."

"Oh, yeah? Didn't know Graham and Melanie were religious. He's changed a bit since we were at school, then."

She gave a wary smile. "I don't think—I mean, I don't know... I think it was just Mel. She felt sorry for Mrs. Reece."

I frowned. "Mrs. Reece...?"

"The parish administrator. Except she's been ill lately, and her husband, of course... That's why Mel was filling in for her."

I nodded. It must be catching. "Must have made it hard for the poor girl to fit in a social life. Did she ever talk about going out? With or without Graham?"

Pip bit her lip. "Sometimes. Well, she had her regular things—prayer group on Wednesdays, Salsacise on Thursdays, and French class on...Mondays, I think. Yes, Mondays. When she wasn't working, that is. And she and Graham always went to her mum's for Sunday lunch."

Bloody hell, no wonder Graham had been pissed off about her going out the night she died. From the sound of it, it must have been their first night in together in a month of Sundays. Of course, if she *had* been seeing someone else, any or all of these hobbies would have made an excellent cover.

"Did you go to any of these activities with her?" Phil asked. Maybe he'd had the same thought as me.

Pip jumped. Maybe she'd forgotten he was there—although how anyone could overlook his brooding, monolithic presence was beyond me. "I—oh, no. I mean... Well, I did go to Salsacise once, but... My husband..." She stared down at her feet.

Okay, this was the second time she'd mentioned the husband not liking her going out at night. My mental image of the nerd was replaced by a beer-swilling, unshaven Neanderthal who thought a woman's place was in the home and wasn't afraid to say so. "You should tell him to make his own tea for once, love," I said. She flicked me a shy smile but didn't reply.

When Phil didn't jump in, I carried on. "I think poor old Graham had to fend for himself a fair bit. Did Melanie ever give you the impression things weren't going too well between them?"

"No—well, she talked sometimes about how frustrated he was getting, looking for work. But I always thought..." She broke off and looked up at me. "You just don't know, though. You might think you do, but you never really know what it's like. A relationship, I mean. Only the people in it know. People are different, when it's just the two of them."

Phil stirred. "Pip, do you think Graham killed Melanie?"

"I don't want to think so," she whispered.

It wasn't exactly the resounding denial we'd been hoping for.

"I knew you'd be a natural at this," Phil said as the door closed behind us.

"What? I didn't find anything in there." Actually, I hadn't even looked. I'd got a bit distracted, first by Cloney Clooney, and then—in a totally different way, I hasten to add—by Pip.

"That's not what I mean. You really got that girl to open up to you."

I shrugged. "All I did was have a chat with her."

"Exactly," Phil said. We crossed the road to head up past the church. "You know how to talk to women." Then he frowned. "I'd have been wondering if you'd suddenly come over all straight, if you hadn't stood there for the first ten minutes with your mouth hanging open, begging Robin East to fill it with his dick." His voice was a low growl as we walked around the Duck and Grouse to the car park.

I just laughed, which seemed to piss him off even more. He certainly slammed his car door a bit harder than necessary. I got in the passenger seat and closed my door with a more reasonable amount of force. "Well, come on—the bloke's gorgeous, isn't he? I wouldn't say no."

"That's the sort of bloke you go for, is it? Smarmy gits flashing their money and their dicks at anyone stupid enough to be impressed?"

"Jealous, are we?"

"You wish." Phil yanked the car viciously into gear and zoomed out of the car park, narrowly missing a Tesco's lorry on the roundabout.

"Steady on—we don't all have a death wish," I muttered. "What did your last passenger die of?"

He didn't answer, and when I glanced over, I saw his knuckles were white on the wheel. Bloody hell, had I hit a nerve? Guilt twisted in my stomach. "So, er, do you like being back around here?" I asked quickly. "Glad you moved?"

The tension eased by about a millibar. "It's all right."

"All right? You've got the whole of Herts on your doorstep, here. If it's good enough for Posh and Becks—"

"Thought they moved to LA."

"Minor detail. They've been seen in one of the restaurants in Brock's Hollow, you know—I won't say seen *eating*, as this is Victoria Beckham we're talking about."

"Good, are they?"

I assumed he meant the village eateries, not the Beckhams. "Not bad. And there's hundreds of places in St Albans and Harpenden too." I ought to get commission from the local chamber of commerce.

Phil nodded, was silent a moment—and then we were back on Graham's estate and pulling up behind my van.

"Thanks for the lift," I said as he parked.

Phil nodded again; any more of this and I'd be expecting him to start going, *Oh, yes-yes-yes,* like the bloody Churchill dog. "How much do you charge?" he asked abruptly.

"Why? Got some pipes you need cleared out?" I leered, but he didn't answer, so I sighed and told him my rates.

"I'm going to Robin East's house tomorrow—got an appointment with his wife. I want you to come along and do your stuff. The mystic crap, that is, not charm the pants off her."

"What, right in front of her?"

"Use your head. You can make an excuse halfway through—say you need a leak or something—and check the place out while I keep her busy."

"Right. Because that couldn't possibly go wrong."

"Come on—what's the worst that can happen? She gets pissed off and throws us out, that's all. No skin off your pretty little nose."

What? "Did you just call me pretty? *Pretty?*"

"Strike a nerve, did it? Sorry. I meant to say, your rugged, manly little nose."

"Arse."

"All right, you've got a rugged, manly little arse too. Happy?"

I had to laugh. "You want to watch that. If you keep complimenting my arse, I'm going to think you're coming on to me."

Phil didn't answer, so I glanced his way. He was staring straight ahead, the smile he'd worn for our banter vanished.

Right. I sighed. Obviously, he'd just remembered who he was talking to. "There's no need to panic; I'm not going to throw a hissy fit if you don't turn up with a bunch of flowers next time and swear eternal love." I opened the door, got out of the car. "See you around."

I didn't slam the door shut. I knew I was just being stupid, getting pissed off about it. I should have known I'd always be scrawny little *Poofski* to Phil bloody Morrison. My hip ached as I walked the few steps to my van. I rubbed it, cursing under my breath. It wasn't as if I needed any more reminders just what a twat I was being. Phil Morrison come on to me?

I'd have more chance with Dave Southgate.

I gave Dave a ring when I got home from work. It'd been a frustrating afternoon of parts that hadn't turned up and fittings that didn't—fit, that was. I was planning to ask him if he fancied going for a pint, but when he picked up, I could tell from the laughter and the clinking of glasses in the background he'd beaten me to it. "All right, Tom?"

"Yeah, I'm good," I said, speaking up so he could hear me over the din. "Where are you?"

"Down the Goat with a couple of lads from the station. Want to join us?"

Not a lot, as it happened. Dave's a good bloke, but coppers en masse are not exactly my favourite drinking buddies. Just imagine a gang of unreconstructed Phil Morrisons, only without the looks, and with the force of law to back up their bigotry. Maybe I'm maligning our gallant boys in blue, but I'd seen the looks they'd thrown me up on Nomansland Common. Psychic and a poof—not a popular combination with that lot. "Tell you what, Dave—you eaten yet?"

"Not as such," he said, which I took to mean he'd had a packet of crisps and some pork scratchings, but nothing with any actual nutritional value. He sounded a bit cautious. Bloody hell, not another one scared I was going to swoon embarrassingly at his feet.

"Don't worry, I'm not inviting you out for a candlelit dinner for two. Just wondered if you fancied grabbing a bite somewhere. I can't be arsed to cook tonight."

"Yeah, why not? How about the White Hart? This lot'll be buggering off home to their wives soon enough." Bit of a sore point for Dave, seeing as Mrs. Southgate had done some buggering off herself six months previously, saying she needed to redefine herself now the kids had left home. I had a vague idea the current definition involved her old personal trainer, who was ten years younger than Dave and about twenty years fitter.

"Sounds good. See you there in half an hour—just got to feed the cats." Merlin was currently doing his best to make sure I didn't forget, winding himself in and out of my legs as if he wanted to tie them in Shibari knots. Arthur, true to form, was sitting regally on the sofa, front paws folded, but he was giving me a mean stare.

The White Hart is an old coaching inn on Holywell Hill, just opposite St Albans Abbey. It's all Ye Olde black beams in a white front, and oak panelled inside. Gives it a cosy feel, although the suit of armour by the door is a bit naff. I don't go in there a lot, and as I pushed open the door from the car park, I remembered why. Definite bad vibes, although they were old and weak. I tamped down hard on my spidey-senses and wondered if I was feeling things more because I'd been deliberately trying to lately.

Then again, the place has a reputation for being haunted. Maybe my psychic so-called gifts were diversifying.

Dave was already there, perched on one of the stools at the bar like Humpty Dumpty about to come a cropper. He hailed me with a wave. "Tom! What are you having?"

"Pint of bitter—cheers, mate. You ordered your food yet?"

"No, I was waiting for you. I'm having the steak-and-mushroom pie."

I quite fancied the roast-pumpkin risotto, but I knew Dave would think that was poncey, so I told the bloke behind the bar, "Make that two." I'd be the same size as Dave if I didn't watch out.

We paid our money and took our drinks over to a table by the window, next to a shelf of books. The inn still operates as a hotel, so I guessed they were there for the benefit of the guests. I picked up one that had an interesting title, *The Archangel and the White Hart.* I thought maybe it was about religious apparitions at the inn, and might explain the vibes I kept feeling, but it turned out to be an anthology by a local writers' group. "Bit too literary for me, that," I muttered, putting it down again quickly. "So come on, Dave, what's got you in a bad mood? Is it the Melanie Porter case?"

From the way he was chugging down his beer, I guessed it was his third or fourth already. "God, I hope your day's been better than mine. We had the boyfriend in for questioning again today. Useless little tosser."

"Oh, yeah?" I tried not to sound too interested, or too pissed off on Graham's behalf. "Still not admitting to it, then?"

Dave took another swig of his beer, then wiped his mouth with the back of his hand. "Thing is, I'm starting to think he didn't do it. Talk about not doing yourself any favours, though.

If it did go to trial, a jury would convict him soon as look at him."

"How do you mean?"

"Well, there he is—supposedly the bereaved lover, innocent of all wrong-doing, et cetera, et cetera. Will he let us search his bleeding flat without a warrant? Will he, my arse. So we have to make it all official, and we take him in to the station so he can't clear the place out while they dot all the bloody *i*'s and cross all the sodding *t*'s, and what do we find at the end of it? Not so much as a dodgy cigarette."

My beer curdled in my stomach. Bloody hell. Phil and I had done Graham more of a favour than we'd known. Thank God we'd got well away from the place before Dave and the boys in blue turned up, warrant in hand.

Dave belched. "Saw your van parked up on the estate—you working up there today?"

"Yeah—just a couple of taps," I lied, feeling like a total wanker.

"Don't suppose you get the big money jobs around there," Dave commiserated.

If he ever found out about me and Phil removing evidence, I'd be in deep shit, and I'd deserve it too. "So, er, what happened about this phone call you told me about?" I asked quickly—then uncertainty twisted in my guts. He had told me that, hadn't he? Christ on a crutch, I was crap at this. It was hard enough remembering not to let on I was a friend of Graham's. "Does that back up the boyfriend's story?"

"Yeah." Dave put down his pint. We were silent a moment as the food arrived and we got busy with knives, forks and a shed-load of salt and vinegar for the chips. "Now," Dave continued around his first mouthful of pie. "I did *not* tell you this, mind—but there was a phone call, all right. From the phone box in the village—you know, the one behind the church. And who the hell uses phone boxes these days? I'll tell you who." He wagged a chip at me. "People up to no good, that's who. Means we're dealing with premeditation, here, not just some poor bastard losing his rag."

"So it couldn't have been Graham," I said, relieved—and nearly choked on my next chip as I realised mid-swallow I'd called him by name.

Luckily, Dave didn't seem to have noticed. "Maybe. Maybe. Or maybe he set that up—got a mate to call."

"That'd mean someone else running around who knows he killed her—if he did, I mean. Why would he want to take that risk? You've got to admit, it's a bit of a favour to ask—*'scuse, mate, mind helping me out with a murder?*"

Dave laughed. "You'd think so, wouldn't you? You'd be bloody amazed at what some of these addicts are willing to get up to, though." He finished his pint. "Same again?"

"Nah, my shout." I was only halfway through my drink, and I was a bit pissed off I'd have to let my food go cold while I went up to the bar, but manners is manners. Luckily, I didn't have to wait to be served—there was hardly anyone else in tonight. I hoped the place did a bit better out of the hotel than they did out of the bar.

Dave gave my lime and soda a dirty look when I put it on the table next to his pint. "What the hell's this? Are you on a diet or something?"

"Got to drive home, haven't I? I don't want to get on the wrong side of the law."

He laughed again. "Yeah, some of those coppers are right bastards. Cheers. Hey, hang on—isn't it time for the match? Oi, Jon," he called to the barman. "You want to switch that telly on so we can watch Spurs getting their arses kicked?"

We didn't talk about the case anymore, which was probably just as well. Dave's drinking slowed down a bit too, which I was equally relieved about. The poor sod was already a heart attack waiting to happen; he didn't need liver failure on top.

We stayed for the match, had a few more drinks, and then I offered Dave a lift home. I dropped him off just as he was getting to the emotional stage. "Y're a good mate, Tom," he slurred, fumbling in his pocket for his door key. "Even—'scuse me—for a poofter. Don't care what anyone says; you're all right by me."

"Thanks, Dave," I said, secure in the knowledge he was too far gone to recognise sarcasm. I went in with him and made sure he had a pint of water to drink; then I legged it before he started telling me he loved me. I was pretty sure our friendship wouldn't survive something that traumatic.

When I got home myself, the cats showed how much they'd missed me by royally ignoring me for the rest of the evening. And a text turned up from Phil, saying he'd pick me up tomorrow at nine a.m. Assuming that meant to go and see Mrs. East, rather to take me out for a cappuccino and a croissant, I texted back, *OK* and went to bed.

I'd like to say I slept the deep sleep of the just, but in fact I kept waking up from nasty little dreams of an upset Dave accusing me of cheating on him with Phil.

Chapter Seven

When Phil turned up next morning, Merlin gave him a hero's welcome, winding round and round his ankles. You'd have thought he'd turned up with a crate of tuna and a can opener. Maybe Merlin just really liked Phil's shoes. They looked like quality—ordinary tan lace-ups, but with the sort of no-styling styling you only get on posh shoes. "Nice shoes," I said, nodding at them.

"Thanks." He looked down at my feet and smirked. "Are you going out in those?"

"Are you dissing my slippers?" They were great hairy brown bear's-feet ones Gary had bought me for Christmas. Complete with fake claws.

"Would I? Just thought it might be a bit hard for the witness to concentrate on her story if you walk in looking like you just trod in a couple of furry animals."

"That's the idea—put her off guard. Lull her into a false— 'scuse me," I stifled a yawn. "Sense of security. Fancy a coffee before we go?"

Phil looked at his watch. "It'll have to be instant."

"I can do instant." I led the way into the kitchen, and he leaned on the counter while I clinked around with mugs, spoons and the coffee jar. "I saw Dave Southgate last night," I said, as I dived into the fridge for the milk. "Asked about your phone call. He said it came from the phone box behind the church."

Phil didn't answer immediately, so when I stood, I glanced back at him. If I'd thought he'd been ignoring me, I'd been wrong. He was looking straight at me. "Thanks," he said, then ducked his head and rubbed his neck with one hand, in a way that really showed off the bulkiness of his arms and shoulders but at the same time, made him look almost vulnerable. It did weird things in the pit of my stomach. "I shouldn't have asked you to do that. I know he's a mate of yours."

I passed him his mug, feeling awkward. "It's all right. He was a bit pissed last night anyhow—I doubt he'll even remember I asked. Wife's left him, poor bastard," I added, because I didn't want him thinking Dave was some kind of alcoholic.

Phil gave a bitter kind of laugh. "Marriage, eh? Sometimes I wonder why anyone ever bothers."

Samantha East, it turned out when we got to her and Robin's house, was slim, blonde, beautiful—and on a mission to prove Phil's cynicism about marriage was well-founded. She opened the door dressed for some kind of fitness class, but she had on a full face of expertly applied makeup and her hair looked like it'd just been blow-dried. She looked down her no doubt professionally sculpted little nose at Phil and me like we were something the cat had sicked up on the mat.

"Mr. Morrison, is it? You didn't say there would be more than one of you."

"This is Tom Paretski," Phil said in his polite voice, the one he never bothered to use when he was talking to me. "He's an associate."

Great. Now we sounded like the Home Counties branch of the Mob. Not that anyone was ever going to take me for the hired muscle. "Pleased to meet you, Mrs. East." I gave her a smile and held out a hand, both of which she pointedly ignored.

"I suppose you'd better come in. Please wipe your feet; the cleaner's just been."

We dutifully shuffled about on the doormat, then trooped into what her husband would probably describe as an extremely well-appointed country residence; price upon request. She led us through an expensively tiled hallway and into a large, airy kitchen, also tiled. I could only conclude she didn't trust us with the soft furnishings.

"Please sit."

We pulled out high-backed wooden chairs from the rustic kitchen table and sat, like the good little doggies we were. As she sat across from us, I looked around. There was a coffee grinder, an espresso machine, and, sitting on the Aga, a posh stovetop kettle with a little birdie on the spout that probably added fifty quid to the price. She still didn't bother offering us a drink.

Phil cleared his throat. "Mrs. East, we just need to ask you a few questions—"

She cut him off. "I suppose you want to hear all about my husband's affair with that little *tart* from the office?" she said, an ugly curl to her lip.

Phil tensed next to me. It was probably the effort of keeping himself from leaping up and punching the air. Even I felt a sort of frisson at this confirmation of what we'd barely suspected— although it was tainted with disappointment on Graham's behalf. All right, so I'd never met the girl, but still, I'd expected better from Melanie. "By which you mean Miss Porter?" Phil asked.

"God, I should hope so. Have you *seen* that scarecrow of a secretary of his? Although he's probably screwing her too—and God knows, I'm sure she'd be pathetically grateful."

"You're certain about this?" Phil asked, leaning forward on the table.

She leaned back, away from him, as if he had raging halitosis and/or the plague. I considered belching loudly just for fun but decided Phil would be more pissed off than she would be. And after all, he was paying for my time here.

Actually, come to think of it, I should probably start earning my keep. "Mrs. East?" I said with my best smile. "Do you mind if I use your loo?"

Mrs. E. looked briefly horrified, so I turned up the smile a bit. "Don't worry—I promise to flush. And wash my hands afterwards." She went a bit pink under her blusher.

"Of course. It's, ah, through the hall, back towards the stairs."

"Oh, I'll find it. I'm good at finding things." I winked, and her expensively pumped-up breasts heaved as she took a deep breath. Result. Bloody hell, though—no wonder Cock Robin had been playing away from home if she was like this with him. I frowned to myself. Or had he? We only had her word for it, and personally, I'd trust that woman's word about as far as I could throw her house.

Which reminded me—I was supposed to be searching the place. I stood still, listening.

Weird.

I could feel the water in the plumbing, of course—but apart from that, nothing. Not a peep.

I found the loo and took a quick peek in the cistern, but all I found was one of those tablets that turns the water blue.

Treading as silently as I could, I crept to the stairs. Once I got there, it was a lot easier to be quiet, as the carpet had the sort of pile you don't so much walk on as hack your way through with a machete. I padded upstairs and tried again with the *mystic crap*, as Phil had put it.

Still nothing.

This was *really* weird. Everyone hides stuff. *Everyone.* Frowning, I pushed open the nearest door and found myself in what looked like the spare bedroom. It was nicely decorated; the bed was made up—but there were no signs that anyone actually lived in it. No half-drunk glasses of water on the bedside table; no rolled-up socks peeking out from under the bed. No vibes, either. I tiptoed out again and went next door.

This room was clearly the master bedroom—or rather, the mistress bedroom, although only in the lady-of-the-house sense. It was still unfeasibly tidy, but there were discreetly expensive pots of face cream on the dressing table, and a bonkbuster by the bed. Well, clearly Mrs. E had to get her kicks between the pages, as I could tell at a glance she wasn't letting poor old Cock Robin in here to give them to her between the sheets. Still no vibes, though, which was weird. The top drawer of the bedside cabinet was open a couple of inches, so I pulled it out the rest of the way, boggled briefly at the variety of sex toys carelessly scattered inside, and shut it again. Didn't she hide *anything*?

I was going to have to hurry up, I reminded myself. I gave up on Mrs. E as a bad job and went looking for where her husband slept. I found it at the other end of the corridor, a boxy little room with a tiny window looking out over the road; clearly Robin thought getting as far away as possible from his lady wife was far more important than having room to swing a cat in.

If this was how the other half lived, I didn't rate it.

Robin's room was the most lived-in one in the house—but even there, I felt nothing. *Nothing.* And that really was odd, because I'd have sworn blind he had secrets. Maybe he'd found somewhere else to keep them. I took a quick look in his drawers, but all I found were neatly paired socks. Not even any porn. Which, to my mind, was the strongest argument yet he was having an affair. Either that or he was a eunuch.

So the question was, where did he keep all his dirty little secrets? I rubbed my chin. He was an estate agent—how hard could it have been for him to set up some little love nest for him and Melanie, or whoever the lucky lady was. He wouldn't even have to buy a place—just set up a rental lease with a fictitious client for an absentee landlord.

When I got back downstairs, Phil and Mrs. E. were standing by the kitchen door—obviously I'd cut it a bit fine getting back. "You were a long time," she challenged me, the previous glow in her cheeks now frozen out of existence.

"Sorry, love," I said with a grimace, rubbing my tummy. "Bit too much of the old Ruby Murray last night. Probably best if you give it ten minutes before you go in there. Still, squirt a bit of air freshener and it'll be right as rain. Are we done here, Phil?"

He nodded, his lips pressed together like he was trying not to laugh. "We're done."

We left her standing there. She didn't look half as pretty with that sour look on her face.

"What did you find?" Phil asked as we drove away.

"Well, she's not human, and he's hiding stuff, but not here. So in other words, bugger all."

Phil swore. "Nothing at all?"

I shrugged. "They're not sleeping together, her and Cock Robin. He dosses in the box room, and she makes her own entertainment with a couple of mechanical friends." Phil snorted a laugh. "So chances are she wasn't telling porkies about him having it off with the staff."

"All of them? Or just Melanie?"

"We don't know it was her." Okay, so maybe I'd only met her the once, and that not exactly socially—what with her being dead and all—but I felt a bit defensive of poor Melanie. It wasn't like she could speak up for herself. "It could have been anyone, not just people at the office. For fuck's sake, it could have been Graham."

"In your dreams, Paretski."

"What?" I'd had as many sexual fantasies as the next man, but sex involving Graham didn't exactly make my top ten. It didn't even make the top ten thousand.

Phil wrenched the wheel around, taking a corner a bit faster than he needed to. "You just want East to swing both ways because you're desperate for him to swing in your direction."

I cocked my head to one side like I was considering it. "Well, I wouldn't kick him out of bed. I mean, come on, he's pretty bloody gorgeous."

"He's a slimy git who cheats on his wife."

"Yeah, but who can blame him?"

"A vow's a vow." Phil's jaw was set.

"Oh, for—you didn't see those rooms. Maybe they made the vows, but you can't tell me what they've got is a marriage. It's a sham. And she doesn't give a toss who knows it."

"I don't give a monkey's. They made their vows; they should stick to them."

"Says the bloke who's never made that kind of promise in his life." When did Phil turn into a bloody Victorian moralist?

"You don't know fuck all about me, Paretski, so get off your fucking high horse and shove it up your—"

"You can turn here," I interrupted. "And I don't think what you were about to say is anatomically possible. It's certainly not legal. Chill, all right?" What the hell was wrong with him all of a sudden? Had the steroids just kicked in or something?

Phil turned into Hatfield Road, crawled along with the Fleetville traffic for a few minutes, then took the left into Regal Road and drew up outside my house. He wasn't ranting anymore, but I didn't think he was all that chilled, either. The handbrake made a painful sound when he pulled it up sharply, and I couldn't help wincing in sympathy. He reached awkwardly into his back pocket.

"Forget the fee," I said. "I didn't find anything, did I?"

"I said I'd pay you for your time."

"Don't be daft."

"I'm not being *daft*; I'm honouring the agreement we made." He pulled out a handful of twenties and thrust them in my direction.

For fuck's sake, were we going to have a row about him paying me, now? I put up a hand. "Keep it, all right? You wouldn't pay an informant who didn't bloody inform, would you? And anyway, we're doing this for Graham. Just...buy me a drink sometime, or something." I hesitated, while Phil slowly put the money back in his pocket. "Who's next on the list?"

"What list?"

"You must have other people you want to talk to." How long had he been in this business? "So you'll be wanting me along for all the *mystic crap*."

He stared at me, and then he laughed like he couldn't help himself.

"What?" I wasn't going to let him disarm me so easily.

Probably.

Phil was still chuckling. "The next one's going to love you and your bloody witchcraft. He's the vicar."

I was about to make some crack about us going to see the vicar like a loved-up couple arranging their wedding, but then I thought Phil might flip out again if I mentioned marriage, and I was kind of liking him in cheerful mode, so I just mumbled something noncommittal.

He leaned back in his seat, obviously taking my mutterings as a sign I wanted to know more. "Remember what Pip Cox said about Melanie filling in for the parish administrator? Got me thinking. Say Robin East *didn't* call her that night. Who else might she have referred to as *the boss*?"

"Nice. All right—you've sold me on it. So when are we dropping in to take tea with the vicar? Can't go tomorrow—Sunday's his busy day."

Phil nodded. "I'll have to give him a call, make an appointment. I'll let you know."

"Okay." I hesitated. "Do you want to come in for a bit?"

He looked at me for a moment, and I'd swear he was tempted—either to take me up on the invitation, or to ask, *for a bit of what?* But then he shook his head.

"Sorry. Things to do. But I'll try and fix the vicar up for early next week, all right?"

"Long as you give me enough notice so I can do a bit of juggling. And if you need me for anything, you've got my number."

He smiled. "And you've got mine. Take care, Tom."

I met up with Gary at the Dyke again that night. I could tell something had happened the minute I set eyes on him—he was, as they say, all a-twitter. And I don't mean he was tapping 140-character pearls of wisdom and/or cattiness into his iPhone.

"Tom! Darling—come and give me a kiss." He proffered his cheek.

I gave him my best impersonation of a blushing virgin. "But Gary—this is all so sudden. I don't know what to say..."

He tutted. "Well, in that case, just sit that luscious little bottom on the chair, here. I have news, my dear. Wonderful, wonderful news. I'm in love!"

I sat and pulled up a beer mat for my pint next to Gary's vodka martini (stirred, not shaken). "Okay, this really is sudden. Who's the lucky bloke? I take it it's a bloke, and you've not started cheating on Julian with another dog?"

"As if I would! He's a greengrocer. A market trader, I should say, shouldn't I, Julian?" Gary ruffled his dog's fur. "He's got a stall in St Albans market. That's where we met, just this afternoon." He fluttered his eyelashes—Gary, that is, not the dog. "He asked if I'd like to feel his plums—well, I could hardly say no, could I?"

"No, I don't suppose you could," I said with resignation. "So how were they? Firm and juicy?"

"Oh yes, and delicious." It was a toss-up as to who was drooling more—Gary or his dog.

I gave Julian's fur a ruffle around his ears, and his eyes closed in doggy bliss. "So how come you're here with me, rather than feeling up this bloke's cucumber?"

"More of a vegetable marrow, actually." Gary smirked, then pouted. "I'm not seeing him until tomorrow. Well, I didn't want to come on *too strong*."

"Who, you?" I said innocently. "Surely not. So, when do I get to meet Mr. Perfect?"

"Next week, if you like. You can come and see him in his element." Gary took a sip of his martini and gave a happy sigh, his eyes closed. Just for a moment, he was the spitting image of his dog.

"You mean on his stall?"

"Isn't that what I said?" Gary picked up the cocktail stick with the olive on from his drink and waggled it at me. "Now, how about you, sweetie? Had any more blonds for breakfast?" He sucked the olive off the stick suggestively.

"I wish," I muttered. "I'm thinking of becoming a Trappist monk—I've heard they get more action than I do."

"Oh?" Gary's eyebrow did its best to chase after his receding hairline. "That's not what I've heard. *I* heard you've been spending a great deal of quality time with a rather magnificent specimen of *homo blondus*. Even," and he leaned forward so far he practically did a nosedive into my pint, "looking at houses together."

I had to laugh. God, Phil would throw a wobbly if he knew we'd been spotted together and Conclusions Had Been Drawn. "Sorry, Gary, but you'd be a bit previous buying a hat for the wedding. That was the bloke who's looking into Melanie Porter's death, and we went into the estate agent's to talk to her boss."

"We? Branched out into the Nosey Parker business, have you? So how much would you charge me for a really thorough investigation? Leaving no stone unturned, and poking into all my little nooks and crannies?"

I put on a phoney Sam Spade accent. "For a good-looking dame like you, five hundred dollars a day, plus expenses. Cheap at half the price," I added in my normal voice. "Nah, this is just a one-off. Phil reckoned he could use my unusual talents." I did the air-quotes thing.

"So go on, tell me about this *Phil.*"

I shrugged. "Nothing to tell, really. He got hired by Melanie's parents, and I'm helping him out."

"On a strictly professional basis? Or is *helping him out* the new euphemism?"

I wish. "Told you, Gary, there's nothing to tell."

"Straight, is he? Never mind, darling—just flash him one of your cheeky smiles, and you'll soon have him joining the sisterhood and eating out of your underpants."

"Sounds a bit gross, that. And what sisterhood would that be?"

"Sisters of Sodom, of course, what else?" Gary beamed. "I've got that on a T-shirt somewhere."

"Yeah, well, he's already a member, as it happens." Although I couldn't see Phil wearing the T-shirt any time soon. "But it's strictly business, me and him."

"For God's sake, Tom, why? From what I've heard, he's *edible.*"

"We were at school together," I reminded him with a sigh.

"Oh—say no more." Gary rested a commiserating hand on my knee and stared into his cocktail for a moment. "If I ever see anyone I was at school with, I run and hide. Force of habit, really. Let's just say it was obvious from a *very* early age the only female heart I'd ever break would be my mother's." He looked up, brightening. "Still, if there were two of you—"

"There weren't. I mean, he wasn't out, back then. Course, I never meant to be, either. But it wasn't exactly a bonding experience, put it that way."

"Let me guess—he joined in the bullying in self-defence?"

"Something like that." I found I was rubbing my hip, so I reached for my pint quickly to give my hand something less revealing to do.

Unfortunately Gary's got a keen pair of eyes on him. "Sweetie..."

I managed half a smile. "Look, just leave it, all right? Water under the bridge and all that."

Gary nodded. "Ooh—did I ever tell you about the time I had sex under a bridge? Mortifying, it was—absolutely *mortifying*..."

And he was off, into a story involving an improbably endowed bloke whose wife drifted along in a narrowboat at the worst possible moment.

Good old Gary. If I ever need cheering up, he's my man.

I spent Sunday doing the shopping, hoovering cat hair off the sofa, and not thinking about Phil. I didn't think about him at Tesco's, when I was staring at their Buy One Get One Free offer on sirloin steak and wondering if I should invite someone round to share it with me. I didn't think about him when I was watching telly in the evening and reflecting that a cat on your lap was all very well, but nothing beat a strong pair of arms wrapped around you. And I definitely didn't think about Phil when I was in the shower, or later when I was in bed, my hand creeping down to my groin...

Nope.

Didn't think about Phil Morrison at all.

Chapter Eight

We went to see Reverend Lewis mid-afternoon on Monday, which I guessed must be his quiet time—after all, you hear about morning prayers and evening prayers, but you never hear anything about afternoon prayers, do you? Maybe the man upstairs likes a nap after lunch.

Like the vicarage he lived in, the Reverend Lewis was tall, austere, and looked like he'd been constructed sometime during the reign of Queen Victoria. Not that he was old—I put him in his early thirties, tops, with his washed-out blond hair and thin, ferrety features. But he somehow didn't seem to fit in the modern world—like he'd be horrified if a girl showed her ankles in front of him, or if anybody swore. He offered us each a limp hand to shake and invited us in. The air inside the vicarage was chilly and damp, which was one way it made a change from the vicar himself. His handshake had been unpleasantly warm and damp.

"Do come this way," he said, ushering us into a front room I guessed had been decorated by the previous reverend's wife—it was all chintzy floral patterns, now faded in parts, and tasselled ties holding back the curtains. This Rev, Phil had told me on the way over, was unmarried. Looking at him, it was hardly surprising. I don't expect my blokes to have film-star looks, but I do like them to have at least a nodding acquaintance with a shampoo bottle, and I'm fairly sure most women would agree.

"Can I get you a cup of coffee? Tea?" At least he had better manners than Samantha East, but then I supposed it sort of went with the job.

"Coffee would be lovely. White, no sugar, ta." I sat down on the sofa, leaned back and crossed my ankle over my knee.

Maybe the Rev had had a big lunch and was feeling a bit dozy this afternoon—he just carried on looking at me for a moment, then jumped when Phil spoke. Loudly.

"I'll have a cup of tea, thanks."

Rev Lewis blinked and turned a bit pink. "Ah. Yes. Of course." He scurried off down the hall.

I looked at Phil; he nodded, so I started listening for vibes. "Nothing here," I murmured after a moment. "But something's definitely calling me upstairs."

"Okay—give it ten minutes or so, then make your excuses."

"You do realise half the bloody village is going to end up thinking I've got incontinence issues, don't you?" I muttered.

Phil laughed. "Bit sad, really—a plumber having problems with his pipes."

"You're all sympathy, aren't you?"

Rev Lewis scuttled back in, carrying three mismatched mugs on a scratched tray with a picture of a fluffy kitten on it. I was a bit disappointed not to see something more overtly religious, but on the other hand, one of the mugs was printed with ~~Coffee~~ *Jesus Makes the World Go Round.* "Here we are. Now, what did you want to ask me, ah, Phil?"

As Phil leaned forward, looking all intent and business-like, I took my coffee and settled back in my seat again. The Rev sat there looking, well, reverend, with his hands clasped in his lap like he was about to start praying or something. His gaze kept sliding in my direction, then zipping back to Phil, as if he'd heard you should make eye contact with people you're talking to but had never actually seen it done.

"I understand Melanie Porter was acting as Parish Administrator?" Phil began.

The Rev nodded, and a lank strand of hair flopped down over his watery blue eyes. When he reached up to brush it back into place, I noticed his shirt cuffs were frayed, and felt a vague sense of guilt that I hadn't put anything into a church collection box since I was a nipper at Sunday School. Which I'd left under a cloud at the tender age of seven after the great Easter Egg Hunt fiasco—well, they'd *told* us to go and find the bloody things, hadn't they? It wasn't my fault none of the other kids had a clue where to look. And you show me a seven-year-old boy who *isn't* a greedy little sod.

"She was indeed." Lewis answered Phil's question and gave us a thin little smile. "A blessing, since poor Mrs. Reece's, ah, indisposition." The way he said it made me wonder if there was something to find out there. "Really quite admirable of her, when she already had a full-time job."

Phil was nodding. "And what did her duties involve?"

"Oh, paperwork, that sort of thing," the Rev said vaguely with a nervous titter that made my skin crawl. "The purpose of the post is to enable the incumbent to keep his mind on higher concerns, of course."

"So... paying bills?"

"Oh, yes. She was an authorised signatory to our bank account, as am I myself, but"—again the teeth-grating nervous laugh—"I try not to become involved in matters fiscal."

"So she could sign cheques? Who are the other signatories?"

"The church wardens, and our treasurer, naturally." I braced myself for another wheezy snigger, but it didn't come.

"And they are?" Phil persisted.

"The church wardens? Oh, Jonathan Riley—but he's off in Africa at the moment, of course—and Mrs. Cox."

"What, Pip Cox?" I butted in.

Lewis blinked in my direction. "Yes—why, do you know her?"

"Met her the other day." Why hadn't she mentioned this when we'd been there? "Nice girl, isn't she?"

Phil cleared his throat, leaning forward even farther. "What about the treasurer?"

"Oh—ah, yes. Lionel. Lionel Treadgood." The Rev had a sour expression on his face that suggested he wasn't over-fond of Treadgood the treasurer. Then again, Treadgood probably wasn't all that keen on the Rev. I knew I wasn't. The vicar in the London church I'd been to as a kid had been an old bloke with a shiny bald head and a perpetual smile, and he'd acted like everyone's granddad. Rev Lewis was more like the weirdo cousin you try and avoid at weddings.

"Would he be willing to talk to us about Melanie?" Phil persisted, seeing as the Rev apparently didn't want to be forthcoming about Lionel.

"I—ah, yes. I'm sure he, ah..." Lewis stared at his wallpaper, which personally I thought was the cheeriest thing in the room, but only seemed to depress him even further.

"And he lives in...?"

The Rev's Adam's apple bobbed as he swallowed, making me think of those nature programs where you see a snake gulping down some poor furry animal. "Fallow's Wood." That was the posh end of Brock's Hollow; half the houses didn't have numbers, only names, which made finding them a bloody nightmare when you were called out. On the plus side, though, the coffee was usually top-notch, and it was often the cleaner who let me in, rather than the lady of the house. That meant I didn't have to worry about her constantly checking up on me— and biccies were usually in plentiful supply.

Phil nodded. "And would you mind—"

He was cut off by the tinny strains of something churchy yet vaguely familiar. I realised it was *Jesu Joy of Man's Desiring*—my mum always liked that one—just as the Rev mumbled, "Sorry," and picked up his mobile phone. "Meredith Lewis. Oh. Yes, I— Well, of course, if you— Actually, I've got some people round— No, no, of course not. I'll be right there." He looked up, grimacing in what I assumed was dismay, although it looked more like he was constipated. "I'm so sorry— I've got to go out. Duty calls..." The Rev made a helpless gesture. "You won't mind me shooing you out, will you? Really, I can't think of anything else I can tell you in any case. I do hope I've been helpful," he added, standing.

Bloody brilliant. That was two failures in two visits. Phil was going to start thinking of me as his bad-luck charm. We stood in unison. "Thank you," Phil said, like the words were being pulled out of him with pliers. "You've been very helpful. I take it we can drop back in to continue this another time?"

"Oh, well—you know how it is. Busy, busy. The job of parish priest isn't a nine-to-five one, I'm afraid." He flapped his hands a bit; I hadn't realised he'd meant the shooing out literally.

"Thanks, Rev," I said, steeling myself to offer a handshake.

He took my hand, moistly. "Oh—please, call me Merry." It was followed by another nervous little laugh. God, he was weird. Even by the standards of a profession that spends most of their working lives in a frock, talking to someone who might not exist and even if he does, they'll never get to meet until they're dead.

"Er, right. We'll see you around, then." I managed not to wipe my palm on my jeans until after the front door had closed behind us.

"What do you reckon, then?" I asked as we got back in Phil's car. "He tried it on with Melanie, she wasn't having it, and he killed her?" I could just imagine the Rev as that sort of creepy stalker type.

Phil turned halfway through putting on his seat belt and stared at me. "Are you serious?"

"Why not?" I asked, nettled by his tone.

He clicked the belt on, put the car in gear and started off down the gravel drive. "The Rev's as bent as a Bishop's crosier. Didn't you notice the way he kept staring at your crotch?"

Merry fancied me? "Bloody hell. Stop the car, I think I'm going to be sick."

"Try and hold it in until we're out of his bloody driveway, will you?" Phil tapped his fingers on the steering wheel as he waited to pull out into the road. "Who do you reckon that phone call was from? Whoever it was, sounded like he had the vicar's nuts in a vise."

"Maybe it was head office," I suggested with heavy sarcasm. "Even God has to move with the times, keep up with technology."

"Haven't you heard? He's got his own website these days. Course, only the faithful can log on..." We swung out into the High Street and headed up the hill towards St Albans. "I think I might start making a few enquiries about the Rev."

"Yeah, well, it's always the closet cases you have to watch, isn't it?" I said idly—then turned to Phil so fast I got a crick in my neck. "That wasn't a dig, all right?"

The tension in his jaw eased, but not all the way. His dentist was going to give him hell next time he went for a check-up.

I managed not to shudder as we passed Nomansland Common and went on through farmland. "Where to now?" I asked. "Seeing as the Rev was a dead loss."

Phil gave me a look I couldn't work out. "I'll drop you off at yours, all right?"

"What, no more interviews lined up?"

"Not right now. I've got a few things I need to check out."

"Like?"

He gave an exasperated-sounding *huff*. "Like Robin East's secret love nest."

"You what? You mean I was right about that?"

"Don't let it go to your head. Yeah, he's got one of those new flats near the river in Harpenden. Pretty pricey, they are—most of them are owned by commuters with flash jobs in London. Don't let anyone tell you money can't buy you love."

"How'd you find out about it?"

"The old-fashioned way. Followed him, then checked through his bins."

I wrinkled my nose. "Nice."

"Says the man who unblocks other people's bogs for a living."

"Like I told Mrs. E, I always wash my hands after." I paused. "Do you think she was right, about him and Melanie having it off?"

Phil shrugged. We were just coming through Sandridge, a pretty little village carved in two by the main road. Not that it's all that main, as roads go, but the place wasn't half as villagey as it must have been in the days of real horse power. Course, it probably wasn't half as whiffy, either. "I haven't seen any other women turn up there, but it's early days yet. But I want to get back there before he shuts up shop tonight. See if he makes a stop there on the way home—and if he's alone."

"Why don't you go over there when he's at work and search the place?" I wondered. "I'd help."

"I'd rather keep my licence, thanks. Anyway, I'm not sure I buy Robin East as the murderer. The wife, now, I'd believe it of her."

"No," I said, thinking about it. "I don't think she cares enough about Robin, or the marriage, to take a risk like that. She might kill *him*, if she was sure she wouldn't get caught, but I can't see her bothering to kill the other woman."

"No? Sometimes it's easier to blame the third party when a marriage goes wrong."

"Haven't you been listening? I told you, she doesn't *care.*"

"Oh, sorry—forgot I was dealing with the Great Paretski, who knows everything about everybody and solves crimes with the awesome power of his mind."

We'd made it into Fleetville. Stung by his sarcasm, I jerked my head towards the halal food shop just down the road. "You can let me out here. I need to get some veg."

"Fine." Phil yanked the wheel round and braked sharply to pull in at the side of the road. "See you, then."

"Right. Bye." I got out of the car, and he pulled away again almost before I'd shut—not slammed—the door.

Why did it always end up going tits-up between me and Phil?

Chapter Nine

Tuesday turned out to be one of those days when everything goes right, for a change. For one thing, it didn't involve Phil Morrison. So, feeling I was probably due to balance the karmic scales a bit, I got in the Fiesta and headed off to Brock's Hollow after work to be a good little Samaritan.

To be honest, I didn't much fancy going to see Graham. It'd been bad enough last time, sitting on his sofa, talking about Melanie...

And how bloody hard must it be for Graham, living there on his own now? Time to stop being such a bloody selfish git and go and do my good deed for the day.

I'd have rung him up, but I didn't have his number and chances were he wasn't answering his phone anyhow. So I just rolled up there. It was pitch-black, and once again a stiff breeze was blowing through the estate like a hail of icy needles on my skin. I wrapped my arms around myself as I waited for him to answer the door buzzer. He was taking his time, but I could see light at his curtained windows, so I pressed it again.

"Who is it?" Graham's voice sounded tired and suspicious— or maybe I was just reading too much into those electronically distorted tones.

"It's me. Tom Paretski. I thought you might—" I broke off as the door buzzed open.

The stairwell seemed even more bleak in the pale light coming from a single, cobwebbed fitting. I jogged up quickly, ignoring the pain in my hip. When I got to Graham's door, he was standing behind it, peering through a narrow gap with the chain on.

"Hi—can I come in?"

He didn't answer, just pushed the door shut. I heard the rattle of the chain, and a moment later, the door opened again, this time fully. I stepped through and closed it behind me.

"Phil said you'd been here. You and him. When I was out," Graham said, his voice flat.

God, yes—the drugs. I'd forgotten he'd have to know *someone* had been there. Presumably Phil had decided letting Graham think the police had found the drugs and were keeping them for later would just be too cruel. "Er, yeah. Did a bit of spring-cleaning in your bedroom." I paused, but he didn't say anything. "You know, you really ought to be careful about that kind of thing."

Graham slumped on the sofa and ran a hand through his hair. "I wasn't using. It was just so I had it, if I needed it. That was all. It's just been so hard—I wasn't sure I could carry on..."

"Course you can," I said heartily. "Listen, have you eaten yet?" He looked at me blankly, then shook his head. "Why don't you come round to mine, then, and I'll cook us something? We can, you know, catch up a bit."

He looked down at himself. "I'm not really...."

He wasn't wrong. He obviously hadn't shaved for days, and his clothes looked like he'd been sleeping in them for at least that long. To be brutally frank, he was starting to whiff.

"Tell you what, I'll see what's on the telly while you grab a shower, and then I'll drive you over to mine. Does that sound all right?" Graham nodded, and I settled down on the sofa and hoped he wouldn't be too long. My stomach was rumbling already.

Maybe Graham's was too, as it was only around twenty minutes later when he came back into the living room to tell me he was ready. He looked a lot better—the circles under his eyes were still as dark, and he looked just as haggard, but without the wild, unstable air that probably hadn't been doing him any favours with the police. "Good," I said and turned off the news quickly before he saw anything upsetting. "Let's get going."

We passed a couple of Graham's neighbours on the way back to my van, two young women with scraped-back hair and plenty of makeup. Nobody said hello. They just stared at us, while Graham kept his head down. "Have things been all right round here?" I asked, suddenly worried.

Graham shrugged, his hands deep in his pockets. "You know. Dog shit through the letterbox a couple of times."

"Bloody hell—have you told the police?"

"What for? They think I killed her too." His shoulders hunched up even further, and he watched his feet like he was worried they might turn against him as well.

We were halfway to St Albans before he spoke again. "I never believed it, you know."

"Believed what?" I asked, pulling out to pass a cyclist.

"About you being a homosexual."

I turned to stare at him before remembering I really ought to keep my eyes on the road. "Graham, I am a, er, homosexual. I thought you knew that." Although now I came to think about it, I wasn't sure just how he'd have known—unless Phil had told him. Bloody ironic he'd suddenly started worrying about my reputation now, when I couldn't give a monkey's. I wondered what Phil was up to right now. Working? Just because he'd spent a lot of time on the murder lately didn't mean he might not have other cases on the go.

I realised Graham hadn't said anything more. "Does that bother you?" I asked. "Me being gay?"

"No, it's fine." He stared straight ahead at the lights of St Albans, his face as unreadable as Phil at his stoniest. "Are you in a relationship?"

"Nah—footloose and fancy free, I am." I gave him my stock answer for that kind of question, then cringed as I realised how it must sound to a bloke who'd just lost his fiancée. I felt like a total tosser. "Shit—sorry." I took a deep breath. "Do you, um, want to talk about Melanie? Or would you rather not?" *Please, God, let him go for the second option.*

Graham made a funny little snorting sound. "Sometimes I think I dreamed it all. Her and me, I mean. And sometimes I think I only dreamed she died—but she's gone. Really gone."

"How did you two meet?" I asked, tapping my fingers on the wheel as I waited for the traffic lights to turn green.

"Through church." He said it like it should have been obvious. Maybe it was—I couldn't think of many other places people from such different backgrounds could get to know each other. Work, maybe, but he didn't have a job. I was still having trouble picturing Graham as a God-botherer, though.

"Yeah, how did you get into that?"

"You know I was living on the streets in London, for a bit? And the drugs?"

"Yeah. Phil said that was how you and him met—met again, I mean. Through Crisis."

Graham nodded. "There's a lot of Christians who help out there. Phil was great, but they made me feel... They were like a family. Do you see what I mean?"

"Yeah, mate, I do." Poor sod—he'd never had a family of his own. "So have they been looking after you since, well, since it happened?"

He was silent for a while, and I glanced over, but we were in traffic, and I had to keep my eye on the road. "Graham?"

"It's not the same, here. People aren't the same. I stopped going to church. People around here don't understand; their lives are too safe and cosy, like they're wrapped in cotton wool. They just get embarrassed when they meet someone with real problems." He hunched down farther in his seat. "I don't want their help, their sodding casseroles. All they ever did was take Melanie away from me."

My hands tensed on the wheel—then I realised he was just talking about all those evenings at Prayer Group and doing the parish paperwork. Still, it bothered me, finding out he had all this resentment bubbling under the surface. He didn't sound like the Graham I'd known. But then he wasn't the Graham I'd known, was he? He was twelve years down the road from that shy, nerdy kid—and by the sound of it, those years hadn't been good ones.

"Well, here we are," I said brightly, pulling up the hand brake. I'd slipped into jolly-the-bloke-along mode again, I realised. "Come on in."

Both cats were there to greet us as we stepped through the front door. "Hello boys," I greeted them, bending down to stroke one furry back and then the other. Graham stood stiffly by the door, and my heart sank. "Shit—you're not allergic, are you?"

"Just...not very fond of cats, that's all."

Not fond of cats? How could *anyone* not like cats? "Well, they don't bite," I reassured him cheerily. This evening was going to be even more of an ordeal than I'd thought. "The fat one's Arthur, and the skinny one's Merlin. Come on through and I'll get you a drink. Beer all right?"

"Just a glass of water, please. I don't drink."

Right. So heroin was just fine and dandy, but not alcohol? Then again, maybe he'd been hooked on that too, back in the day. I got him a glass of water—from the tap, because I pay enough on my water rates already, I'm not shelling out for bottles of the stuff on top—then checked what was in the fridge. "Do you fancy pasta? I can do a carbonara, or something with tomatoes if you'd rather."

"Whatever you want." He didn't offer to help, so I sent him to the living room and got some water on to boil, then chopped up an onion as quickly as I could before I keeled over with hunger.

I've always quite liked cooking. It's all self-taught, but you can pick up bits and pieces if you watch cookery programmes on the telly. I've even tried making my own pasta a couple of times, since seeing a bloke on *Masterchef* make his own ravioli from scratch, but it's a bit of a faff unless there's someone you're trying to impress. And even then, most people can't tell it from store-bought stuff. That's if you buy a decent brand, obviously—I'm not talking Tesco Value dried wallpaper paste, here. But I didn't reckon Graham would be handing out any Michelin stars tonight whatever I served him—he probably wouldn't even notice if I opened a can of Heinz spaghetti hoops and dumped it on his plate—so I just concentrated on getting something tasty and filling on the table as quick as possible.

I made a quick salad with rocket and parmesan—can't stand lettuce that doesn't taste of anything—and called out, "Grub's up."

Graham poked his head warily around the door.

"Here you go, mate—dinner is served." We dug in, which was fine for a while, but to be honest, I prefer my meals with a little more conversation, if I'm not actually on my own. What the hell had we used to talk about, when we were at school together? Computer games, probably. Oh—and girls. Graham, like a lot of sixteen-year-old boys, had been a bit obsessed with the relative bust sizes of the girls in our class. And while I might not have had his level of interest in the subject, I'd argued and joked along with him because, well, you did, didn't you? Hmm. Maybe it wasn't so surprising he'd thought I was straight.

I tried to remember what other sorts of thing he'd been into back then. "Still playing chess?" I asked.

"No. Not for years." He looked down at his plate for a moment, then roused himself to make an effort. "Are you still playing football?"

I grimaced. "Nah—not since the accident." I gave my hip a slap, to show it I hadn't forgiven it for letting me down. It twinged right back, as if to say *oi, you're the one who ran out in front of a four-by-four.* "I'm in the darts team at the Rats, though."

"The Rats?"

"Rats Castle—it's my local." There's no apostrophe in the name; I've always assumed the greengrocer round the corner nicked it for his grape's. "We passed it on the way in; it's on Hatfield Road. We could go for a drink there sometime—um, if you go to pubs?"

Graham stared at the few congealed bits of pasta left on his plate. "Not really."

Bugger. "Nah, s'pose not… Seen any good films, lately?"

The conversation limped on, worse than a one-legged man at a dance marathon. I'd never been so relieved in my life to hear the doorbell ring. "Better get that," I said, trying not to look

115

too eager for an interruption as I jumped up from the table. If it was the Jehovah's Witnesses again, maybe they'd be able to make a better job of talking to Graham than I was.

It wasn't them. It was Phil. I blinked up at his tall, broad-shouldered figure in surprise, and realised he was holding a bottle of wine. "Did we have a date or something?" I blurted out. Wishful thinking, maybe.

His expression, which had been warily optimistic before I spoke, hardened. "Come at a bad time, have I?"

"No! God, no—come in. Graham's here. I asked him round for a meal—thought sitting alone every night with a takeaway couldn't be good for him."

The tension around Phil's eyes relaxed, and he nodded. "Decent of you. I'll leave you to it, then." He thrust the bottle of wine at me. "Here. I wanted to apologise for yesterday."

"Oh, right." I didn't quite know what to say.

"You know. In the car. I know I pissed you off. It's just... There's stuff you don't know about me..." He half shrugged. "Anyway, I'll get out of your face now."

"Don't be daft!" Okay, so maybe I was just a little bit desperate not to be left on my own with Graham any longer. I grabbed Phil by the arm not holding the bottle and practically dragged him inside—dropping his arm in a hurry when it occurred to me he might mistake my eagerness for something it wasn't. Honest. "Graham will be pleased to see you," I added.

I led him through the hall and into the kitchen. Graham had got up from the table, probably because Arthur, the big bully, had scented weakness and jumped up on top of it. "Arthur!" I yelled, clapping my hands. "Get down!" Haughtily, and in his own good time, Arthur left off hissing at Graham and jumped down via one of the chairs.

"Sorry about that," I said. "If he does it again, just shove him off, all right? Actually, why don't we go through to the living room?"

"Want me to open this?" Phil asked, holding up the wine. It was a French Merlot; looked expensive, like his leather jacket. Looked tasty too.

The wine, I meant.

Honest. Again.

"Um—best not, maybe." I glanced over at Graham. He roused himself to say *no, go ahead,* but of course we didn't. "I'll put the kettle on," I offered.

We all ended up sitting in a row on the sofa, with Graham in the middle like a Victorian chaperone, although I wasn't sure quite whose virtue he was protecting. His own, most likely. Arthur jumped on my lap (he winded me, but I was used to it) and Merlin again flirted shamelessly with Phil.

It ought to have been easier to find stuff to talk about, with three of us there, but somehow it was even harder. I realised all Phil and I ever did was talk about the case, argue or swap innuendo, none of which seemed very appropriate with Graham there. Luckily I remembered there was a League Cup match on telly tonight. I grabbed the remote and switched it on to find Chelsea had scored already. I groaned. "Come on, you Reds," I muttered despairingly.

Phil gave me a dirty look. "I might have known you'd be a Man U. supporter."

"And I might have known you'd be a fan of the boys in blue. But what was that supposed to mean?"

"Have you ever been up to Manchester in your life?"

"Yeah, I've been there. I've even seen a home match or two."

"But basically, you've got about as much connection to the place as my left nut."

I grinned. "I wouldn't know. You tell me what your left nut's been up to these last twelve years." I wouldn't have minded listening to the edited highlights, anyway.

Graham stood up suddenly, startling Arthur off my lap. "I ought to go."

"Nah, it's early yet," I protested, feeling guilty but at the same time, a little bit miffed. Phil and I weren't being *that* gay.

"Thanks, but... I think I'd like to go home. Thank you for the meal."

Phil got up, and then both of them were looming over me, one skinny and scruffy if freshly washed, and the other big and bulky in all the right places. "I'll drop you off," Phil said. "No need for Tom to turn out again."

"Okay. Bye, Tom." They trooped off, leaving me with two cats, a load of washing up, and a bottle of wine I wasn't sure whether to open or not. Was Phil coming back? He hadn't said either way. But it really was early yet, so maybe...

I washed up, bunged some clothes in the wash, watched the rest of the match (United won 3:1—take that, Phil Morrison) took the laundry out, bunged it in the dryer, and eventually had to accept I was on my own for the rest of the night.

So I took my nagging sense of failure upstairs and went to bed.

Chapter Ten

I'd arranged to meet Gary outside the Merchants Café in St Albans at eleven the next day, so he could show me his new light of love. He was a bit late, and I was about to nip inside for a cappuccino when I saw his cuddly teddy-bear figure lumbering towards me. "All right, Gary?" I called, waving. He gave a cheery grin and let Julian drag him in my direction.

"Fantastic, darling. Found anything interesting in the drains this morning?"

I'd had a loo to unblock. "Only a toilet duck and half an Action Man," I said, hampered by the huge, hairy paws that had landed on my chest. Julian's paws, that was, not Gary's. "God, you're a ton weight," I told the dog. "What has your daddy been feeding you?"

"Tender young virgins, of course. It helps keep his coat glossy. Shall we?"

Leaving the café behind us, we elbowed our way through the crowded streets of market-day St Albans. The market's a jumbled mix of food and clothing, leather goods and bolts of fabric—something for everyone, and everyone seems to turn out for it. We passed a fishmonger's stall and were nearly knocked flat by the whiff—the cats would have been in ecstasy. Stall holders assaulted our ears with cries of "Two fer a pahnd, when they're gone they're gone," and I felt a sudden burst of nostalgia for my London childhood.

"So are you going to tell me about this bloke of yours?" I asked, dodging a couple of tracksuited mums pushing armoured buggies.

"Darren? Oh, he's just *adorable*. You'll love him. Very good-looking. Actually—" Gary broke off and glanced around furtively before whispering in my ear. "He's an ex-porn star."

"Yeah?" I tried not to sound too staggered. Gary's a great bloke, and I love him to bits, but I'd never have expected him to land a porn star. "Oi, I hope you're using protection," I added.

"Sweetie! We've hardly done more than *kiss*, so far."

"And how long's that going to last? Make sure you've got some on you at all times; then you won't be tempted to take a risk."

"Tommy, darling, I may be besotted, but I'm not silly. Of course I'll use protection. Scout's honour."

"You were a Boy Scout?" I was having a lot of trouble picturing it. Girl Guides, maybe, but Boy Scouts?

"For about a month. The uniform was lovely, but the other boys were terribly rough. And going camping wasn't nearly as much fun as I'd thought it would be. Here we are," he added, his voice suddenly breathless. "This is Darren's stall."

Even though I was gagging to see what the porn star looked like, something about the way Gary said it made me glance over at him, instead of at the stall. There was a faint flush on Gary's cheeks, and his eyes were shining, his lips parted in a tender smile.

Bloody hell. I'd never seen him like this before. It must be love. I stared for a moment, then dragged my eyes round to the stall.

Gary's bloke was currently selling fruit and veg to an old dear with a bag on wheels. As she shuffled away, her place was taken by a Boden-wearing lady who looked at the bowls of mixed veg ("pahnd a bowl, three bowls for two pahnd") as if she'd found a cockroach in one of them. "I really only want a cauliflower," she said doubtfully, in ringing middle-class tones.

"Here you go, love," he said, his tones slightly nasal as he unabashedly tipped the contents of the bowl into a paper bag, twirled it shut and handed it to her. "That'll be a pound for the cauli, and just for you, I'll throw the carrots in free."

She paid up, either overpowered by the force of his personality or just not too strong on logic.

I studied Darren carefully. He had dark hair swept back from his face, and a neatly trimmed goatee. There was certainly something arresting about his looks. I could see why he'd got a job in film—although to be honest, I reckoned a handsome face was probably an optional extra in the sort of films he'd been in. He towered over us from behind the stall, but I got the weirdest feeling something wasn't quite right. It took me a moment to work out what it was. His proportions were all wrong, for a big bloke. His arms were too short, and his body was as well, unless...unless he was standing on a box.

A big box, I decided. "Gary!" I hissed furiously. "You didn't tell me he was a dwarf!"

Gary looked like he was about to pitch a fit. "Well, if that's all you can think of to say—"

He was interrupted with a cheery call of, "Gary! All right, mate?" We'd been spotted. Gary's face transformed as he turned to the (fresh, juicy, four-for-a-pahnd) apple of his eye.

"Darren, sweetie, this is Tom," he said, having apparently forgotten he was pissed off with me.

I was given a brief but thorough inspection by the undeniably good-looking man behind the counter. "This the one you was telling me about?"

"The same," Gary cooed. "Thomas Paretski, plumber *extraordinaire.*"

Darren's eyes narrowed. "Bit of a short-arse, ain't he?"

My jaw dropped, as Gary shrieked with laughter beside me.

Sod Rome—apparently these days, all roads led to Brock's Hollow. At least, I found myself driving through the village again that afternoon, after a sandwich lunch in the Merchant's with Gary, taking the not-quite-direct route to a cracked kitchen sink in Harpenden.

I wasn't the only one paying the place a visit. Dave Southgate and his boys in blue were parked in the lay-by outside the church, the one the hearses always parked in so they could take the coffin in through the lych-gate. Looked like today it was Robin East's funeral. He crossed the road between Dave and a uniformed officer, his face flushed but his head held high. George Clooney starring in a remake of *Papillon*, maybe.

Bloody hell. Had it been him after all? There was a gaggle of old dears and young mums gawking at him from outside the WI shop, and they obviously had him tried and convicted already— arms folded, noses in the air, they might as well have been shouting *I always knew he was a wrong 'un* for everyone to hear. Standing in the doorway of the estate agents was a pale, hunched-over Pip Cox.

I didn't think twice—just turned the van into Four Candles Lane and parked in the car park behind the pub. The kitchen sink could wait. They could always bung a bucket under it. By the time I got to Village Properties, the lynch mob had taken their disapproval elsewhere, and Pip had disappeared inside. The sign on the door had been turned round to *Closed*, but I went in anyway.

Red-eyed, Pip looked up from her desk. The pale green cardi she was wearing cruelly highlighted how blotchy her face was. "W-we're closed," she stammered, sounding an inch away from tears.

"I know, love. Just wanted to make sure you were okay. I saw what happened." I leaned against the door frame, my hands in my pockets, so she wouldn't feel I was barging in on her. Looking round the office, I saw a kettle in the corner. "Want me to make you a cup of tea?"

She stared at me silently for a moment, then bit her lip and nodded.

I smiled encouragingly and closed the door. "Bit of a shock, I expect, having your boss carted off by the police. Have they arrested him, or is he just helping with enquiries?" I checked the kettle, decided the water in there would just about do, and switched it on.

"They didn't—they didn't say he was under arrest. Just that they wanted him to come down to the st-station." Pip swallowed.

"Might just be a routine thing, then," I suggested, trying to cheer her up.

"They said—" She broke off for a minute, then rallied. "He told them he was working late, the night Melanie... But they said someone had told them it wasn't true."

"Oh?" I turned round, mugs in hand. "Milk and sugar?"

She shook her head, so I carried her black tea and my white one over to her desk. "Wouldn't have been the missus, by any chance, would it? Because I've met her, and she's a right—

sorry." I made a zipping motion by my lips. "Forgot she might be a friend of yours."

Pip's mouth twitched into what was trying to be a smile. "No. We're not friends. But I don't think... They said they'd been told there were no lights on. The inspector—"

"Dave Southgate, yeah, I know him."

"He asked Robin if he'd been working in the dark. I know who told them about it," she surged on, suddenly fierce.

"Yeah?" I parked my bum on the corner of her desk, and tried to look casual as I took a sip of my tea. Hmm. Maybe I could have done with using fresh water, after all.

"It was that *hateful* old woman next door," Pip said, looking surprised at her own venom.

"What, the Women's Institute lady? Her with the homemade chutney and the crocheted dollies?"

She nodded. "But it's not true. I know he didn't kill Melanie. I *know* it."

I sighed. "I know you don't want to believe it, love. *I* don't want to believe it. But if he's innocent, why would he lie to the police in the first place?"

Pip burst into tears. She put down her tea with wobbly hands and sobbed like her world had just ended.

There was nothing else for it. I shuffled round to her side of the desk and put my arms around her, patting her back, stroking her hair and muttering soothing phrases. To tell the truth, I felt a bit of a bastard for what I'd just said. If being willing to lie to the police was a sign of guilt, we all ought to be banged up. Everyone makes bad decisions when they're scared.

I held her for a long time, until the sobs died down into sniffles and my shirt front was unpleasantly soggy. "Hey," I said, once I reckoned she'd hear me. "Why don't you go on home? No point you trying to hold the fort here. All you're going to get is Nosey bloody Parkers."

Pip lifted her head. Her face was blotchier than ever, but she seemed a bit calmer. Not as much as I'd have liked, mind. "I can't go home."

"If you need a lift, I've got the van round the back of the Four Candles."

"No—I mean, thanks. It's not that."

A nasty little suspicion clouded my mind. "Him indoors, is it?"

She didn't answer, just stared at the table.

"How come he's not at work?"

"He—well, it's been hard for him. Finding work. Since he got laid off, he's... It's been hard."

I nodded sympathetically. "And now you've got him moping round the house all day, making the place look untidy. Tell you what—why don't I take you out for a proper cuppa? Something stronger, if you like—they serve all sorts down the Four Candles."

Pip looked down and mumbled something embarrassed and incomprehensible. I reckoned I had a fair idea what she was worried about.

"Hey, I'm not trying to chat you up or anything. You're a married lady, and I'm—well, let's just say I might have my eye on someone. And nothing personal, but he's a lot more my type than you are." I gave her a smile while she worked it out. "So just a friendly drink, all right?"

She bit her lip, but she was looking a lot happier. "All right."

I took the mugs out back for a rinse while Pip got her coat, pulled down the blinds and shut up shop.

"So what's Pip short for?" I asked as we headed down the road. "Philippa?"

She looked at her feet. "Persephone."

"That's a nice name. Suits you. You should use it more. Or if you don't fancy using the whole thing, there's lots of ways you could shorten it—Seffy, maybe? Or how about Persie? Or Phoney?"

She almost giggled at that.

"That's better," I said, pleased to see her looking a bit more cheerful. I linked an arm in hers. "Right, let's get—"

I didn't finish my sentence, because right then an angry-looking man with a dark beard came round the corner in front of us, stared for a second, then launched a fist at my face.

Just because I'm small and I've got a duff hip doesn't mean I just stand there and take it when someone lays into me. I was a bit hampered by Pip being so close on one side, but I still managed to dodge the punch and land one of my own, right in his flabby gut. He doubled over, and I was going in for the knockout when Pip grabbed hold of my arm and tried to pull me back.

"Stop! It's my husband!"

This was Mr. Pip? "What the bloody hell did he want to hit me for, then?" I demanded.

"I'm sorry, I'm so sorry," she gabbled—whether to me or to him, I wasn't sure. I was keeping my eye on the bastard as he staggered and wheezed, his eyes sending death threats in my direction. "He must have thought—I'm so sorry." Obviously deciding it was safe to let go of me, she went over to Mr. Pip and tried to put an arm around him. He shrugged her off viciously.

"Nigel, he was just—just looking after me. Robin's been arrested, and I was upset, so he was going to take me for a drink, but there's nothing going on, I promise."

I didn't much like the pleading tone in her voice. Far as I was concerned, he was the one who ought to be apologising, not her. "Maybe Nigel should go and cool off somewhere," I suggested—I'd have been very happy to throw him in the river, personally—"and I'll take you for that drink?"

"No, I'm sorry. I'd better—we'll go home, Nigel, all right?"

Nigel wiped his mouth with his sleeve, glaring at me all the while. "You stay away from my wife," he snarled. I got a waft of beery breath as he spoke.

Apart from wrinkling my nose a bit, I ignored him. "Pip, are you sure you're going to be all right with him?"

She nodded. "It's fine. Nigel just—it's fine."

It wasn't my definition of fine, but at the end of the day, what could I do? "If you need anything—if you *ever* need anything—give me a call," I told her. "I'm in the book—Tom Paretski. Or look in Yellow Pages under plumbers. Promise?" I added, because I didn't want her to think I was just being polite.

"I'll be fine," was all she said, as her husband grabbed her hand and pulled her away.

I felt like kicking something, hard, but I'd only end up knackering my hip. So I headed back to my van and sat there for a moment, thinking about what she'd said about relationships, and nobody really knowing what they were really like except the people in them. Had that been a cry for help? Or her way of saying despite appearances, she was happy with Mr. Pip? God, there was no accounting for the bastards some people ended up with.

Which reminded me, I'd better call Phil and let him know what had happened.

He picked up on the first ring. "Tom? Good to hear from you. Between jobs?" He sounded cheerful and chatty. It was a bit unnerving.

"Uh, yeah, but I didn't ring up for a chat. Listen, have you heard about Robin East?"

"Heard what?" His tone went from relaxed and playful to sharply focused.

"He's been—well, not arrested, exactly, but Dave and the boys went and picked him up from the estate agent's. Very publicly. And apparently some old dear's trashed his alibi for the night of the murder."

There was sharp intake of breath on the other end of the line, but he didn't say anything.

"Phil?" I asked.

"Thinking." He was silent a bit longer, but just as I was about to say bye and leave him to think in peace, he spoke again. "Just because he wasn't where he said he was, doesn't mean he's the killer. Secret love nest, remember?"

"Yeah. Do you think the police know about that?"

He laughed. "They may do after today. Be interesting to see where he heads when they let him go—*if* they let him go. How'd the secretary take it?"

"Pip? Badly. I met her husband, by the way. Nice bloke—I'd known him for all of half a second when he took a swing at me."

"Are you all right?" Phil's voice was even sharper now, and his obvious concern for me sent warmth flooding through my chest. I'd been expecting something more like a joke about how I had that effect on a lot of people.

"I'm fine—he never touched me. I winded him, though. Course, I didn't know who he was, did I? She went home with him afterwards." I let my tone tell him what I thought about that.

"Did he have a reason for attacking you? Or do you just have that effect on some people?"

Ah, there it was. "Very funny. He told me to stay away from his wife, so he must have thought I was after her."

"Interesting."

"Which bit?"

"The bit where he just assumed there was something funny going on as soon as he saw you together."

"Ah. Well, I sort of had my arm in hers at the time, so I s'pose it did look a bit suspect."

There was a stifled sound on the other end of the line. "Christ, Tom, do you ever stop?"

"I never even started! I was just looking after her, that's all. She was in a right state."

"Fine. I'll believe you; thousands wouldn't. Right—I've got stuff to do. Thanks for calling; I appreciate it." He hung up before I even had a chance to suggest we meet up for a pint or something.

Feeling a bit let down, I put the van in gear and headed over to Harpenden.

Where I found a pissed-off Post-it on the front door, with *Waited over an hour for you. Don't bother to call again,* scrawled on it in angry biro.

Swearing under my breath, I dug in my pocket until I found a stubby pencil. I wrote *Sorry* at the bottom of the note, then I turned back around and headed home.

Chapter Eleven

It had been bugging me, not being able to check out those vibes at the vicarage. The one time I'd known there was something to find—and I hadn't been able to get to it. I needed to get back there and see what it was. The trouble was, how?

I wasn't proud of what I came up with, but I just couldn't think of any other way. I thought about telling the Rev I was offering a free plumbing check-up to houses in the area, but trouble was, people who wear shirts with frayed cuffs are generally of the if-it-ain't-broke-don't-fix-it persuasion. He'd just have told me thanks, but no thanks, and I'd have burned my boats for any other kind of approach. So I went the God-bothering route. I had a look at the church website—got to be a first time for everything, hasn't there?—and gave the Rev a ring, saying I'd like to have a talk with him about the Alpha course they were running for new Christians.

He seemed glad to hear from a possible new recruit and asked me over the following afternoon. Like I'd thought, mornings and evenings were his busy time. So I stood on his doorstep at half-past two, wiped my palms on my jeans and rang the doorbell.

The Rev's ferrety face lit up like a baptismal candle when he saw me. "Tom, so good to see you again," he said, ushering me in, his hands all a-flutter.

"Good to see you too, Merry," I told him with the sort of smile I usually save for the housewives.

He went bright pink. "Let me put the kettle on."

"Cheers. Actually, mind if I use your loo? I've just come from a job." Was lying to a vicar in his vicarage as bad as lying in church, or only as bad as any other lie? I'd have crossed my fingers, but I didn't want Jesus thinking I was taking the mick.

"Oh—of course, go ahead. I'll make the drinks—coffee again? White, no sugar?"

"You remembered. Cheers, Rev, that'll be lovely."

He disappeared down the hall to the kitchen. I bypassed the downstairs loo and legged it upstairs, trying to keep my steps as light as possible. I was on the right track—I could feel it. Smell it, almost. A thick, greasy, shameful trail of repressed desire and guilt.

Luckily, the Rev wasn't one for keeping bedroom doors shut, so I could see at a glance which was his room. The others were either bare, or half full of boxes, presumably of church stuff. It seemed a shame, all this space going to waste, but I supposed the Rev wouldn't stay here forever, and the next bloke might have a family to fill the place up a bit.

Of course, Phil might have been wrong about old Merry, and he might one day have a family of his own. I wouldn't be holding my breath, though.

The trail led straight under Merry's bed. I brushed aside a couple of crumpled-up tissues and socks in a sad state of repair—clearly holeyness really was next to Godliness. There was a shoebox that had once held a cheap pair of unbranded trainers, half price in the sale. Bingo. I opened it up and stared at the contents.

Out magazine from July 2010. Some dry-looking book about ancient Greeks. A copy of *Maurice*, looking fairly well-thumbed, and one of *The Lord Won't Mind.* A few faded snapshots, the most risqué of which featured a pigeon-chested bloke with his shirt off. Some old letters—way too old to have anything to do with Melanie.

This was it? This was the Rev's secret shame? Poor sod—all that guilt over this? Anyway, it was time I went back downstairs. I put the lid carefully back on the box and was about to slide it back under the bed when a floorboard creaked behind me. I spun round guiltily, the box still in my hands.

Merry was standing in the doorway, and he wasn't living up to his name. "You didn't come here to talk about the Christian faith, did you?" he said quietly and with a sort of sad dignity. "May I ask why you wish to expose me in this manner?" His voice shook, and I realised his hands were shaking too.

I felt like the lowest form of pond scum, crouching down there rooting through his private life. I stood up, my stomach queasy. "I'm not going to expose anything. I'm sorry." I took a couple of deep breaths as he just stood there, staring at me. "I was just curious, that's all. I thought—last time I was here, with Phil, I thought maybe you were interested in me. But I wasn't sure, you know? I just wanted to...check out the theory." My heart was pounding in my ears, and Jesus and all his angels were probably busy right now preparing a special hell just for me.

"Why?" the Rev asked and gave that nervous laugh of his. Somehow it didn't seem quite so slimily funny anymore. "Because you were...interested in me too?"

I drew a breath, but I didn't get to answer.

"No," he said, turning away from me. "No, that's not it, is it? How silly of me, to suppose someone like you..." His thin lips wobbled, then turned white as he got them under control, pressing them even thinner.

Shit. "I'm sorry," I said helplessly. "I just—I'm a mate of Graham's, all right? I don't want to see him go down for something he didn't do. And I could tell you were hiding something, so I wanted to see what it was. That's all. God's truth." I was silent for a moment, but he didn't say anything, and the words came bursting out of me, unstoppably. "But for fuck's sake, why don't you just come out and be honest about it? Even I know you're not the only gay priest in the Church of England. It's supposed to be all right, isn't it? As long as you don't, you know, do anything about it. I mean, reading a couple of books, that's nothing, is it?"

The Rev gave a deep, deep breath and let it out again audibly. "I hope you won't take it amiss if I ask you to leave." His voice was barely more than a whisper.

"Course not. And look, mum's the word, all right?" I clapped him on the shoulder as I walked out of the room and felt even shittier when he flinched away from my touch.

I thought about checking Pip was okay, so after I'd left the vicarage I drove down the village High Street and parked in a lay-by. But although we were heading for dusk, the estate agent's window was unlit, and there was a sign on the door that said *Closed due to unforeseen circumstances.*

It was probably just as well. I'd most likely have buggered that up as well.

I knocked off early that day, had beans on toast for supper and headed straight down to the pub.

There were a few old regulars in the Rats Castle, plus some loud lads from an office somewhere. I ignored them as best I could, and they bogged off just after seven, which left me in peace to get rat-arsed.

How did Phil do this? All the lying, the sneaking around behind people's backs?

I suppose I'd got pretty good at switching off my dubious talent over the years. Ignoring all the stuff I didn't want to know about. Even when it's mates—especially when it's mates—there's always stuff they don't want you to know about, and generally speaking, they're right. Some things you're just better off not knowing.

But Phil's job was to rake up all that dirt, just on the off chance it might have some bearing on the case. How could he do this, day after day?

I think I must have texted him to ask him at some point, because when I looked blearily up at the shadow falling over my sixth or seventh or eighth pint, I saw it was Phil.

"What do you think you're doing, Tom?" He had a smooth voice. Flowed all over me like whiskey. No ice, just tingling warmth.

"Turning it off. See?" I held up my pint, struggling to work out whether to focus on the glass or Phil, and eventually giving it all up as a bad job. A fair amount of beer sloshed onto the table, ran along the surface and started dripping onto my jeans. "Buggrit. 'S working, though. Couldn't find the Thames right now from a standing start in Docklands." I laughed. All right, maybe I chortled. "Couldn't find my arse"—I belched— "with my elbow."

"Yeah, well, I think you'd find most people have a problem with that one. Come on, I think it's time you went home."

"Am home," I protested. "An Englishman's pub is...is his castle," I said, sweeping my arm to indicate the interior of the Rats. My jeans got even wetter, and I was worried for a moment I might have embarrassed myself, until I realised I was still holding my pint. What was left of it, anyway. "Oops." I was about to move the beer to the safety of my stomach, but it disappeared. I looked around for it and saw Phil was holding a glass. I frowned. "Did you just nick my pint?"

"Trust me, you don't need it." He put it on the table and reached down to grab my arm. "Come on, time for bed."

I sniggered. "Think I'm easy, do you?"

"No, I just think you're rat-arsed."

"Rat-arsed. In the Rats." I sniggered again. "That's a...that's a... Whassat?"

"It's about time you got some fresh air. Not to mention fresh jokes." Phil took a firmer hold of my elbow. "This way."

It got cold, suddenly, and I realised that somehow we'd left the pub and gone outside. "'S cold," I muttered, shivering.

Phil heaved a sigh, and then something warm yet light draped itself around my shoulders. It smelled nice. Woodsy. Like Phil. I pulled it closer around me and breathed in deeply. "'S nice."

"You throw up over my gilet and you're buying me a new one."

"Gilet?" I snorted in laughter. "Nobody says *gilet*. How bloody gay is that?"

"Probably just gay enough to get us a kicking, around here, so how about you watch your mouth, all right?"

"You dissing my neighbourhood?" I frowned blearily up at him. "When was the last time you got a kicking, anyway? You're all...big and butch and 'timidating."

"On the other hand, I've got my hands full at the moment, haven't I?"

"I bet you've got a handful and a half," I said, batting my eyelashes at him. Then I laughed so hard I nearly pissed myself.

Phil didn't join in. "Come on, let's get you home and you can tell me what's brought this on."

Was he stupid or something? "I think," I said slowly and clearly, "it might have been the beer." I belched, just in case he still hadn't got the point.

"You don't say? Right—here we are. Where's your key?"

"'S in my pocket." I sniggered. "Is that a key in my pocket, or am I just pleased to see you?" Phil rummaged around in my jeans, the randy bugger, and I laughed some more. "Tickles."

"Turns out it was a key." Phil held it up. "See?"

He opened the door. "'S dark," I said. Then it wasn't. "Ow." I blinked.

"Let's get you on the sofa. Here you go. Now, don't go to sleep yet."

"Got plans for me, have you?" I tried to look flirtatious, but it was a bit hard as both of him kept slipping off to one side.

Then he left. "He's left me, Arthur," I said sadly. Arthur didn't reply, so I prodded him and realised I'd been talking to one of the sofa cushions.

"Not yet, I haven't," a blurry shape said in Phil's voice. "Drink this. All of it."

"Had 'nuff," I muttered into the pint glass under my nose.

"Not of this, you haven't. It's water. Trust me, you'll thank me for this in the morning."

I sniggered, spluttering water. "That good, are you?" Then I yawned. "Sleepy."

"I'm not surprised. You lie down, and I'll get you a blanket. And a bucket, if I can find one, just in case."

"Don't go." I had to tell him something. It was really important. Couldn't remember what it was, but I had to tell him. I grabbed his arm. "Phil?"

"Yeah?"

I blinked at him. "I'm not Polish. Not even a little bit."

"Well, I'm sure England's vastly relieved we can justly claim you for our own. Now go to sleep."

"Yes, Mum." I closed my eyes. Just as I was about to drift off, I thought I felt the touch of his lips on my forehead. "Love you too," I muttered.

Chapter Twelve

I was lying on my back underneath a bath in Jersey Farm—that's a big council estate between St Albans and Sandridge, by the way, not an actual farm—when he rang me next day. "Paretski Plumbing," I answered chirpily, recognising his number.

"You don't sound Polish," Phil's voice rumbled in my ear, its tone light. Flirtatious, even—or was I just reading too much into it? I hoped not.

"Would you like me to?" I countered, hoping the customer was still busy downstairs and wouldn't (a) hear me flirting back or (b) come up and notice I was semi-aroused. I'd had a restless night—sleeping on the sofa has never done wonders for my hip—with a certain PI playing a prominent role in my dreams. I'd finally woken up late, feeling horny as hell and with no time to do anything about it.

My memory was a bit fuzzy about what had happened the previous night after Phil had got me home, but I'd woken up wrapped snug in a blanket, with a pint glass of water and a bucket (thankfully unused) by my side. I'd felt, in a word, cared for. It was a good feeling, and I'd carried the good mood it gave me all the way to work.

"Maybe some other time. Are you free at all today?"

I was tempted to trill *I'm free!* like John Inman playing Mr. Humphries, but I resisted. After all, they might not have watched *Are You Being Served* reruns in his house. "Depends what for."

"How about a visit to the Honorary Treasurer, Mr. Lionel Treadgood, esquire?"

"You take me on all the best dates, don't you?" There was a silence, which I rushed to fill. "What time?"

"Any time this afternoon, he said."

"Sounds like we're dealing with a member of the leisured classes. Nice work if you can get it."

There was a sharp breath down the phone line that might have been Phil smiling. "He's got his own construction firm, so I guess he takes time off when he wants to. House up in Fallow's Wood; makes the East place look like a council flat."

Which meant my house, by comparison, was a condemned garden shed with both wet and dry rot. "Do I need to put my Sunday frock on, then?"

"Twinset and pearls will do just fine."

"Shame my tiara's in the wash."

There was another short silence. "Thought you might be feeling a bit hungover after last night."

"Nah, someone got me to drink a gallon of water before bed. And I don't really get hangovers. Well, not that bad, anyway."

"Lucky bastard."

"Hope I didn't say anything too daft last night."

"What, dafter than usual?" There was a pause.

I was expecting him to ask why I'd drunk so much—I was fairly sure I hadn't got round to telling him last night—but maybe he didn't want to get into anything heavy over the phone. I thought about bringing it up myself, but then again, the customer (*call me Angie, love*) was only two flights of stairs away, and though I seriously doubted she was a regular at St Anthony's Church, Brock's Hollow, loose lips sink ships and all that.

"Thanks for taking me home," I said, when he didn't say anything.

"No problem. It was only up the road." He cleared his throat. "Right. How about we meet up at the Four Candles in Brock's Hollow, and you can leave your van in the car park, and we'll drive up together?"

"Works for me. Okay, I've got a quote to do around twoish—might need to go up in the attic—so how about I meet you in the Four Candles at three?"

"See you then." He rang off, and I got back to work just in time for when Angie came back up.

"I brought you a cup of tea, Tomasz," she said with a fair attempt at a Polish pronunciation, at least as far as I could tell. "Or is it Tomek?"

"Just Tom, love," I told her, trying not to sound too long-suffering.

She crouched down to my level. Given how short her skirt was, it was probably a bit more of a revealing move than she meant it to be. Then again, maybe not. "Two sugars all right?"

"Lovely," I said and gave her a wink. "Thanks, love. Just put it down there, and I'll drink it in a mo."

I could always tip it down the sink.

I was just finishing up my Diet Coke when Phil walked into the Four Candles. I was sitting in a corner, surrounded by photos on the walls of Brock's Hollow in Days Gone By. Most of the buildings in the pictures were surprisingly recognisable, except every other house in the High Street seemed to have been a pub those days. Perhaps that was what old people meant when they talked about making their own entertainment in the pre-TV days.

Phil was looking good, in tailored trousers and a different cashmere sweater, one I hadn't seen before. Did his wardrobe have its own mortgage? Mind you, you can get cashmere in Tesco's these days.

I was fairly sure he'd have shopped somewhere a bit more upmarket, though. "Who says you can't take the council estate out of the boy?" I joked, appreciating the view.

He flushed—and not in a pleased way. "Some of us work hard to get away from our roots, all right?"

"Keep your hair on! You're going to take someone's eye out with that chip on your shoulder. I just meant you're looking good, that's all." Okay, so now I'd overcompensated and I was probably going just as red as he was.

"Oh. Well, you too, obviously."

"Yeah, right." I hadn't had time to change, so I was in my dusty work jeans and shirt, and when I'd nipped into the Gents a few minutes ago, I'd found cobwebs in my hair—no reflection on Jersey Farm standards; *nobody* hoovers under the bath, for God's sake. Or in the attic. "Old Lionel's going to think you found me sleeping under a hedge."

"You look fine." He coughed. "Are you ready to go?"

I nodded and stood. "So is this bloke a suspect, or do you just want to sound him out about the Rev?"

I'd said it quietly, but Phil still darted a gaze around before glaring at me. "We'll talk about it in the car."

"Oh, come on, you don't think—fine, let's talk about the weather. Bit nippy for the time of year, isn't it?"

He didn't answer. Maybe that cashmere sweater was really good at keeping him warm, and he didn't like to disagree with me. I chuckled to myself—quietly, so Phil wouldn't hear. "How are you getting on with the new place?" I asked. "Got all your stuff unpacked yet?"

"I wish. Still living out of boxes, mostly."

"I could come and give you a hand some time, if you like," I offered, surprising myself a bit. Usually I get my second thoughts a bit sooner than that.

Still, Phil looked pleased, so I was glad I'd said it. "Thanks. Yeah, that'd be great." He frowned. "Have I told you where it is?"

"No—I was going to ask you about that, but I thought you were enjoying being a man of mystery. Either that or you were worried I'd turn up and uncover all your secrets."

"I've got my secrets, but my address isn't one of them. And it's not like I've been living there long enough to get the skeletons moved into their cupboards. I've got a flat out on London Road." He gave me the address.

"Hey, we're practically next-door neighbours! You must be what, half a mile away from mine?"

"Something like that."

"You never did tell me how come you moved back out here," I reminded him as we got into the Golf.

"No. I didn't." Phil started the engine.

"Oh, yeah, I forgot. Man of mystery and all that. Fine—have it your way. So can we talk about Lionel now?"

He nodded. "He's church treasurer, right? So he'll know a lot about the way the church conducts its business. We can ask him about that night—see if he thinks it's feasible Melanie might have meant the vicar when she talked about her boss. If it's likely the Reverend would have called her out in the evening." Phil peered cautiously out of the narrow entrance to Four Candles Lane, saw both oncoming cars were politely waiting for him, and pulled out onto the village High Street. He gave a pinched-looking smile. "See if he knows the vicar's dirty little secret, and if he's got any of his own."

"Still think being gay's a dirty little secret, do you?"

"It is if you're a vicar. He should grow a pair and come out. Half the persecution of homosexuals done in the name of the church could be avoided if people like him weren't too shit scared to stand up and be counted."

I stared at him, speechless for a moment. I'd been about to tell him about my trip to see the Rev, but right now I was damned if I was going to betray that sad collection of books and keepsakes. When I finally found my voice, it wasn't pretty. "You fucking hypocrite! What about when we were in school together? You never stood up to be counted then."

Phil flinched back for about a hundredth of a second, then turned on me angrily. "That was then. Do you still define yourself by what you believed when you were seventeen?"

I thought about it. "Pretty much, yeah."

"Well, spare a thought for us poor mortals who have to learn by experience, all right? Not everyone gets it right first time."

I couldn't help it. I had to laugh. "You think I get everything right first time? 'Scuse me, but have we even met?"

He threw me a look, but it was gone before I could work out what it meant. "You really haven't changed, you know," he said, and I didn't think he meant it as a compliment.

We took the left turn off the main road, towards Fallow's Wood. It was all scrubby forest either side of us for a short

way—if you come here in the spring, the bluebells are lovely—
then we got to the first of the houses.

Fallow's Wood isn't much of a village, more a collection of
posh houses, some with gardens measured in acres, scattered
around a golf course. Opinions differ as to whether it's part of
Brock's Hollow or a separate address in its own right. Me, I'm
on the fence, which around there is around eight feet tall and
made of freshly painted wrought iron with pointy gold bits on
top. The place has got its own pubs, which is a point in its
favour, but no corner shop. It'd piss me right off if I had to get
in the car every time I needed a pint of milk, but I suppose the
Fallow's Wood residents have got to justify their three or four
motors per family somehow.

Lionel Treadgood's house was set at the end of a private
road, which was un-surfaced and had more potholes than I've
had hot dinners.

"You'd think with all the money floating around here, they'd
do something about this," I said as we rattled along in Phil's car
at ten miles an hour. "I suppose maybe they just see it as sort
of low-tech traffic calming,"

"Or maybe they're just tight-fisted bastards," Phil muttered,
his face set. Probably worrying about what the road was doing
to his tyres and suspension. We'd have been better off bringing
my van—it might not be smart, but it's robust. When we got to
Lionel's wide driveway, Phil parked the Golf with a crunch of
gravel and a vicious jerk on the hand brake, and we got out.
The house in front of us was large, but it looked more like it'd
been built for practicality and added to when necessary—at
least, "necessary" by rich people's standards—than
architecturally designed to tone in with the surrounding
countryside, or whatever the usual estate-agent guff was.

"Going to do your stuff?" Phil asked softly.

"What, out here? With that?" I nodded towards the swimming pool on the right of the house. Shielded by a high hedge, it hadn't been visible from the road. "And I reckon they've got the river down the bottom of their garden. It'd be needle in a haystack time. Must cost an arm and a leg to keep a pool that size heated this time of year." I pursed my lips, looking at the steam rising gently from the water. There was a sort of summerhouse thing to change in, and a decking area where you could sit out with drinks when it was warm.

"Nice if you can afford it," Phil murmured, pursing his lips. "Wouldn't mind one of those myself."

I shivered. "You can keep it."

Phil turned to stare at me, an incredulous look on his face. "Don't tell me you're scared of water? A plumber with hydro-bloody-phobia?"

"No," I said, a bit indignant. "I'm not scared. I just don't like swimming pools. Too much dead water. The vibe's all wrong."

"And it's got your sat-nav on the blink?"

"I'll be fine in the house. It's just interference, that's all." We crunched up to the front door, and Phil rapped on it with the old-fashioned door knocker.

"Okay, remember—same drill as at the Easts', all right? Except this time, pull your finger out and get back before he starts getting suspicious."

"Tell you what, why don't you shove a broom up my arse, and I can sweep his floors while I'm at it?"

"Stop being such a touchy little—"

I was saved from hearing the rest of it by the door opening.

Lionel Treadgood wasn't quite what I'd been expecting. He was tall—around Phil's height, but narrower across the shoulders and broader in the waist, without actually being fat.

He looked like he kept himself in shape the old-fashioned way, with long walks in the countryside in between rounds of golf and persecuting small furry animals. Probably in his late fifties, or a well-preserved early sixties, he still had a full head of thick, iron-grey hair, darkening to steel in the middle. He wasn't bad looking, if you like that sort of thing—not a patch on Robin East, mind. Even though Lionel was at home, he had on a proper shirt and tie. I wondered if it was for our benefit, but decided he'd probably been wearing it anyway. He was the sort who never took his tie off unless it was to put on his flannel pyjamas to go beddy-byes.

"Mr. Morrison? Good to meet you. Dreadful business about poor Melanie." He shook hands with Phil, then turned to me with a polite question in his eyes.

"Thanks for agreeing to talk to us," Phil said in his impressing-the-punters voice. "This is my colleague, Tom Paretski."

I was a colleague, was I? Maybe I'd insist on getting paid this time.

Lionel grasped my hand in a firm, cool handshake and frowned. "Paretski... That sounds familiar, somehow. Have we met?"

"I don't think so. But I've got family in the area." I was willing to bet none of them moved in his sort of circles, though.

"Ah! Maybe that's it." More likely he'd seen the van around, but I didn't want to ruin Phil's little we're-all-professionals charade by mentioning the day job. "Well, do come in—don't let me keep you standing on the doorstep."

We trooped inside, my work boots clattering loudly on the tiled floor of the hall. Even Phil's smart shoes made a little squeak as he trod, but Lionel's expensive leather-soled brogues made no sound at all. I felt like I'd blundered in while looking for the tradesman's entrance, and wondered if I should tug a forelock or something. "This way, please," Lionel said firmly, interrupting my gawping at the grandfather clock and the antique hunting prints on the walls.

He ushered us into a sunny room that wouldn't have looked out of place in a five-star hotel. It was nice, actually—I mean, of course it was nice, but it didn't just look posh; it looked comfortable too, with the old wing-back chairs and antique tables carefully placed so you'd always have somewhere to put a cup of tea.

"Tea?" Lionel asked, making me jump. "Or would you prefer coffee?"

"Whatever you're having," Phil said politely.

"Tea it is, then," Lionel said genially. "Do take a seat—I shan't be a moment." He swept out of the room.

I glared at Phil. "I was going to ask for a coffee."

"Tough. It's the witness we need to keep sweet, not you. And don't forget to do your stuff," he added in a lower voice.

"Fine," I huffed. While he sat down in one of those comfy-looking chairs, I wandered around the room, listening for vibes. It was odd—there was definitely nothing in the room, but I was picking up a faint trail from somewhere. Every time I grabbed for it, though, it trickled away.

"Found something?" Phil murmured.

"Not sure. I—" I broke off as Lionel came back into the room, bearing what looked like a solid silver tea tray with a matching teapot, sugar bowl and milk jug, plus some dinky little tea cups with saucers. There was even a plate with homemade shortbread fingers on it. My opinion of Lionel went up a notch.

We all sat down, and Lionel poured the tea like we were at a Women's Institute meeting, about to discuss the jam-making rota. I took a piece of shortbread and tried not to groan obscenely in pleasure at the way it melted in my mouth, an explosion of butter and sugar. The tea, afterwards, was a disappointment—nothing wrong with it, but it wasn't anything special, either, and those bone-china cups were way too fiddly.

"I have to say," Lionel began, "I'm a little surprised you're investigating poor Melanie's death. Isn't this sort of thing best left to the police?"

He seemed to have a lot of faith in Dave and his boys. I wondered how they were getting on. Seemed to me if they'd come up with anything, we'd have heard about it.

"I'm sure they're doing an excellent job," Phil said smoothly. "But it never hurts to have an extra pair of eyes looking out for things. A fresh perspective."

"I shouldn't have thought any fresh perspective were necessary. There's no doubt in my mind who's responsible for this dreadful business. I told Melanie she was making a mistake, tying herself to that drug-addled layabout, but poor girl, I'm afraid she refused to listen to the voice of experience."

I bristled, but Phil carried on with an even tone. "My information is that Graham had been off drugs for over a year at the time of Melanie's death."

"There's no such thing as an ex-addict," Lionel said, shaking his head. "It's an old saying, but a true one."

"What, like *give a dog a bad name and hang him*?" I asked, deciding that tasty shortbread fingers notwithstanding, I wasn't a huge fan of Lionel Treadgood.

Phil gave me a look like he wished we were sitting around a table so he could kick me in the shins. Hard. "I imagine you worked quite closely with Melanie on church matters," he said, losing the glare as he turned pointedly to Lionel.

"Oh—well, to some extent, yes. Of course, a lot of it gets accomplished without face-to-face contact, of course. I'd drop off things for her attention at the vestry, and she'd do the same for me."

"But you had regular meetings?"

"If you mean the PCC meetings, then yes. But there would be between ten and twenty of us at those, depending on other commitments."

"And the vicar, I assume, would attend?"

"Meredith? Oh, yes." Lionel's mouth twisted a little as he said the Rev's name. I got the feeling he didn't have all that high an opinion of poor old Merry.

On the other hand, it could just be that utterly crap name he hated. Seriously, what had the Rev's parents been thinking? Had they secretly wanted a hobbit?

Phil leaned forward. "How well did Meredith and Melanie get on?"

"Oh, Melanie got on well with everyone, poor girl. She was such a lovely young lady—always willing to help out. And never had a bad word for anyone." He sighed. "She's a sad loss to the parish. But then I always did question the wisdom of her...personal choices."

"You mean Graham?" I asked sharply.

Lionel spread his hands in a smugly eloquent gesture. I had half a mind to give him an eloquent gesture of my own. "Even his best friends could hardly claim he was any great catch. And now—well, it seems he's shown his true colours."

"Graham Carter hasn't actually been charged with murdering Melanie," Phil put in mildly.

"No, but really, who on earth could it have been, if not him? Nine times out of ten—more, I've no doubt—it *is* the lover." Lionel shook his head. "I feel sorry for him, actually—he was bound to suffer from an inferiority complex, with a fiancée like Melanie."

The fact that I'd been wondering myself what on earth she'd seen in him didn't make me hate Lionel any less. I drew in a breath.

"Want another?" Phil asked pointedly, thrusting the plate of shortbread in my face.

I blinked, startled. It brought me back to myself. I had a job to do here. "Oh—no, thanks. Actually, Lionel, do you mind if I use your loo? 'Fraid that tea's gone right through me."

"Of course. In the hall, next to the front door."

"Thanks."

I didn't, of course, follow his directions. I tiptoed upstairs as quietly as I could, wishing I'd thought to change into trainers. At least the stairs were carpeted, with a thick crimson runner. I couldn't work out why it made me feel vaguely uneasy until I realised it was exactly the colour of blood, as if a river of the stuff was pouring down the stairs like in some cheap horror-schlock film. I shuddered, then told myself not to be so daft. Blood's actually quite a nice colour, as they go, and it went well with the William Morris Thistle wallpaper.

There was an oak sideboard on the landing between the two flights of stairs, with a massive dried flower arrangement on it, presumably in case you got bored halfway up and wanted something to look at. The window behind it was made of that antique glass that looks like old bottles, and you couldn't see through it. The whole place smelled of wild roses. Once at the top of the stairs, I listened carefully. Again, all I got was a faint trail that slipped away from me teasingly every time I tried to get a fix on it.

All the doors on this floor were either shut or just barely ajar. Hoping like hell there'd be no one in there, I opened the door to the nearest bedroom and peered inside. It was a good-sized room but very clearly not used for sleeping in—there was a sewing machine set up on a table by the window, a dressmaker's dummy, and bits of fabric everywhere. It looked like the current project was curtains, in a pale floral fabric that looked like it cost more per yard than all the ready-made curtains in my house put together.

There was nothing in there. I closed the door.

Then a soft, musical voice asked, "Can I help you?"

Chapter Thirteen

I nearly jumped right out of my skin. I whirled to see a woman several inches shorter than me with silver-blonde hair. It was hard to tell how old she was, with her big, blue eyes and waiflike figure. She looked beautiful but fragile, as if she'd been made out of the same bone china as Lionel's little teacups.

I gave a nervous laugh. "Sorry, love—I was looking for the loo. Think I must have taken a wrong turning somewhere." I smiled at her, trying to hide the pounding of my heart.

She smiled back. "The bathroom's just down the hall, the second on your right. You've come to see Lionel, haven't you?"

I nodded. "Are you, er, Mrs. T?"

"Patricia, please." She held out one tiny hand, and I took it carefully, paranoid I'd crush it with my plumber's grip. "Delighted to meet you."

"Yeah, same here. Oh—I'm Tom, sorry. Tom Paretski. Did you make those shortbread fingers? Because they were lovely. Best I've ever tasted." I managed to stop babbling, eventually.

A tiny flush of pink appeared in her cheeks, and her smile deepened. "I only followed my mother's recipe. But I'm so glad you enjoyed them."

There was a moment's pause.

"Still, I mustn't keep you." Her cool, soft fingers slipped away from mine, and I carried on mechanically towards the bathroom she'd pointed out. Bloody hell, she was unreal. Unearthly. She was the sort of woman you could imagine slaying dragons for, or launching a thousand ships... I shook my head. What kind of effect did she have on a straight bloke, for fuck's sake?

The bathroom was big and plush, and completely bare of dirty secrets, unless you counted that Lionel didn't bother to clear his pubes out of the drain after a shower. Mrs. T—Patricia—was still audibly pottering around upstairs, so although I stood on the landing for a moment, listening, I didn't try and look in any more rooms.

God, Phil was going to love me.

When I got back downstairs, I got the feeling the interview was over. Lionel and Phil were standing by their chairs, and all the shortbread was gone. Bastards.

Lionel shot me a sharp look. "I hope you didn't get lost?" The implication *and steal a few priceless knickknacks on your way* hung in the air between us.

I gave him a carefree smile. "Ran into your missus, actually. Lovely lady."

Lionel's expression softened, though he still looked a bit wary. "She is indeed. Her father was a High Court judge, you know."

I wasn't sure what that had to do with the price of fish—did he wish he'd married the judge?—but I nodded and tried to look suitably impressed.

"Well, as I was saying to your colleague, I'm afraid I have to ask you to leave. An appointment with my solicitor, you know how it is. Sorry to cut things short—but, well, I'm sure the police can only be days away from arresting that young man in any case."

Phil didn't look happy. "Before we go, could I just ask you—"

Lionel cut him off. "Sorry—I really do have to go." He steered us firmly out into the hall, managing without any of the little shooing motions the Rev had used. There was no doubt about it, the bloke had presence.

"Are your guests leaving so soon, Lionel?" Again, the melodic voice seemed to come from nowhere, without warning.

We all turned to look up at Patricia, who was standing halfway down the stairs as if she'd been posed there by MGM. I glanced at Lionel. As he gazed up at his wife, he gave a gentle, seemingly unconscious smile that made him look about ten years younger. "Oh, you know, darling. That wretched appointment with Cameron."

"Oh? I thought that wasn't until four thirty."

"Change of plan, my dear. He has another client who's being difficult, so..." He shrugged.

"Of course." She wafted down to stand on the bottom step. "Well, it was lovely to meet you, Mr. Paretski."

"Tom," I said, stepping up quickly and taking both her hands, because weirdly, it seemed the only proper thing to do.

She smiled. "Tom, then. And your friend...?" She glanced over at Phil.

"Morrison," Lionel said. "He's a private investigator."

Patricia's eyes widened. "That must be very exciting."

"Mostly routine," Phil said, like he couldn't give a toss what she thought. I wondered what the hell his problem was.

"Mrs.—Patricia," I blurted out. "Don't suppose I could trouble you for that shortbread recipe?"

"Of course you may. Would you like me to get it now?" She looked delighted.

Lionel, on the other hand, wasn't a happy bunny. His bushy eyebrows lowered like storm clouds over eyes that were getting ready to shoot out lightning bolts. "Darling, I really—"

"Nah, that's okay." I didn't want to cause any domestics. I dug in my pocket for a card. "All my contact info's on that. Don't want to make your hubby late for his appointment."

I pressed the card into her cool little hand, and we left.

"Bloody hell," Phil muttered out of the side of his mouth as we crunched back to the car. "Did you see Treadgood's face when you were chatting up his wife? Enjoy living dangerously, do you?"

"I wasn't chatting her up! But I'll tell you what, if I was straight..." I sighed. "She'd still be way out of my league."

"She's just a woman," Phil said, sounding amused.

"No, she's a lady. There's a difference."

"Yeah, and it's made of paper and lives in a bank. Come on, Romeo, time to bugger off before the lord of the manor sets the dogs on us."

"You know, class is nothing to do with money," I told him as we strapped ourselves into the Golf.

"So what are you trying to say? We should all know our place and not get above ourselves, is that it? *Can't take the council estate out of the boy?* Thanks a fucking bunch." The gears complained as Phil put the car in reverse a bit too viciously.

"That's not what I meant. I just meant... Patricia Treadgood's a lady, that's all."

"Fine. I hope you'll be very happy together." We drove out onto the road to play hunt-the-pothole again. "Course, you might have to bump off *hubby* first, but I'm sure she'll forgive you for that. It'd be the classy thing to do."

"You know, right now I'd like to do something really classy to your arse."

There was an excruciating silence that lasted through several potholes. Okay, so maybe I hadn't meant it to come out *quite* like that.

"Listen," I said quickly, trying to break the tension that was crackling through the air. "There's something I ought to tell you."

"Like what?" Phil sounded cautious, but then we were just getting to the worst bit of the road.

"It's about the case. And the Rev. I went to see him again yesterday—I wanted another chance to search the place." I paused. If I was waiting for a pat on the back, it was a good job I wasn't holding my breath.

"You what? On your own? You twat!" Phil's face darkened, its lines hard. "Have you forgotten this is a murder investigation? And the Rev's a sodding suspect?"

"He didn't do it," I said earnestly. "I found what he was hiding, and it's nothing to do with Melanie or her death."

"And how the bloody hell do you know that? If you've got something to hide, you can be blackmailed about it. That's how it works."

I was shaking my head. "You didn't see it. It was, well, it was a bit pathetic, really. Just a few really tame gay books and some old letters and pictures."

"Who were the letters from?" Phil asked.

I shrugged. "Dunno. I didn't read them. They were old. They obviously weren't anything to do with Melanie."

"Have you even been listening? People have been blackmailed over stuff that's fifty years old."

"You what? The *Rev* isn't even fifty years old."

"You know what I mean. Please tell me you at least looked at the photos to see if there was anyone in them we know."

"Look, I'm sorry, all right? They weren't rude or anything. It just didn't seem relevant."

"Nobody knows what's relevant or not, at this stage. I can't believe you didn't look at them."

"I don't like prying, all right?"

"Don't like... It's what you *do*, for fuck's sake!"

"No, it's what *you* do. I've got a so-called gift I never asked for. I didn't choose this—not like you did. You're the one who decided to make a business out of poking your nose into other people's lives."

"So basically," Phil said, a frown creasing his forehead and an edge to his tone I didn't much like, "what you're saying is, my job disgusts you."

"That's not what I..." I trailed off. Maybe it was what I'd meant. "I don't know, all right? All I know is, I don't feel comfortable doing it."

"Feel more *comfortable* watching Graham go down for his girlfriend's murder, would you? While the bastard who did it looks on and laughs? Would that be all right with your holier-than-fucking-thou conscience?"

"Oh, for fuck's sake! That's not what I'm bloody saying, and you know it." We'd turned onto Brock's Hollow road, and I'd had enough. "You can let me out here. I'll get a bus back or something."

"Don't be so bloody stupid. I'm not leaving you stranded here on your own," Phil snapped, as if I was a none-too-bright ten-year-old who'd never quite got the message about stranger danger.

"Worried the Rev's going to pop up to have his way with me and bury me in the churchyard? Actually, hang on a minute," I said, my anger draining away as I thought about it. "If the Rev killed Melanie, why wouldn't he do just that? Why not hide a body with a whole lot of other bodies? Wouldn't it be way riskier taking the body somewhere else? I mean, he'd have to get it there, and it was always going to get found eventually, up on Nomansland Common. The whole bloody village walks their dogs up there. Even the Girl Guides go up and build dens there."

Phil's knuckles were still white on the steering wheel, and he took a couple of deep breaths before he answered. "You might have a point," he said, like it was being dragged out of him along with his fingernails. "But you've got to remember, people don't always do the logical thing when they've got a body on their hands. Most murderers don't plan to kill."

"Yeah, but you said this one did, didn't you? The phone call, I mean. That had to be planned in advance."

"*If* it was the murderer who made the call."

"Oh, come on—it'd have to be a bit of a coincidence, otherwise."

"Coincidences happen. That's why there's a word for them."

"There's a word for unicorns too, but I haven't seen a right lot of them prancing down the High Street lately."

"There's a word for smartarses, come to that." Phil's tone was still grim, but he'd eased up on the death-glares, and he was keeping to the speed limit as we drove into the village.

I relaxed a bit. "Only one? I thought you had a better vocabulary than that. You need to stop reading the *Sun* and start buying yourself a proper paper. You know, one where you don't just look at the pictures."

"I can find all the words I need to describe you in the *Sun*, thanks."

"What, like *cor, what a stunna?* I'm flattered—I never knew you saw me that way."

Phil just shook his head, but he was smiling.

"Hey, are you doubting my abilities as a glamour model?"

"You do seem to be lacking a couple of essential qualifications," he said, glancing at my chest.

"You haven't seen me with my kit off. At least, not since school. I like to think I've filled out a bit since then."

Now he was laughing. "To page three model standards? I bloody well hope not."

"If you hate tits that much, how come you spent so much time at school hanging around with Wayne Hills and that crowd?"

"God knows." There was a beat. "You know I—"

"Don't," I said. It was all water under the bridge, now. "That was a long time ago, all right? You're not the same bloke you were then, and neither am I."

He glanced at me as we turned into Four Candles Lane. "You reckon? Because I don't think you've changed all that much."

"Great, so now you think I never grew up." And presumably, never got over that stupid crush I'd had on him.

"No, that's not what I mean. You just... Forget it." I opened my mouth, about to push him on it, when he beat me to it. "Do you—fuck." He shook his head again. "Sod it...I know this is a daft idea, but do you want to get dinner some time?"

I stared at him. After about a minute, I realised I still had my mouth open, so I shut it, quick. Then I opened it again. "You what? Are you asking me out?"

"Maybe."

I couldn't seem to get my head around the idea.

I think my silence got to Phil. "Look, forget it, I said it was a daft—"

"No!" I blurted. "I mean, yeah, I'll go out with you. Um. For dinner, you know, I'm not saying I want to be your boyfriend, because obviously..." My mouth still wasn't working properly. Or my brain, come to that, so I shut the one and hoped the other would sort itself out PDQ.

Phil looked a bit shell-shocked. I wasn't sure if it was down to my babbling, the fact he'd asked me out, or that I'd said yes. It was probably just as well we'd got to the Four Candles, as I had a nasty feeling if we talked any longer, we'd bugger it all up again. "Right," he said, as he parked the car next to my van. "Tomorrow all right?"

Probably didn't want to give either of us too long to have second thoughts. "Yeah, that's fine. Why don't I come out to yours, for a change, and we can walk into town from there?"

"My place is a bit of a mess..."

"So? What am I, a domestic goddess? Have you got any pets?"

"What? No." He sounded baffled.

"So you win over me on the cat-hair factor, at any rate."

"Fine, fine. Just don't expect much, all right? I've only just moved in. You still got the address?"

"Yes, Mum."

"Call me that while we're out and you'll be paying for your own dinner."

I'd thought I would be anyway. God, this really was going to be a date. Phil Morrison was Taking Me Out For Dinner. An embarrassing little shiver ran through me at the thought, as if I was still at school, lusting after him from afar. Bloody hell, I was going to have to watch myself. At this rate, I was going to start doodling little hearts on my invoices and putting *Tom loves Phil* inside. I shook my head to clear it of the frightening image.

"Are you all right?" Phil asked.

"Yeah—fine. Um. See you around seven, seven-thirty?"

He nodded. "Whenever you can get there."

"Right. I'll see you then, then." I got out of the car, still not quite believing it. Me and Phil, going on a date.

I might even have something to tell Gary about, next time I saw him.

Chapter Fourteen

I wasn't working on Saturday, so I had plenty of time to wonder what the hell I thought I was doing, agreeing to go out with Phil. I cleaned the house a bit, did some food shopping, watched the football on the telly. By six o'clock, the butterflies in my stomach had mutated into flying elephants all flapping around like Dumbo drunk on champagne. It was daft—after all the time I'd spent in Phil's company over the last couple of weeks. But that had been business—his business, at any rate. This...this was dinner, with a chance of sex.

At least, I hoped there was a chance of sex.

Well... I thought that was what I hoped. To be honest, I wasn't entirely sure what the best-case scenario was in this situation. Phil was...well, basically I fancied the pants off him, but every time we spent more than half an hour in each other's company, we ended up yelling at each other. And not in the porno way. It was so bloody frustrating—every time I got a hint he might actually like me, it all seemed to go tits up the next time we met.

I wasn't even sure what to wear. He'd only seen me in my work clothes—scruffy jeans and dusty shirts. Would he be disappointed if I dressed up? Did he like to see me as his little bit of rough? Then again, if I turned up like that and he was all smart in his posh shoes and his cashmere, wouldn't it just look like I couldn't be arsed to make an effort?

It was weird—back in school, *he'd* been the bit of rough. Maybe he'd had a taste for the good life back then, but his parents certainly hadn't had the money to indulge it. My dad had made bank manager by the time I was in my teens, so my stuff was always brand-new. God, I hoped this wasn't just some twisted way of getting his own back on me, of rubbing it in how well he'd climbed the social ladder, while I'd slipped down a rung or two.

In the end, I went for a fairly new pair of jeans and a lambswool sweater Gary always tells me makes my shoulders look bigger. Of course, sod's law it'd be warm in the restaurant so I'd end up taking it off, and be back to my usual skinny-runt-in-a-T-shirt look, but at least I'd tried. Then I gave the cats an early tea and set off on foot.

Phil's flat was just up from the old Odeon on London Road. They've tarted the outside of the cinema up a bit recently—supposed to be restoring the inside as well. I wasn't holding my breath, but at least they weren't just letting the place fall down anymore. I'd even chipped in the odd fiver to the fundraising myself. From the location, I'd expected Phil to be living above a shop, but as it happened, the whole building had been converted into flats. His was on the top floor—in fact, when the house had been built, it would've been the attic. I wondered how he was getting on with the sloping ceilings—at his height, I'd have thought they'd have been a bit of a challenge. I grinned to myself. Maybe that was why he was so grumpy all the time— he had a permanent headache from constantly banging his head on the ceiling.

It looked like I wasn't going to have to wait to find out, as he buzzed me in on the first ring and opened the door to his flat just as I reached the top of the stairs. He smiled when he saw

163

me, which sent the butterflies into overdrive. He looked relaxed, in jeans and a soft blue shirt the colour of his eyes. "Want to come in for a drink before we head out?"

Dutch courage? I was all in favour of that. "Yeah, sounds good." I stepped inside and looked around. The place had been modernised recently—it was all open-plan, with bright white decor and light-coloured wood, making the most of the space. In daylight, it'd probably be light and airy, but the downside was a faint smell of fresh paint which didn't seem to sit too well with my empty stomach.

It was also...bare. And full of boxes, many of them open at the top and showing signs of frustrated rummaging. "Still not unpacked yet?" I asked, because there's a rule you have to state the obvious in this sort of situation.

"Not even close." He grimaced. "Half the trouble is, I've got no cupboards or shelves to store stuff when I unpack it—the London flat was furnished, and I've been concentrating on buying the essentials. Like a bed." It was good to know he had one of those. A decent night's kip is very important. "I've got a sofa on order," he carried on, oblivious to my filthy mind filling in what else his new bed might be good for, "but for now, you'll have to park your arse on the garden furniture."

There was a set of green plastic chairs and a wobbly looking table next to a large, square window, all of them covered in either boxes or the contents of boxes. I shifted a few things and pulled up a chair, glad to sit down. "I'm guessing you don't do a lot of entertaining?"

"Not as such, no. Beer? Or would you rather have wine?"

"Whatever you're having," I said, his uncharacteristic politeness obviously having rubbed off on me. "Beer, for preference, but I'm not that fussy," I added a bit more honestly.

"Beer it is, then." He grabbed a couple of bottles from the fridge, opened them and handed me one.

"Cheers," I said and took a swallow—realising too late the gassy stuff wasn't really what my stomach was set up for right now. Maybe it was just nerves, but something was definitely making me feel queasy. "Mind if I open a window?"

"Be my guest."

Even though it was fully dark and had been for an hour or two, Phil hadn't drawn the curtains. I supposed that this high up, he wasn't worried about people looking in. I leaned on the windowsill and drew in deep breaths of fresh, cold air, but the nausea didn't go away.

"Are you all right?" Phil asked, looming a bit, which didn't help me feel any better.

"Yeah...uh, well, I'm feeling a bit off. Maybe I'm coming down with something." I turned from the window and paced through the room. Was this just nerves? As I tried to walk it off—whatever *it* was—I trailed my fingers along a stack of boxes against the wall. "Maybe dinner's not such a great—bloody hell!"

I snatched my hand away from the boxes. It felt like I'd had an electric shock, one that sent greasy jolts right into my heart.

"Tom? What the hell happened?"

"I don't know. I think..." Almost without meaning to, I let down my barriers and listened. The pulse of guilt and shame that slammed into me brought me to my knees, my stomach turning and a white hot ache in my head.

"Tom!" Phil was by my side, was helping me up. "Christ, what is it?"

"Something…something in one of those boxes," I managed. "Bloody hell, Phil, have you got a dismembered corpse in there?" I was joking. It wasn't that kind of feeling at all.

"You're…reacting to some of my stuff?" His bewilderment seemed genuine, but the greasy darkness from the boxes was calling him a liar.

"Yeah." I tried to smile. "Badly."

"I can bloody well see that. Come on, come and sit down." He parked me in the one free chair, then marched over to the boxes I'd touched. "Which one was it?"

"The one on the top—third stack along. But you don't have to show me. It's not like I go round telling you all my dirty little secrets."

"That what you think this is?" Phil's fist clenched, and for a moment, I thought the offending box was about to be pummelled within an inch of its cardboard life. At least, I hoped it'd be the box. "I'm not having you thinking I've got kiddie porn in there."

Actually, I'd been thinking more along the lines of BDSM and/or amputee fetishes, but yeah, kiddie porn could have accounted for the way it'd hit me.

Possibly.

I'd never reacted to *anything* this badly before. I didn't say anything more, because despite what I'd said, I was bloody desperate to see just what it was.

Phil turfed through the contents of the box, laying them out on the boxes to either side. There were ancient packets of photos, what looked like school books—why the hell would anyone keep those?—and then an envelope. A bog-standard brown manila envelope that nearly made me throw up at the sight of it.

"That's it," I rasped.

He was looking at the envelope like he'd never seen it before—and I saw the exact moment when he realised what it was. His eyes widened—then narrowed dramatically. "Okay. I know what this is. It's not porn. Can I put it away?"

"It's your stuff. You can do what you want." My voice was strained.

He gave me a sharp look. "It's still bothering you?"

"Yeah. Still hidden, see?" I nodded at the envelope and nearly fell off my chair.

Phil stared at me for a long, long moment. "Fucking hell." His tone was resigned as he opened up the unsealed flap of the envelope and drew out a few bits of paper. He handed them to me, and the relief was so great it felt like euphoria. I couldn't even focus for a moment.

"Oh, God, that's so much better," I breathed.

"Well, take a look at them; you might as well." Phil turned abruptly away and strode over to the window I'd opened, staring out into the darkness.

I looked. Then I looked again. There wasn't much there. The first was a clipping, yellow with age, from a newspaper: *Local boy in serious car accident.* I read on automatically. *Thomas Paretski, 17, was seriously injured when he was hit by a car...* I put it down. I didn't need to relive that story. The next was a grainy photo. Of me. Or rather, of my teenaged self, badly cut hair, less-than-perfect skin and all. The last was a picture of the school under-eighteen football team. I'd played in defence. We were all grinning madly and gurning for the camera—looked like we'd just won a match.

I didn't even remember the occasion. But Phil had kept these mementoes.

"Why?" I asked, my tone over-loud and harsh in the tingling silence.

"You mean, why did I keep those?" Phil was talking to the window, his tired voice making a circle of condensation on the glass. "What do you think?"

"You felt...guilty about the accident? *Really* guilty?" I couldn't believe that was all it was.

Phil turned, his face dark. "Oh, for— Yes, I felt guilty. But I fancied you, all right? Back in school."

"But—I thought you hated me!"

It was like lighting a firework. In your living room. Phil exploded, and it wasn't pretty. "I *did* fucking hate you, okay? I hated the things you made me feel, made me want... Christ, don't you realise I didn't have a bloody clue I was gay until I noticed you drooling over me after games? I wanted to fucking *kill* you for making me feel that way."

He was breathing hard, his fists clenching and unclenching. I got slowly to my feet, then wondered if that just made me a bigger target. "Um, I think I'd better go," I said uncertainly. I realised I was still holding the photos and stuff, so I put them down on the chair. This was just too weird.

Phil had fancied me—by the sound of it, as much as I'd fancied him. Maybe more, even. And he'd kept the photos, the clipping, for a dozen years, even through a move.

But he'd still hated me.

Halfway to the door, I turned. "Why did you keep them?"

"Because I never wanted to forget the way I felt when that car hit you."

I swallowed. "That wasn't—I'm hoping that wasn't because it was such a *good* feeling?"

"No. It wasn't." He gave a tired smile. "You're right. This was a crap idea. I'm sorry. I'll see you, Tom."

Now, of course, I wasn't sure I wanted to go. I was pretty certain Phil didn't want me to stay, though, so I nodded and closed the door behind me.

I called up Gary on my way back into town and begged him to meet me up the Dyke. For one thing, I was starving, and if I tried cooking with all this on my mind, I'd probably end up burning the house down. For another, I couldn't face going home alone, where I'd just sit on the sofa and obsess about the god-awful bloody failure of my date with Phil. I needed distracting, and Gary was nothing if not that.

Of course, I hadn't realised that these days, Gary was a buy-one-get-one-free offer. When I got to the Dyke, an ache starting in my head to match the one in my hip, he was curled up in a corner seat gazing at a certain market trader like the sun shone out of his proverbial. I got myself a pint, gave Flossie a pat in passing and joined them, trying not to let my smile curdle on my lips. "All right, Gary? Darren?"

Gary was his usual effusive self, bless him. "Tommy! Sit down and tell Uncle Gary *all* about it. What *did* the nasty man do to you?"

"Did he rest his pint glass on the top of your head, that sort of thing?" Darren asked. I couldn't tell if he was trying to be sympathetic or just taking the piss. Although my money was on him taking the piss.

"Sorry, Gary, I'm not sure I really want to talk about it," I began, with a glance in Darren's direction.

Gary *tsked*. "Darling, don't be silly! Darren and I have no secrets from one another, so you might as well tell us both."

169

Right now I wasn't sure I wanted to spill the beans to either of them, but they *had* come out specially to cheer me up. "It just got a bit weird, that's all. You know that accident I had when I was seventeen, right?" I found I was rubbing my hip, and picked up my pint instead.

Annoyingly, they both nodded.

"Well, it sort of happened when I was running away from Phil and his gang—we didn't exactly get on, back then. Turns out he's been feeling bad about it all these years. Guilty. And he, you know, kept newspaper clippings and photos of me and stuff."

"Oh. My. *God.*" Gary looked like he was worried his face was going to fall off, and he was trying to hold it on with both hands. "Tommy! You've got your very own stalker!"

"No I haven't! Come off it, Phil's not like that." I took a gulp of beer to steady myself.

"Oh? After all these years, he comes in search of you—"

"He came in search of Melanie Porter, actually."

"—finds he can't stay away from you—"

"He asked me to help him out a couple of times, that's all."

"—finally, he entices you into his secluded lair—"

"It's a bloody loft conversion on London Road!"

"—and confesses his obsession."

"He didn't confess, I..." I glanced at Darren. He stared back, poker-faced. "I found the stuff he'd kept, that's all." Except that wasn't all, was it? I put my pint down. "He said he hated me."

"He didn't!" Gary cried.

"Yes, he bloody did. He said he hated me, back when we were at school, because I made him fancy me." God, I was going soft. I'd started to wish they hadn't left Julian at home, so he could put his head on my knee, soak me in slobber and make me feel better.

Instead of a wobbly pair of jowls, a small but meaty hand landed on my leg. Darren's hand. "Course he hated you. Always bleedin' do, don't they? Sodding closet cases. Don't like the message, shoot the fucking messenger. You're better off without that tosspot, ain't he, Pumpkin?"

Pumpkin?

Gary nodded and didn't even blush. Then again, I'm not sure he even knows how. "Absolutely, Sweetie-Pie."

Not the least bit embarrassed either, Darren leaned forward. "Tell you what, I've got a mate out Hemel way—well, ex-colleague, if you know what I mean. Him and his partner are looking for a third. Say the word and I'll give 'em your number."

"Um, thanks," I managed. "I'll let you know. Want another drink?" I was only halfway through my pint, but I was pretty sure I'd be needing another.

I left Pumpkin and Sweetie-Pie cooing over one another and escaped to the bar, where Harry herself was serving. I'd have preferred one of the harem—they're a bit less intimidating, as a rule. She raised a bushy eyebrow at me.

"Two pints of best and a dry martini, please," I asked politely.

"Stirred, not shaken?" Harry queried in that gravelly voice that always makes me fancy a cigarette, even though I gave up smoking a dozen years ago, which was around two weeks after I'd started.

"That's the one. Kitchen still open?" I asked, suddenly catching sight of a packet of pork scratchings and remembering I was starving.

She nodded. "Pie's good tonight."

"Ah, but isn't it always?" I smiled. "All right, you've sold me on it. Pie and chips, please, and whatever veg is going. Got to keep up my vitamins."

She nodded, bellowed my food order to Marnie in the kitchen and got busy pulling pints.

I handed over twenty quid, thinking I really needed to make time for a bit more actual paid work in the near future. And maybe take up running, to burn off all this beer and pub grub. Harry gave me a tray to take the drinks over—it's easy enough carrying three pint glasses in your hands, but you try it with two pints and one of Gary's dinky little cocktail glasses. He'd have been well pissed off if I'd dropped his olive.

"Lovely, sweetie," Gary said when I plonked them on the table. He and Darren had fallen silent when I'd got back.

"Talking about me, were you?" I asked, sitting down.

Gary shrugged. "There's nothing wrong with being the centre of attention, I've always thought. Anyway, you can get your revenge by talking about *me* now while I pop to the little girls' room."

Once Gary was out of earshot, Darren leaned over the table, fixing me with what's usually described as a gimlet stare, although I wasn't too sure what it had in common with Philip Marlowe's cocktail of choice. "He talks a lot about you, my Gary does." There was a definite emphasis on the *my*. "I hope this bust-up with the closet case don't mean you're going to start looking nearer to home. You ever lay a finger on my Gary, I'll nut you in the nadgers." He cocked his head to one side, giving me a speculative look. "Actually, in your case, I reckon I could knee you in the nadgers."

"Whoa!" I threw up my hands. "Gary and me are just mates. Cross my heart and hope to...get kneed in the nadgers. Anyway, haven't you noticed he's about this far from getting your name tattooed on his arm?" I gave Darren my own hard stare, one I'd copied off Harry from that time she caught someone making homophobic jokes in her bar. "So make sure you treat him right."

"Or what?" he taunted, in a you-and-whose-army sort of voice, but he was smiling.

"Or I'll come round in the night and fix it so your sewer backs up in your kitchen sink."

Darren burst into hearty cackles. "You're all right, aintcha?" He took a long swig of his beer. "Did Gary tell you I used to be in films?"

I toasted him with my pint. "What do you reckon? Think Gary would keep quiet about something like that?"

"Bless 'im. Have you seen any of them?"

"Well, none that I remember... But then again, I probably wouldn't have been looking at your face." It seemed a bit more tactful than just saying *Sorry mate, I don't watch dwarf porn.* "What was your stage name?"

"Ever see the *Man from UNCLE*?"

I nodded, wondering where this was going.

"You're looking at the one and only Napoleon So Low." He leered as he said it, and I spluttered into my pint.

"So have you given Gary a private showing?" I asked.

"Depends what you're talking about, don't it?" Darren put down his pint, just as Gary returned.

"Ooh, what have I missed? I hope you two haven't been talking about me." He was lying through his teeth. Gary *loves* people talking about him.

"Would we?" I said, just as Darren chipped in with, "Only the good stuff." Then his face softened. "Course, that's all there is, innit?"

"Aw, bless him!" Gary cooed, looking worryingly moist around the eyes. "Isn't he adorable?"

"Darren was just telling me about his career in films," I went on quickly, before any of us could drown in the slushy stuff. I turned to the man in question. "So how come you gave it all up? The acting, I mean," I clarified before he could come up with some ripe innuendo on the subject of *giving it up*.

He made a face. "Had to, din't I? Industrial accident." He shook his head sadly, and Gary joined in.

Call me a coward, but I *really* didn't dare ask. Good thing my pie turned up at that point.

The food was lovely, bless Marnie's nimble fingers, although I had to edge around the table a bit to protect the chicken filling from Flossie's hungry gaze. She stayed on the alert for a moment longer, ears pricked and nose twitching in my direction, then settled back down on her well with a reproachful air. I didn't feel guilty. I knew for a fact Harry fed her two square meals a day, plus all the rowdy drunks she could chew on.

I'd no sooner set my fork down for the last time than Sweetie-Pie and Pumpkin were making their excuses.

"Sorry, Tommy." Gary pouted. "Darren and I need to get an early night. I need to be up bright and early tomorrow morning to ring in the faithful."

Darren leered and nudged me painfully in the ribs. "And after that, he'll be coming home and ringing my bell."

Gary shrieked with laughter and pretended to slap Darren. "Sweetie-Pie! You are *terrible!*"

As far as I could see, the only good thing about that evening was getting home to find a chatty, friendly email from Patricia Treadgood, attaching both her shortbread recipe and one for ginger snaps.

Chapter Fifteen

Sunday morning, I woke up way too early for someone who had neither bells to ring nor a boyfriend to shag. Granted, it hadn't been a particularly late night, but this was my chance to have a decent lie-in, and I hated to waste it. Still, once you're properly awake, there's no point fighting it. It was either get up or lie in bed having a lonely, maudlin wank over Phil Morrison. I got up.

I had some part-baked croissants in the freezer, so I bunged them in the oven, made a cafetière of coffee and sat down on the sofa with the cats, warbling a little Edith Piaf as I went. A perfect lazy Sunday morning. At least, that was the intention, but the cats buggered off because they hate my singing and the words didn't fit anyway, seeing as I was regretting a bloody sight more than *rien*. I thought, sod this for a lark, so I had a shave, put on something respectable and went to church.

No, I hadn't suddenly got religion. It'd just occurred to me that everyone mixed up with Melanie's case was also mixed up with Brock's Hollow parish church. Apart from Graham, obviously, but I was trying *not* to treat him as a suspect. And all right, Robin East and his wife probably weren't much into the God-bothering business either, but the rest of them were. I didn't really have a plan in mind, but I thought it couldn't hurt to see them all together, watch how they acted with one another.

I felt a bit bad about turning up on the Rev's doorstep like the proverbial bad penny, but then again, maybe it'd reassure him if I went along and didn't do anything to out him?

When they built St Anthony's Church, Brock's Hollow, which according to the signs was sometime in the thirteenth century, for some reason they didn't think to put in a car park. I ended up parking next to the Four Candles and hurrying breathlessly into church just after the service had started. My shoes clattered like hob-nailed boots on the flagstones, and the Rev faltered in the notices he was reading out. I mouthed *sorry* in his general direction, hoping the rest of the congregation would get the message too, and looked around for a spare pew. It wasn't as easy as you'd think. For all the talk in the papers about declining church attendances, this place was pretty well stocked with worshippers. Looked like the better schools in the area still had a church-attendance requirement to get your kids a place.

"This way—there are some seats in the Lady Chapel," a reedy voice whispered in my ear, and I turned to find a wiry old dear, so bent over with age she had to peer up sideways at me, offering me a chirpy smile and a hymn book.

I beamed back at her, relieved to see a friendly face. "Thanks," I whispered, following her doll-like steps around the side of the main pews and up towards the front. The church was built in the shape of a cross, and I ended up in one of the arms, staring at the side of the Rev's head. A family of four obligingly shuffled their bums over to make room for me on the end of their pew, and I sat down as quickly and as quietly as I could. "Thanks," I whispered again. The old lady beamed and toddled off again.

Across the way, I was surprised to see Robin East was here after all. No sign of Samantha. Maybe Sunday morning was her time for bathing in the blood of freshly squeezed virgins.

The Rev finished droning on—something about an extension project, and the forthcoming Advent Carol service—and announced a hymn. Everyone opened their hymn books, and I flicked around frantically in mine trying to find the right page as the organist started up.

"Tom, how lovely to see you here."

I looked up, startled, into Patricia Treadgood's face. She was in the pew in front, next to her husband. The glare Lionel shot me over a ramrod-straight shoulder left me in no doubt how lovely *he* thought it was to see me. I smiled at Patricia, mostly because I was glad to see her, but also because it'd annoy him. "Hey, you too. I didn't see you there. Thanks for your email."

"My pleasure." She turned back to the front just as the organ intro finished and everyone launched into the first verse. Everyone except me, of course, as I was still trying to find the bloody thing. Maybe this was what I'd missed out on after they'd kicked me out of Sunday School: advanced hymn-finding. I hunted on, trying not to curse, until a small hand tugged at my sleeve. The little girl next to me shoved her hymnbook under my nose, one grubby, nail-bitten finger pointing out the place they'd got to.

"Thanks," I whispered yet again, and did my best to join in the tune. By the time we'd got through seven verses, I had an aching back and a crick in my neck from leaning down awkwardly to share the book with her. I'd also remembered I was tone deaf, and by the appalled and/or amused faces around me, quite a few people were now in on that little secret. Maybe I'd just lip-synch from now on.

Then again, the row in front had shifted slightly and Lionel Treadgood was right in front of me. I couldn't think of anyone else I'd rather torture with my off-key attempt at religious worship. I needed something to amuse me, because frankly, I was disappointed. I'd come here for a game of spot-the-suspect, and I'd clocked half of them in the first five minutes. Still, it wouldn't hurt to keep my eyes peeled and check out the rest of the congregation.

As the Rev droned on some more, I let my gaze wander around the church. It was pretty big, and all bare, pale greyish stone—no interior paint to brighten the place up, although someone had got their sewing kit out and made some bright felt banners to hang here and there. Nice flowers too. Hefty pillars blocked the sight lines in several directions, but I was able to spot Pip sitting between a tired, worried-looking woman and a scowling Mr. Pip. I was fairly sure he wasn't thinking pious thoughts as he glared at me. Pip herself kept her eyes fixed on her knees.

Everyone seemed very white, although I suppose most places in Hertfordshire would be a bit like that after Fleetville. There were quite a lot of old dears, most of them in hats, but then it was a bit nippy. There seemed to be some kind of under-pew heating system, which meant my bum was nice and warm but the rest of me was shivering even in my padded jacket. I couldn't see half as many men as women, and most of them were old too, their liver-spotted heads peeking through wisps of white hair. There were just a few young, male heads—and oh, shit. One of them was Phil's. He looked up just at the wrong time too, and I got a jolt in my chest as our eyes met.

The pillar he was sitting next to looked soft and insubstantial next to his granite glare. Bugger. For some stupid reason, it hadn't even occurred to me he might have had the same idea I did and rolled up here. Although the fact I'd been trying to avoid thinking about him all morning might have had something to do with my lack of getting a clue. I wished I could work out what that look he was giving me was all about. Then I wondered what he could see in my face, and if he'd tell me if I asked, because I was buggered if I knew how I felt about him and his little obsession. Was it an obsession? It had only been a couple of photos, for God's sake. And a newspaper article...

I dropped my gaze hurriedly, just as everyone around me shuffled a bit and bowed their heads. Time for the serious God-bothering, I guessed. I tried to look like I was as into it as they all were. At least it gave me an excuse not to look at Phil anymore.

We didn't have to kneel, which was a relief. There were hassocks or cassocks or whatever it is you call those cross-stitched kneelers hanging from hooks on the back of the pew in front, but nobody seemed to be using them. Unless you counted the little girl who'd shared her hymn book with me, who was playing a game with them with her brother, swinging them together like conkers.

I felt like a right fraud, pretending to pray. Luckily, they gave you all the words, rather than make you sit there like a lemon and think up your own. There was a bit where they prayed for people who'd died, and I thought of poor Melanie Porter. It felt weird to think she might be up in heaven now, looking down on all this. If you believed all that stuff, anyway. Then I started thinking, if there was a God, why didn't he just send down a thunderbolt on the bastard who'd killed her, and save me and Phil the trouble?

It occurred to me about then, though, that depending on your views about the whole thing, God (if he was there) might not look too kindly on blokes like me and Phil, and might think we were pretty good candidates for the thunderbolt treatment ourselves, so I decided maybe I'd just keep my head down in here and not draw attention to myself.

When the service was finally over, Patricia turned round to me again. "Are you staying for coffee, Tom?"

"Er..." Actually, I'd been planning on making a quick getaway before Phil had a chance to ask me what the bloody hell I thought I was doing here.

"Oh, do stay. It's all Fair Trade, you know."

I wasn't sure how that was supposed to persuade me, but I found myself nodding. Lionel looked pretty pissed off about the whole thing, which was a plus. "Well, seeing as it's you asking," I told her with a smile, and she glowed a bit in response. So after the organist had played the retreat for the blokes in frocks—with the choir as well, there were quite a lot of them—I joined the queue for the coffee urn, which was handily set up just inside the area I'd been sitting in.

The coffee was all right, but the Fair Trade biscuits turned out to be not a patch on Patricia's shortbread. I turned to tell her so, but while I'd been exchanging a few words with the ladies serving coffee, it seemed Lionel had whisked her away. Instead, I found myself face-to-face with Phil. Well, all right, given the height difference I was face to throat with Phil, but that didn't make things any easier. Neither of us spoke. Then both of us spoke at once.

"You all right—"

"Sorry about last—"

We fell silent again. Set into the floor by my feet was a stone slab like a tired gravestone; I could just make out the words, *Here lyeth ye virtvovs body of...* The name had been worn away by generations of Christian feet, but whoever it was, I envied them briefly.

"Hello, again. You're new, aren't you? Welcome to St Anthony's." I looked up from my feet and into the wrinkled face of the old dear from earlier. "Are you two together?"

I was momentarily floored. Did she mean *together*, together, or just together?

"Um, we're, um..." I managed.

"No," Phil said flatly and walked away. It felt like he'd slapped me in the face.

"Well, he wasn't very friendly, was he?" It was delivered in high, ringing old-lady tones, which had to have been heard by half the congregation and must have left Phil's ears burning. I was glad he couldn't see my smile.

"Maybe he's just not a morning person," I suggested. "Thanks for the welcome. I'm Tom, by the way, and yeah, it's my first time here. Nice church—those flowers are lovely." I nodded at a big, fancy spray of red and white blooms and greenery that'd almost taken my eye out a couple of minutes ago.

Her crepey cheeks bloomed with a rosy glow. "Thank you! I do my best with them, but of course, it isn't easy in the winter. I'm Edith Penrose, but please, call me Edie."

"Lovely to meet you, Edie. Would that be Miss or Mrs.?"

"Mrs., you cheeky young man, although I lost my dear Albert twenty years ago. He's out by the lych-gate. I'll be paying him a visit after I've finished my coffee."

Just as I was wondering if she was going to invite me along to say hi to the late Mr. P, and if she'd be expecting him to say hi back, a familiar voice battered my eardrums from around three inches away. "Tom! Darling, what on earth are *you* doing here?"

I turned to see Gary beaming at me. "Came to hear the church-bell concerto, didn't I?"

"I hope you haven't been leading our Edie astray. Watch him, Edie, he's a total heathen. And the *worst* flirt."

She gave me a roguish smile. "I might have known you'd turn out to be a *friend of Gary's.*" She made it sound like a euphemism. "Well, it was lovely meeting you—I do hope we'll see you here again soon." As she twittered off, I could just make out a sigh, and the words, "Such a waste."

"Hey, I'm not a flirt," I protested.

"And I'm the Pope, sweetie. Now, why are you *really* here?"

I sighed. "It's complicated. Phil's here too, by the way."

As I'd thought, that got Gary's attention off difficult questions right away. "Ooh, where? Where is he? Tall, blond..." He scanned the coffee crowd feverishly.

"By the door, about to bugger off."

Gary looked, just as Phil half turned, displaying a firm-jawed (some might say gittishly stubborn) profile. "Oh, my *God!* Is that him? He is *gorgeous!* No wonder you're such a mess about the whole thing."

"I'm not a mess!" Anyone would think I was a love-sick schoolgirl, the way Gary was going on about it.

"Don't argue with your Uncle Gary. Now, have you finished your coffee? Good. Let's get out of this crush before Merry signs you up for choir practice."

"Not much chance of that," I muttered darkly.

"Why do I get the feeling there's a lot you're not telling me?" Gary asked, shepherding me past the milling faithful like a little lost lamb. We emerged blinking into the sunlight, which gave me a good excuse to pretend I hadn't seen the Rev. He was waiting at the door to moisten everyone's palms, a sort of final baptism before they headed out into the wicked world again. "Now, I wonder... Ooh, there he is!" He waved frantically, and I saw, with a sinking feeling, that Darren was here. He was leaning on a tombstone, but as I watched, he pushed himself off it and started ambling towards us. "He said he might come, if he wasn't too tired after last night."

"Thought you and him were getting an early night?" I said, a bit distracted. I should have known, really I should.

Gary's elbow impacted sharply with my ribs. "Oh, but we *did*. Very early. And *very* exhausting!" He giggled.

Darren caught up with us. "Oi. I thought I told you to stay away from my bloke," he said, but he was smiling, so it looked like my nadgers would live to nadge another day.

"Want to tell me exactly what you think we might have got up to *in church*?"

He gave me a look. "Ah, but how do I know you were in church? You can get up to all sorts in that belfry of Gary's."

"I wouldn't know," I told him.

"Of course he wouldn't, Sweetie-Pie," Gary put in. "I've never *had* Tom up in my belfry."

"You've had me up there, though, haven't you, Pumpkin?" Darren gave a filthy laugh. "Several times, now."

I might not be religious, but I was a bit scandalised, all the same. "Gary! You can't do that kind of stuff in a church!" I hissed.

They burst out laughing.

"What?" I said, miffed.

"Darren was speaking, ah, euphemistically. We weren't talking about the *actual* belfry."

Thank God for that. "Right. Fine. But keep it down, yeah? The volume, I mean, in case you thought I meant that euphemistically too. There are people still coming out of church." I turned to indicate the open door, just as the Rev poked his head out.

He saw our little group, and for a moment, I thought he was having a heart attack. His face, pale to begin with, turned grey, and he literally staggered where he stood. A group of die-hard churchgoers surrounded him then, and he was lost to view.

I felt sick. Christ, what had I done to the poor bloke?

"Well, well, well," Darren said. "Who'd have thought it?"

I wrenched my attention back from the concerned knot in the church porch. "Thought what?"

"I'd never have reckoned I'd see that face above a dog collar." He laughed. "Not that sort, anyhow."

"Ooh, do you know our Merry?" Gary trilled.

"Darren," I said carefully. "If you're about to tell me you used to work with the bloke, I think my head's going to explode. Fair warning and all." Bloody hell. The Rev's little episode hadn't been about me at all. It'd been about Darren.

Darren laughed. "Nah—but he was a fair old goer in his day. Years ago, it was, back in London, when I met him. There was this party, see—we was celebrating, 'cause we'd just finished filming..." He frowned. "Sod it, which film was it? Might have been *A Taste of Mud Honey*—or hang on, was it *Hope and Glory Holes*? You'd have liked that one; it had a plumber in it. Goes to fix a public lav in Clapham, and when he bends over to shove in his plunger, he gets—"

"And the Rev?" I whispered, impatient.

"Yeah, he was—oh, I know which one it was we'd just done. *The Horniness of the Long-Dicked Cummer.* Good film, that was. I had some great reviews for that one."

I looked around nervously, but luckily all the old dears from church were already doddering off to their Sunday lunches or their online bingo or whatever it was they did with their time, not listening in to Darren's potted history of British gay porn. "So this party, what happened?"

"Well. Me and the lads turn up at this place—it was at the director's house, nice place it was too, very nice—and we was still in costume, so we was in a fair bit of demand. I had on this leather harness—"

Gary's face lit up. "Ooh, Sweetie-Pie, have you still got it?"

"Nah, sorry, Pumpkin. Weren't mine to start with—I had to give it back after the party. Tell you what, though, I know a bloke with a garage in Camden—"

"Can we get back to the bit about the Rev, here?" I interrupted. "You can sort out your kinky love lives later."

"Bit of a prude, are we?" Darren asked in an *Ooh, get him!* kind of voice.

"Just think of me as the saddo who isn't getting any, so doesn't want to hear about people who are," I muttered.

"You won't want to hear about the Rev, then. When I saw him, he was sucking off Wayne—he was the long-dicked cummer—and getting his arse pounded by Rudy. Course, Rudy just had a small part in the film." Darren cackled with laughter. "Had a big part in your Rev, though, din't he?"

My gob was well and truly smacked. I stared at him, open-mouthed. Then I closed it quickly, because the mental image of a spit-roasted Merry wasn't doing wonders for my stomach.

"I don't believe it!" Gary actually sounded genuinely shocked, which is not an easy feat to accomplish. "Merry?"

"He was that night, anyhow. Totally off his head. Anyone's and everyone's, he was."

"You *didn't!*" Gary gasped, his hands to his mouth.

"What, me personally? I'm wounded, Pumpkin. I thought you knew I've got taste." He winked. "I know a few more who did, though."

God, Merry must have been easy prey for that lot, with all his pent-up desires and his repressions wiped out by the alcohol and whatever else he was on. Maybe Darren read my expression. "What? He was old enough to look after himself, wasn't he?"

Gary made a sort of apologetic face.

"Course," Darren carried on thoughtfully, "now I come to think about it, maybe it ain't so surprising. I used to live near Lambeth Palace, and you wouldn't believe what a load of randy buggers some of them was. They never admitted they was church, mind, but you can tell."

I didn't need to hear any more. "Listen, I've got to go, all right?" I said. "I'll catch you later." I half ran out of the churchyard. I had to tell Phil about it. This was just what he'd been talking about, wasn't it? Blackmail—at least, the possibility of blackmail.

It didn't make sense, though. Even if Melanie had somehow found out about the Rev's wild youth, would she really have blackmailed him? I didn't want to believe her capable of something so, well, heartless. And it was an even bigger leap of faith to imagine the Rev killing her. After all, when he'd found me poking around his stuff he hadn't gone ballistic with the fire irons, had he?

I shivered a little, though, as it finally sunk in what a risk I'd been taking, going there on my own. Phil was right. I'd been a twat.

I got in my Fiesta, made sure my seat belt was nice and tight, and drove back to St Albans, bypassing my house and heading straight for London Road.

Chapter Sixteen

I was relieved to see Phil's Golf parked outside his building—for all I'd known, he might have been off investigating something, or even just out at a pub somewhere for Sunday lunch. I found a space halfway down the road, glad the restrictions didn't apply on Sundays. Parking in St Albans is a bloody nightmare. I pulled on the handbrake, wiped my palms on my jeans and went and knocked on his front door.

Phil didn't look happy to see me. Then again, he didn't look all that unhappy either. Basically, he was back doing his impersonation of a slab of rock. "Tom," was all he said.

"Yeah. Can I come in?" I asked, shifting my weight from my bad side.

He stepped aside, leaving the door wide open, and set about clearing one of the garden chairs. There was noticeably more mess around than last night; he'd obviously spent the evening working on his box collection. Maybe he'd wanted to make sure he'd unearthed all potential skeletons before the next time I came round and blundered across them. "Coffee?" he offered.

"No, thanks. Just had some," I reminded him.

"Want to sit down?"

I didn't, really, but it seemed a bit impolite not to seeing as he'd cleared the chair specially. I sat, and he loomed over me like one of the monoliths at Stonehenge gone rogue, while I shifted on the chair, trying to get comfortable.

"Listen," I said. "I found something out today. After you left. Darren—that's my mate Gary's new bloke—he used to know the Rev."

"And?"

I took a deep breath. "And it looks like I should have read the letters, after all. Turns out the Rev's got a bit of a secret past."

"What kind?"

"The open-to-blackmail kind. Darren called him, and I quote, 'a right goer' in his day. He said he'd seen him at some kind of sex party, and it wasn't so he could tell people the error of their ways." I hesitated, then blurted it out anyway. "But I still don't think he killed Melanie. She'd never have blackmailed him, and he's not the violent sort. No way."

Phil stared at me—then looked away. He grabbed another chair and shunted the boxes onto the floor, then sat, leaning towards me with his elbows on his knees. "Tom, you've met the vicar twice. All right, three times, if you count this morning. You never knew Melanie at all. Do you really think you're qualified to decide what either of them is capable of?"

I opened my mouth to argue, but he carried on.

"You're letting yourself get too close to these people. Nobody wants to believe crap like that about people they know—but it happens every bloody day. Maybe Melanie was one of those Christians who think being gay's a sin; have you thought about that? She might have told Lewis he had to resign or she'd expose him. And you've no idea what kind of pressures the Reverend's under. Sometimes people just snap. Christ, Tom, you need to be more careful."

"No," I said. "You're wrong. I don't know how I know it, but you're wrong."

"What is this, more of your special talents? Turned into a bloody polygraph now, have you?" Phil turned away with a muttered curse and stared out of the window. "Sorry," he said without turning. "But have you got any basis for believing what you do?"

I stood up and walked around, trying to ease the ache in my hip. Bloody church pews. "No," I admitted. "Sod it, I don't know. Anyway, I've told you now, all right? So you can do what you like with that little bit of information."

Phil turned back to me. "This Darren, you got a full name and address for him?"

"Sorry. I can give you Gary's address, I suppose. Darren seems to have more or less moved in there. Or you can catch him at the market; he's got a stall. You can't miss him— shortest trader, loudest voice." God, I hoped Gary would forgive me for sending Phil round to ruffle the feathers in their little love nest. I wandered over to the window, having noticed a picture of a good-looking, dark-haired bloke that hadn't been on the sill last night. "Who's this?" I asked, picking it up.

"My husband."

Shock stabbed me in the chest and I spun round so bloody fast I nearly fell over. "Your what? You mean all this time, all this dancing around me you've been doing, you're sodding well *married*? Does he know you bring blokes home when he's away? Or is it that sort of marriage anyway? Forget it—I don't give a monkey's. Just leave me out of it, all right?"

I was halfway to the door, breathing hard, my heart beating furiously, before Phil spoke. "He's dead."

This time, I turned slowly, feeling cold inside. "Dead?" I said stupidly. "Really dead, or just as in *he's dead to me*, dead? Because you've been sending out some pretty mixed signals—"

"He died in a car crash. Seems there's a lot of it about." There was nothing humorous about his smile. "It was a couple of years ago, now, and we were separated, anyway."

"But you still wear the ring. Why the bloody hell did you lie about it?"

"I didn't lie. I told you I wasn't married, and I'm not. Not anymore."

"Yeah, but you made me think—"

"Think what? That I was an arsehole? So what? No skin off your pretty little nose, was it?"

There was that phrase again. Did it mean anything, him calling me pretty, or did he say that sort of thing to everyone? "I don't like people lying to me," I said. Because whether or not he'd said the words, he'd lied.

"And I don't like telling the whole bloody world about me and Mark, all right?"

"I'm not the whole bloody world!" I snapped, stung.

Phil rubbed his face with both hands. "No. You're not—now. But back then, you might just as well have been. For all I knew, you still hated me for what happened when we were seventeen."

Had I hated him? I wasn't sure anymore. "You don't like it, do you? Letting people in. Letting them find stuff out about you."

Phil looked up but couldn't seem to meet my eyes. "Knowledge is power."

"Bollocks. That's just what people say when they're paranoid Google's logging their porn."

"Is it?" Phil took a step forward, and for a moment, I thought he was going to grab me by the shoulders, but then he let his hands fall. Just as well—I didn't fancy getting into a knock-down fight with him. I had a feeling it'd be me who'd end up getting knocked down. "You're telling me, if no one had ever found out about you being queer at school, you'd still be walking with a limp?"

It hit me like a body blow. "I don't limp," I said weakly.

His face was twisted in what looked like anger, but his eyes were lost, somehow. "Yeah, right. Ever seen yourself on CCTV?" He looked like he wanted to kill someone, and I realised with a shock it wasn't me.

My stomach felt hollow. "It's all right. It doesn't even ache, much, in the summer. And it wasn't your fault. It just happened."

He didn't say anything.

"Look, I don't blame you for it," I said. "Everyone does stuff they regret when they're young." He was doing his made-of-granite act, but he wasn't fooling anyone. Well, he wasn't fooling me, at any rate. I stepped up to him and lifted a hand to his face.

Phil twisted away from me. He didn't actually tell me to bugger off, but then he didn't need to. I sighed. "Fine. I'll see you around, all right?"

I went home to the cats hoping for some simple, uncomplicated affection, but they were facing off in the hall, hissing and spitting at one another. It looked like Merlin had got on all six of Arthur's kitty tits this time. I grabbed Merlin and carried him out of harm's way, sitting on the sofa and stroking him until he started to purr.

Then I remembered I hadn't given Phil Gary's address. I picked up my phone to call him—then thought better of it. He knew where I was, if he wanted to ask me.

I wasn't trying to avoid Phil by going to the Rats for a bit of Sunday roast. I just didn't have anything in the fridge I fancied eating.

Honest.

I was surprised to see Dave there, sitting in a corner with his paper and a plate of fish and chips. The Rats was a bit off the beaten track for him. I gave him a friendly wave, and he beckoned me over. "Tom? I was hoping to catch you here. A word, if you wouldn't mind."

I could tell by the serious tone he wasn't just after help with the *Mail on Sunday* scrabblegram. "Course, mate. What's up?"

"Branching out, are you? Your job got a bit boring, so you're trying to do mine as well?"

Shit. "Has someone been saying stuff about me?" I pulled up a stool and sat down.

Dave wagged his fork in my direction. "I've been getting all kinds of grief about you and your mate Phil Bloody Morrison harassing witnesses in the Melanie Porter case."

"Harassing... We went to talk to a few people, that's all." I hoped I didn't look as guilty as I felt. If it was the Rev who'd complained, he might actually have a point—but would he really risk letting the cat out of the bag like that? "Who's been giving you grief?"

"Lionel Treadgood. Said you've been pestering his wife too."

"*Pestering?* I asked her for a bloody recipe! Now come on, no way did Mrs. T complain about me—and Phil didn't even speak to her."

"That's not what her husband says."

"Well, have you tried asking her about it?"

"No, because then he'd be on *my* back about police harassment." At least Dave was looking less pissed off and more amused now. "Seriously, Tom, swapping recipes? Did you ask her where she got her hair done too?"

"No, but we're going shopping on Saturday, and then we're going to do each other's nails. You know, there are plenty of straight blokes around who don't think it's sissy to cook. Try telling Gordon Ramsay only nancy boys hang around the kitchen—he'd panfry your nuts and serve them up as a starter."

"Yeah, well, that's different. He's a chef."

"Oh, I see—it's all right, as long as you're wearing a silly hat and getting paid for it. Not every single bloke likes to live on a constant diet of pub grub and takeaways, you know." I felt a bit bad for him even as I said it—although on the other hand, maybe Mrs. S wouldn't have been so quick to skip out on him if he'd been a bit keener to help with the cooking. "I bet I could even teach you a few meals, you know," I added.

Dave shuddered. "Thanks—but old dogs, new tricks. I can manage beans on toast; that'll do me."

He was probably right. Plus, if his mates on the force ever found out I was giving him cookery lessons, the poor sod would never live it down. "So anyway," I said, hating to get back to the subject but knowing I had to. "Has anyone else complained?" I crossed my fingers.

Obviously Jesus was the forgiving sort, as Dave shook his head. "No, but I don't like seeing you get mixed up in this kind of thing."

"You're the one who called me in to find her," I reminded him.

"Yeah. Find her. And then leave the rest of it to the professionals."

"Phil's a professional," I said slyly.

"He's a loose bloody cannon, that's what he is. Trampling all over my investigation."

"Bit hard for a cannon to trample. No feet."

Dave's eyes swept briefly heavenwards. "Fine. He's rolling all over my investigation, then. With his cast-iron bloody wheels. Crapping out cannonballs."

"Sounds painful."

"Trust me, it will be if I find out he's bollocksed up my case."

"So have you got a case, then?" I asked innocently. "Is it against Robin East?"

"Nice try, sunshine. You're not getting word one out of me—not while you're in bed with the bloody enemy. I wouldn't even give you the time of day."

I was a bit miffed. I'd thought we were mates. "Anyone would think we weren't on the same side here."

"And I wonder why that might be?"

"Hey, we all want justice for Melanie, don't we?"

"The best way of getting that is by letting the police do their job. Not by running around putting people's backs up."

"The only one that's happened to is Lionel Treadgood. And I reckon his back's permanently up." I hesitated, then plunged on. "Dave, why have you never got me in when you're searching a suspect's house? You know, looking for evidence."

"Because there's no point finding stuff if we can't use it to get a conviction. There are rules about conducting searches, and they're there for a reason." Dave put down his fork. "Look, Tom, I'm getting enough bloody grief with this one going cold on me. Don't make it worse, all right?"

It sounded like he wasn't going to be arresting either Graham or Robin for it in a hurry, which was good, wasn't it? Wasn't Graham's safety all I was after? It didn't feel right, though—leaving Melanie unavenged. Maybe Phil was right, and I was getting too close to it all. I nicked one of Dave's chips while I thought about it.

"Oi! That's my dinner."

"Thought you'd finished," I said with a grin. "So how come you're not having the roast, then? Do you know something I don't?"

"Gravy." Dave sighed. "No one makes gravy like my Jenny used to."

Jenny was the ex-Mrs. S. It looked like Dave still missed her, poor sod. "Guess I'll join you in the fish and chips, then," I said to show solidarity. "Another pint?" He nodded, and I went off to the bar to place my order.

I half expected the pub lunch with Dave to turn into a whole afternoon, but after he'd finished his second pint, he stood up and belched. "Right, I'm off. Got better things to do than sit about drinking all afternoon like a bloody layabout."

"Oh, yeah?" I teased. "Hot date, is it?"

To my delight, he blushed. "Maybe."

"You can't leave it at that!" I protested. "Who is she, then, and how long have you known her?"

"First: none of your beeswax, and second"—Dave went even redder—"I don't know her yet. Met her on one of these online dating sites, and if you breathe a word about this to anyone, I'll bleedin' kill you."

"Better watch out," I warned. "She'll probably turn out to be at least ten years older and three stone heavier than her profile picture."

"Yeah, but everyone does that, don't they?" He gave an embarrassed smile. "It's practically compulsory. I put in my profile I was late thirties, with an athletic build."

God help the both of them, I thought, but I just raised my glass and wished him luck.

Chapter Seventeen

At half past ten on Sunday evening, I was just puttering around, getting ready for bed—had an early drain next day—when the doorbell rang. Generally, when that happens, you don't expect good news—but when my heart sped up a little as I went to answer it, it wasn't only for the bad reasons. There was a little voice in my head saying maybe, just maybe it was Phil.

It wasn't. It was Merry, in mufti—at least, he'd left off the dog collar—looking about as relaxed as, well, a closeted gay vicar visiting a bloke who knew all his dirty secrets.

Or, say, a murderer about to commit crime number two. I suddenly wished I'd thought to put the chain on. "Er, hi, Merry. Bit late, isn't it?" I managed to get out without too much stuttering.

Merry glanced around furtively, which didn't do a lot for my nerves. "Please, can I come in? Just—just for half an hour."

I couldn't think what to do—but he looked like he was at the end of his tether. His skin was paler than ever, with an unhealthy sheen, and his hands were shaking. "All right. But just for half an hour." I opened the door fully, Phil's inevitable verdict of *You twat* ringing in my ears, and motioned him in. "You can go through to the living room," I said, gesturing at him to go in front, partly because I was brought up right and partly because that meant I'd be able to keep him in sight.

"Um, I'd offer you a coffee, but..." *But I'd like you to go as soon as possible.* All right; maybe the upbringing didn't take all that well.

The Rev, halfway through parking his bum on my sofa, made a jerky motion with his hand that presumably meant *No, ta, it keeps me awake this time of night.* At least, I hoped it meant that, and not *Actually, I'd rather not leave DNA traces on your cups.* "I need to speak with you," he said once he was fully seated. "About this morning."

I perched on the arm of the chair opposite him. The illusion of superior height would have been more comforting if it hadn't been just that—an illusion. "What, in particular?" I asked cautiously.

Merry looked like he was about to cry. "What do you want?"

"I... What?"

"You brought him there, to, to denounce me. To expose me." Merry gave a sickly smile. His hair was plastered to his forehead in thick, greasy strands, and his top lip glistened. "I'll do anything you want, you know that, don't you. Anything."

"What? No!" I leaned forward. Christ, had he meant...? I hoped he hadn't meant what I thought he'd meant. I folded my arms, trying to hide a shudder. "You've got it all wrong. You don't have to do anything. Darren was there for Gary. They're an item. No one's going to expose you." I thought about it a bit. "Although, you know, you could save yourself an awful lot of grief if you just came out. What is it the Good Book says? *Christians aren't perfect, they're just forgiven?*"

Merry was obviously relieved enough to give a pedantic little frown. "That was a car bumper sticker, actually."

"Ah. Sorry. But wouldn't Jesus approve, you know, of the sentiment?" I stood up and rubbed my hip. Then I realised

Merry's eyes had fixed a bit manically on my pelvic area, and I sat down again hurriedly.

"I can't come out," Merry muttered, his hands wringing one another damply. "You don't understand. I did terrible things when I was younger."

I stood up again. "Crimes?" I asked, my voice a bit high.

"Against God, yes."

I wished I hadn't turned the dimmer switch down. In the low lighting, his face was marred by sinister shadows. "But...would they be things you'd go to prison for?" I prodded, moving so the armchair was between me and him. Darren's party hadn't got *that* wild, had it?

"The conscience...the conscience is its own prison," he mumbled vaguely.

Did I have my phone in my pocket? Maybe I could call Phil. Or Dave.

I cursed under my breath as I realised I'd left it charging in the kitchen. "But you don't do that kind of thing anymore, do you?" I said as soothingly as I could manage.

"But I want to!" he said so fiercely I jumped. His eyes glittered darkly.

Maybe some straight talking was called for. "Have you ever considered that maybe, just maybe, you're not really cut out to be a vicar?" I asked.

"Leave the priesthood?" Merry sounded like the idea had never even occurred to him. But at least it seemed to have got him thinking of something other than his dark, forbidden lusts.

"Well, yeah. Because you don't seem all that happy right now. Maybe you're just asking too much of yourself. Maybe," I added, inspired, "God doesn't want you to suffer so much. He's supposed to be loving, isn't he?"

"But my vocation…"

"There's other stuff you could do, isn't there? And still be, you know, serving God and all that? There's…charity work. Or missionaries," I added eagerly, because somewhere like Africa would be nicely far away from Regal Road, St Albans.

Merry stood. I edged away a little bit. "You…you've given me much to think about. Thank you."

"You're going to do it?" I asked, now worried I'd gone a bit too far with the careers advice to a bloke I hardly knew and didn't want to.

"There are things… I need to put things straight. Yes. The path is clear now. Thank you." He smiled, his face transformed. I'd never seen anyone look at one and the same time so innocent and so bloody scary. "God truly works in mysterious ways." He carried on smiling and muttering to himself as he walked out of the house.

Once he'd gone, I bolted the door, put on the chain and took a deep, shuddering breath.

Then I grabbed my phone from the kitchen and called Phil.

He didn't bother with hello. "What is it, Tom?"

"I—uh, can you come round? Sorry."

"Tom? Has something happened?"

"Yeah, kind of…" Now I had to explain it, I felt stupid. "No, I'm just being daft. Forget I called."

"I'll see you in five minutes." He hung up.

This time when the knock came on the door, I didn't take the chain off until I was sure it was Phil.

"You look like you've seen a ghost," he said ominously.

"Either that, or just narrowly missed becoming one," I muttered. Phil didn't laugh—if anything, his frown deepened—so I hurried on. "I just had a visit from the Rev. It freaked me out a bit, that's all. I shouldn't have bothered you about it, though. Sorry."

"Stop fucking apologising. What happened? And how did he know where you live, anyhow?"

I stood back so Phil could get his broad shoulders inside and wipe his size-eleven feet on my doormat. "From the phone book, maybe?" I tried to rein in the sarcasm. "I do have a business to run here. Are you telling me you're ex directory? Do your clients have to hire someone just to find you?"

"I've got an office on Hatfield Road." Phil stayed put, just inside the house, so I had to sidle past his reassuring bulk to shut the front door. I wasn't complaining.

"With a sexy secretary in six-inch heels and bright red lipstick?" I quipped, feeling better already for his presence.

He folded his arms, but it didn't come across as a defensive gesture. It came across more as a *just in case you've forgotten the size of my biceps* gesture. I hadn't forgotten, but the reminder didn't hurt one bit. "No, as it happens. Why? You want to apply for the job?"

"Heels, with my hip? And red's really not my colour. No, ta. Look, come in properly." I shepherded him through to the living room. "Do you want a drink?"

He nodded. "I'll have a beer, if you've got some."

I got us a bottle each; opened them up. Nearly dropped them when I looked up and realised Phil had followed me into the kitchen in those stealth moccasins of his. I flushed and waited for the sarcastic comment. It didn't come, so I handed him his beer.

"That's better," he said after a long swallow. "Want to tell me all about it, now?"

Somehow it was easier to talk to him in the kitchen, leaning against the counters opposite one another while the cats milled around our legs. Where had they been when Merry was here? Staying out of the way due to some sixth sense of their own? Thanks, guys. Trading them in for a pair of Rottweilers was looking more appealing all the time. "You know what I said about Darren recognising him? Well, he came round in a right paddy. The Rev, I mean, not Darren. He thought I'd set it up, thought I was after something."

"And?"

"I told him I wasn't, obviously. Then he went on and on about the terrible things he'd done when he was younger—that was his words, *terrible things*—and how he still wanted to do them. And that he knew what he had to do now." I shook my head, not looking at Phil. "Go on, rub it in about how bloody certain I was this morning he hadn't done it."

There was a *clunk* as he put down his beer, and then the dark, cashmere-clad bulk of him intruded in my vision. I looked up to find him only inches away from me, and took a sharp breath. Phil smelled warm and solid, with a hint of spice. "Why did you call me?" he rumbled. "Why not DI Southgate?"

My smile was as weak as the rest of me felt right now. "Call the police? Christ, I don't know. If I sic them on the Rev, they'll dig up all the stuff he wants buried, but if I don't... Do you really think he's a danger?"

"I think it wouldn't hurt to give your mate Dave a call. You don't need to go into details. Just tell him the vicar's been acting a bit odd, and you're worried."

"Yeah. I guess." I grabbed my phone from my pocket, and dialled Dave's number. It went straight to voice mail, so I left a long, garbled message and hung up. "Great. Now he'll probably call me for details at three a.m."

Phil had an odd expression on his face. I couldn't quite work it out, and then it hit me—he didn't look stony in the slightest. He looked younger, less cynical—almost fond. My chest felt warm and tight, and I had to take a deep breath, which I managed to turn into a yawn.

"Need your beauty sleep, do you?" Phil asked. "Guess I'd better be going, then." There was a definite hint of disappointment in his voice.

"No—don't go." I swallowed. "I mean, if you'd like to stay…" My heart raced.

He froze. "Just what are you offering, here? Because I think we ought to be clear on this."

He was probably right—but the band around my chest tightened at the thought of laying myself bare. "Do you want me to be offering anything?"

"Let's not play games, Tom. You know I want you."

I did? "Then…that's what I'm offering," I heard myself say.

There was a moment of absolute stillness. I swear my heart stopped beating. Any minute now he'd say something like, *Are you sure?* And then I'd bottle it, tell him *nah, daft idea*, and that'd be it.

He didn't. His warm hands slid around my waist, and he pulled me close. I felt his hardness grow against my belly and shivered. He didn't ask if I was all right, thank God. He just bent his head and kissed me.

Phil tasted of beer, and bitterness, and regret. But as our tongues moved together, the bitterness faded away, leaving a new taste of want and need. I still had my beer bottle in one hand, and I fumbled blindly behind me for the counter, setting my beer down heedless of whether it stayed upright or spilled its contents onto the floor. Phil's hands dropped to my arse and cupped it, lifting me up against him. God, that felt good. My hands now free, I slung them around his neck, pressing his mouth into mine. Lips and teeth clashed bruisingly. Despite my efforts, he broke the kiss. "Are we going to do this here?" he asked roughly.

"Wherever you want," I mumbled into his neck, his stubble scratching my lips, my face.

He chuckled, his hand still kneading my arse. "Can't help noticing you haven't got any blinds. Don't want to frighten the neighbours, do we?"

"Well, maybe Mrs. F. at number ten. She's a right miserable old cow." I bit at his neck, just above his collar.

Phil gasped. "Come on—upstairs. Or do I have to carry you?"

He would too, I didn't doubt. "Can't take the caveman out of the boy, eh?"

"Something like that." He gave my arse one last squeeze.

We stumbled out of the kitchen, still half-entwined, and up the stairs, Arthur doing his best to trip us up on the way. "First door on the right," I told Phil, because my hands were a bit busy right then to open the door. So were his, but he shouldered it open anyway. "Sorry about the mess," I muttered, trying not to think about how many days' worth of old socks were littered around the floor.

"Forgotten what my place looks like already, have you?" Phil countered.

I didn't want to think about Phil's place, with its guilty secrets and its photo of the man he'd loved, so I pushed Phil down onto the bed and landed on top of him. He laughed, and twisted somehow, and suddenly he was on top, his weight crushing the breath out of me and making me dizzy. "This all right?" he asked sharply, lifting up on his arms.

"Fuck, yeah," I breathed, wondering what he was on about.

"I mean, for your hip."

"Oh—yeah, it's fine." It wasn't aching any worse than usual, and my cock was being a bloody sight more insistent about wanting attention. "Don't worry about it."

He gave me a look like he didn't believe me, and knelt up over me, straddling my legs. I was about to complain until I realised he'd done it so he could get his kit off. The cashmere sweater hit the floor to hobnob with my manky old socks, and half a second later, his shirt joined the party. I was struggling to follow Phil's example, but then he undid his trousers and completely robbed me of the ability to think straight.

Yeah, of course I'd seen his cock before. School changing rooms. Showers. But it had been a bloody long time ago, and back then, it hadn't been stiff and erect and pointing straight at me. He was big—bigger than I remembered. God, I wanted to taste him. I could smell him from here, musky and male, with a strong hint of salt from the wetness that glistened on his exposed head.

I didn't even realise I'd licked my lips until Phil smiled. "Want a taste of that, do you?"

"Oh, God, yes."

"Lie down. Put a couple of pillows under your head."

I did what he said, my cock now screaming at me for a touch, or at least to be let out of my jeans. I ignored it and waited, breathing hard, for Phil to get his trousers off properly and get himself into position to fuck my face.

He was a bloody tease about it, holding his cock in one hand and rubbing the end of it all over my face and neck before he finally touched it to my lips. Good thing I'd had a shave today. Or maybe he liked a little pain, anyway. I bucked up, trying to get my mouth around him. "Greedy, aren't you?" he said, sounding fond. "Say please."

"Please," I said, making a rude gesture at him at the same time.

"I ought to spank your arse for that," he muttered, but he lowered himself down on me anyway.

I opened wide for him, shielding my teeth with my lips. Salt exploded across my tongue as I flicked it over the head of him, and he moaned. He pushed in, and I circled him with my tongue, the circles getting smaller and smaller until I poked the tip of my tongue into his slit, because I bloody love it when blokes do that to me.

Phil swore. Looked like we had something in common. I brought a hand up to fondle his balls, rolling them around in their soft, hairy sac. Phil made tiny thrusting motions into my mouth, obviously holding himself back. His arms, as he gripped onto the headboard, were tense and shaking. "Bloody hell," he said and pulled out of my mouth.

"I was enjoying that," I protested.

"So was I. Too bloody much." He knelt just out of reach for a moment, breathing heavily, then swung his leg away. "Time you got some clothes off, Paretski."

I sat up and took my shirt off a bit more slowly than I needed to. I was trying to think how to do this.

I didn't want Phil to freak out when he saw my scars.

They're not terrible—I'm not the bloody Elephant Man—but it's obvious I've had surgery. I could pretend I was shy; ask him to turn the light off, or get under the duvet, but wouldn't that just make it more obvious? In the end, I thought, *sod it.* "Don't freak out when you see the scars," I said, pushing off my jeans and underwear all in one go.

Phil drew in a sharp breath, staring down at me. He could have been looking at my hip or my cock, but I had a sinking feeling I knew which it was. He was back to stone-face, and he didn't make a move to touch me, either.

Sod it. "Hey, I've got an ache right here that needs some attention," I said, stroking my cock as a visual aid. "If you like, you could kiss it better," I encouraged him.

Phil's gaze lifted to meet my eyes. I dared him silently to say something about the scars, about the accident. To apologise.

He didn't, and I breathed again as he dipped his head to kiss his way down my chest, all the way down to take me in his mouth. The intensity of it made my head spin—Phil Morrison, with his lips wrapped around my cock, and God, he knew a trick or two with his tongue. My eyes kept trying to clench shut, but I was bloody determined to keep them open, to drink in the most beautiful sight I'd seen in a long time.

Phil's fingers ghosted across my balls, but they didn't linger, heading to that bit just behind them. An American bloke I went out with for a while used to call it the *taint*, but I never did find out why. For some reason, I'd kept getting distracted every time the subject came up. Whatever it was called, it was a gateway to heaven. Phil teased it gently, rubbing back and forth, getting closer and closer to my entrance all the time, until—fuck—he slipped a finger inside me.

He took his mouth off my cock so he could speak. "Like that?"

"Fuck, yeah." I gasped involuntarily as he pushed in deeper. He sucked me some more, probing ever deeper with his finger until I was bucking and cursing, then he pulled off and shifted position. I didn't resist as he rolled me on my side and spooned up behind me, his cock jabbing between my thighs, hitting my balls. "You can fuck me, if you want," I said, hoping he wouldn't take the shake in my voice for reluctance. "There's stuff in the drawer." He was silent so long I started to worry. "Phil?"

"Yeah. Fuck, I want that." His words went right to my cock. I leaned over to scrabble in the drawer, and tossed him a condom and a packet of lube.

"Just bear in mind it's been a while, okay?" I warned him.

"I'll take care of you," he rumbled. He caressed my arse cheek for a moment, then slithered down the bed. Oh God. Was he going to do what I thought he was going to do?

He was. His grip on my arse so hard I knew I'd have bruises in the morning, he spread my cheeks wide and dived in with his tongue. How did he know? How the fuck did he know what this did to me? So fucking intimate. I was shaking so hard he must have barely been able to hold me, as that teasing, wet warmth bathed my crack and circled my entrance, then jabbed inside. Again and again he tormented me, until I was so bloody desperate I'd have given anything, *anything* if he'd only get inside me now. I struggled to form the words to tell him. "Need you in me," I begged. "Want you now."

The wait while he rolled on the condom and slicked himself up was agony. I felt a moment's fear as the huge, blunt tip of him pressed against me, and then the burn as he forced his way inside. "Oh, fuck!" I gasped. "Don't stop."

He didn't. He kept pushing, slowly but unstoppably. Stretching me out and filling me. It hurt, yeah, but somehow it was right that it hurt, the physical pain driving away all the mental hurts of all those years ago. Like the operations I'd had when I was seventeen, and the rehab afterwards, where I knew all the pain was doing me good. And then it stopped hurting, and I could feel his balls against my arse, his bruising fingers on my hips, and it was fucking wonderful.

Then he started to move. Slowly at first, then speeding up, he pulled out of me and slammed back in, changing the angle until I cried out, and then hitting that spot again and again. "Christ, Tom," he groaned. "Touch yourself—I can't..."

I barely had to lay one shaking hand on my cock before I was coming, a blinding white flash of pleasure searing through my whole body and leaving me limp and trembling. Phil let out a huge, wordless groan that rumbled through my chest and I knew he was coming inside me, shooting out his own ecstasy. His harsh breaths rasped in my ear, and he let go my hips and wrapped his arms around me, pulling me to his chest. "So fucking beautiful," he whispered. I melted back against him, moulding to his body.

I didn't realise we'd fallen asleep like that until I woke, hours later, my back warm but my front half bloody freezing. Seeing as that was the half with the important bits, I roused myself to try and work the duvet out from underneath Phil's gently snoring body. Thankfully he woke up just enough to give me a hand, as his solid, muscular bulk seemed to have tripled in weight since I'd had him lying on top of me last night.

We'd made a right mess of the sheets—they were definitely feeling a bit crusty—but that could wait until morning. I pulled the duvet up over us both and surrendered to oblivion once more.

Chapter Eighteen

I woke up, the way I often do, just a couple of minutes before my alarm was due to go off. Right. Early drain. I turned the alarm off quickly, not wanting it to ring and wake Phil up. He was lying on his back, his mouth slightly open, breathing softly. I had it on good authority that if I tried that, I snored like a foghorn. His face was softer in sleep, more vulnerable, the blond hair mussed up and boyish. I briefly wondered about waking him up with a kiss or possibly a morning blowjob, then regretfully decided we probably weren't at that stage yet.

Yet. That was implying things were going to carry on from here. We hadn't done a whole lot of discussing things last night—maybe Phil didn't want to carry things on? Maybe last night had been his way of getting me out of his system? My chest felt uncomfortably tight at the thought as I swung my legs out of bed and got up. My bum was aching a bit. I'd be thinking of Phil all day whether I wanted to or not.

Coffee. That'd make me feel better.

When I got downstairs, Merlin greeted me like I'd been gone for a week, winding in and out of my bare legs like I was a kitty slalom course. Arthur just yawned at me from his perch on top of the fridge, the big lump. I got the kettle on and filled up the cafetière; then I took pity on poor, skinny Merlin and filled up his food bowl. That finally got Arthur's attention, so I fed him as well.

"Bloody hell, aren't you frozen?"

I straightened to find Phil standing in the doorway, fully dressed, which made me feel twice as naked, if that's possible. "You could come and warm me up," I suggested.

He gave me a speculative look, then, just as I'd convinced myself he was going to make his excuses and leave, possibly forever, he moved. Four silent steps, and his arms slid around my waist, pulling me close. I hadn't realised I was cold until I felt the warmth of him against my skin. I breathed out into his cashmere sweater, the soft fibres tickling my nose. When did the smell of him get so bloody familiar? His hands dropped to my arse, kneading it gently.

I took that as an encouraging sign he probably wasn't finished with it yet, and pushed him away gently. "I'm going to have to cut and run," I said. "Customer's expecting me. Just got time for a bit of breakfast."

He smiled. "God forbid you go without your food. All right, what's on the menu?"

"Toast," I said. "But I've got some bacon and eggs in the fridge if you want to cook yourself something and let yourself out after."

"Toast's fine," he said, running his hands up and down my hips. Then he stepped back, away from me. "Suppose I'd better let you get on with it."

I made toast and marmalade, and we ate leaning against the kitchen counters. I still felt naked, but it looked like Phil appreciated the view. Scars and all. "Thanks for coming round last night," I said as I bunged my plate in the dishwasher.

Phil handed me his plate. "My pleasure." He took the opportunity to grope my arse a bit more, and when he pulled me back against his body I could feel his erection growing.

"Some of us have got work to do," I said, moving away from him with regret.

He raised an eyebrow. "What, you can't spare five minutes?"

"Only five? Is that all?"

"I bet I can get you off in five minutes."

My dick jumped up to say it'd take that bet, and against my better judgement I let him pull me against him once more, this time face-to-face. His lips were salty from the butter on his toast, there were a couple of tiny crumbs in his stubble, and I was in way over my head, here. He kept on kissing me like the toast had just been the first course and it was me he really wanted for breakfast, while one hand kept on massaging my arse and the other worked on my cock. Pleasure surged through me in pulses, making me gasp into his mouth.

Five minutes? It was more like two and a half before I was coming helplessly, my spunk shooting out in an arc that landed on the kitchen floor, narrowly missing the cats. Merlin gave me a disgusted look, then carried on chowing down.

Phil backed off a couple of inches, looking smug. "Better wipe that up before anyone slips in it," he suggested. "Oh, and Tom?" he added as I reached a limp arm over to the kitchen roll.

"Yeah?"

"I'd think seriously about getting some blinds in here. The neighbours are getting a right eyeful, and I think they're getting a bit pissed off about it."

I darted a panicked glance to the window. There was no one there, of course. "Stop winding me up, you git," I muttered as I bent down to clean up the mess.

"Now there's a sight I could get used to," Phil murmured.

"Since when have you been into looking and not touching?" I said over my shoulder, with my best come-hither look.

He stayed thither. "I can wait till there's time to do the job properly. And that arse is *definitely* worth doing properly."

I waggled it at him, then went upstairs to get dressed with a smile on my face.

When I came down again, he gave me a look. "I've haven't got any other clothes here—what's your excuse? Forget to do your laundry, did you?"

I looked down at my clothes. All right, I'd worn them last night, but they didn't look *that* crumpled. "I'm not putting on clean clothes to go shove my head down a blocked drain. Trust me, no one's going to even notice if *I* pong a bit."

Phil shook his head. "All the jobs you could have done—rat catcher, traffic warden, dustman—and you chose to go wading around in other people's shit for a living."

"It's a labour of love," I said, straight-faced.

We parted company at the front door ten minutes later, and Phil went off back to his place for some clean socks—actually, come to think of it, socks were the one item of clothing I could actually have lent him. It wasn't exactly a sentimental farewell; just a nod and a "See you later." I had to get a shift on, over to the other side of St Albans for Mrs. R. and her blocked drain. Still, at least I was pretty certain I *would* see him later. All of him. My good mood lasted all the way to her house, and even through lying on the ground with my arm down a foul-smelling pipe to the shoulder—then disappeared down the plug-hole when Dave called.

He was another one who didn't bother with *hello*. "What's all this about the bloody vicar, then?"

"Kind of in the middle of a job, here," I protested, trying not to drip slime on my clothes from the hand that wasn't holding my phone, while Mrs. R. wrinkled her nose at me. In the cold light of day, it all seemed a bit daft, me getting so creeped out by the Rev.

"Put that on your gravestone, shall we?"

"What? Look, you've got it all wrong. He was just acting a bit odd, that's all." I glanced at Mrs. R., who was cleaning her glasses on her sari and trying to pretend she wasn't listening in. "Look, I can't talk right now. I'm with a customer."

"How soon will you be finished?"

"Half an hour, maybe? Depends."

"Soon as you can get away, I want you down the station."

"You what?"

"You heard me. I want a proper statement from you about what the vicar told you—none of this *oh, he was acting a bit odd, but I'm sure it's nothing.* I want the facts, that's all. And then *I'll* decide if it needs following up."

"Fine." I might have huffed a bit.

"And you can leave off the martyred tone, all right? This isn't a bloody game. It's a murder investigation. So we do things my way—no, bollocks to that, *I* do things my way. *You* don't even breathe funny without a court order and a note from your mum."

"That'd be you, then, would it? All right, all right, I'll be there, keep your hair on. What's put you in such a bad mood— did she stand you up last night or something?"

There was a heavy sigh. "Oh, she turned up, all right. Bit older than I was expecting, but we had a great evening—went out for a meal, talked for hours. I told her all about Jenny and the job and everything."

"But?" because there was obviously a *but.*

"But, at the end of the evening, she says *Sorry, Dave, you're a nice bloke, but you're too hung-up on your ex-wife.* So that was that."

"Her loss, Dave," I said kindly. Then I hung up and got back to the serious business of sorting out Mrs. R.'s drain.

I don't know if you've ever tried to remember a conversation you had the day before, word for word. I found myself making a right hash of it, although it probably didn't help that every time I shifted on the hard chair in Dave's police interview room, a twinge in my arse sent my mind skipping happily back to last night with Phil. I'd headed straight round to the police station after Mrs. R.'s, thinking if Dave was going to make such a song and dance about the whole thing, he could bloody well put up with me whiffing a bit, but I was starting to wish I'd nipped home for a shower and a change of clothes first. Apparently, the police force weren't big on windows that opened. Funny, that.

"Right," Dave said wearily. "So the Rev's a bit limp-wristed. No surprise there. And he did a few things when he was younger he wouldn't want the bishop finding out about."

Of course, from what Darren had said, there was a good chance the Bish might have got up to some of the same tricks, but I wasn't going to mention that to Dave.

"And," Dave went on, "he had his knickers in a twist about the whole thing, but after he'd talked to you—you being, apparently, Hertfordshire's new gay Agony Uncle—he'd decided what to do about it, and was feeling a bit better. Is that it?"

From the tone of his voice, I could feel a caution for Wasting Police Time coming on. "It...look, you had to be there, all right? He just seemed a bit, well, off."

Dave massaged his temples. "Can you give me a for-instance?"

I screwed my face up so hard, thinking, I could feel a headache of my own coming on. "Sorry," I said in the end. "I did try and tell you on the phone it was just a feeling."

"Feelings. Gawd help us." Dave sighed heavily and pushed back his chair. "Just leave the investigating to the professionals, all right?"

"Sir?" A uniformed constable hovered at the door, although from the look of him, he ought to have been in school studying for his GCSEs. I had a vague idea that probably meant I was getting old, if the policemen started looking younger—but sod it, the kid had *acne*. "You're wanted. There's been a development."

Dave looked round sharply. "What kind of bleedin' development?" The constable's eyes flicked over to me. "Fine, fine, we're done here anyway. Tom, you can go—come back and see me when the Reverend gives you his signed confession, all right?"

PC Puberty's eyes went wide. "Um, sir, you might want to hear about this before you let the witness go."

"Oh?" Dave's voice went sharp. "Hear about what?"

He wasn't looking at Constable Kid. He was looking straight at me.

"Er, well, there's been another incident."

"Another murder?" My voice cracked. Was this what Merry had meant about stuff he had to take care of? Oh, God.

"Well?" Dave demanded.

The kid swallowed. "They found the Reverend Lewis dead in the vicarage this morning."

An ice-cold pain shot through my chest. "Merry's dead?" I asked, my voice sounding like it was coming from another room. I wondered why they were looking at me strangely.

"How?" Dave barked.

"Hanged himself, it looks like, sir."

"Suicide?" My voice was a croak. Oh, God. He'd killed himself after speaking to me. That meant it was my fault, didn't it? "I thought he was feeling better... Oh, God."

It shouldn't have hit me so hard, I suppose. I hardly knew the bloke. I hadn't even *liked* him.

But I'd felt sorry for him. He'd had such a crap life. The only time he'd managed to get a few kicks, he'd ended up regretting it for—fuck—the rest of his life. Bloody hell, from what Darren had said about that party, he hadn't been in much of a state to even remember what he'd been so ashamed about. "He seemed so much happier," I kept saying. *My fault, my fault* ran through my head on permanent loop, and I bit my tongue to keep from blurting it out.

Dave took pity on me and got the constable to fetch me a cup of tea. I found myself wondering if he'd got a grown-up to help him with the kettle, and almost gave a really inappropriate giggle at the thought. He'd put two sugars in it, and I drank half of it down before I even noticed.

We had to go over last night's visit again, of course. And this time, make it official, with a signed statement. I might have been the last person to see the Rev alive. *My fault, my fault.*

It helped, actually, going over the conversation again. Reminded me he'd already been in a right state when he'd got to my house. Maybe I hadn't helped him like I'd meant to—but I'd done what I could. I began to breathe a bit more easily.

"Right," Dave said at the end, leaning back in his chair with a heavy sigh. "So Lewis left you shortly before eleven, and you called me, then went straight to bed after that?"

"Um," I said. "Sort of."

Dave narrowed his eyes. "Want to expand on that?"

I took a deep breath. Best to get it over with. "I called Phil, and he came round and stayed the night, all right? Left just before eight."

"Phil...Morrison." Dave looked unhappy. "So you and him are...?"

"Um," I said again.

"Well, are you or aren't you? How bleedin' hard is it to tell?"

"We slept together for the first time last night," I said in a rush, trying to get it over with. I wasn't feeling too happy myself about the way the conversation was going. Dave and me, we were friends—but there was a sort of unwritten rule I wouldn't go shoving my homosexuality in his face. I'd always reckoned he was fine with me shagging blokes, just as long as he never, ever had to think about it. And I'd been okay with that. Like I said before, some things you're better off not knowing, even about your mates.

I didn't want to find out Dave was a bigot. I was ninety-nine-percent certain that any prejudices he had were a product of his upbringing, and he was struggling to overcome them. But if I ever found out for certain they existed, well, it'd change things between us. It'd have to.

Because there was always that one-percent chance he really meant them.

Dave was rubbing his face again. "Tom... Look, don't take this the wrong way, all right?" He paused like he was waiting for me to cross my heart and hope to die. Just like poor old Merry.

I'd got it all wrong last night. I'd reckoned he'd hoped to finally start living.

"What?" I asked a bit sharply. I wasn't promising Dave anything.

"I don't think it's a good idea for you to be involved with Phil Morrison," he said bluntly.

I stared at him. "Why?"

"You told me yourself he was a bully at school. That sort never change. Christ, Tom, he could flatten you as soon as look at you. And all right, it suits him to be nice to you right now, but sooner or later, that's going to change."

"What do you mean, it suits him to be nice?" And what did he mean, *now*?

"You know. Your little talent. The *finding* thing. Gift from the bloody gods to a PI, aren't you? I bet he's like a kid with a new toy right now. Just you wait, though. Sooner or later, he's going to end up chucking you out of the pram."

I wished I hadn't drunk that sugary tea. I felt sick. "You think he's sleeping with me just so I'll find stuff for him?" That couldn't be right, could it? We'd done all the finding stuff well before he'd made a move, hadn't we?

"I just mean, it's in his interests to keep you sweet at the moment, that's all." Dave rubbed his neck, looking more tired than ever. "The thing about you is, you only ever want to see the best in people. And that's great, Tom. Makes you a good bloke to be around. Trouble is, though, you work in this job a few years, you get to realise most of humanity is a load of bleedin' tossers you wouldn't want to piss on if they were on fire."

"You're wrong," I said, but my voice sounded funny. "It's not your fault—like you said, it's the job. But that's not—he's not—"

"Tom," Dave said, leaning forward over the table. "I know you don't want to hear this right now. But take care, all right? Don't be too ready to trust him." He pushed back his chair and stood. Guessing the interview was over, I did the same. Dave was halfway to the door when he turned and spoke to me again. "Oh, and Tom?"

"Yeah?"

"For God's sake, take a shower and get some clean clothes on before you get pulled in as a public health hazard. You stink like a bloody sewer."

By the time I finally got out of the police station, I was late for one customer and I'd missed another altogether. I made a few damage-limitation phone calls to the clients, then went home, threw my clothes in the washing machine and stepped wearily into the shower.

The hot water seemed to wash some of the fog out of my brain, and I realised what I should have done as soon as I got home. I should have called Phil and told him about poor old Merry. But after I'd towelled myself off and pulled on some clothes—even when I was standing in the living room, phone in hand—I couldn't seem to make myself dial the number.

Was Dave right about Phil? Was he just using me?

No. That couldn't be true. What about that hidden stash of photos and the bit cut out of the paper? I gave a twisted smile as I pictured myself telling Dave about, in Gary's words, *my own personal stalker*. Yeah, right. That'd really reassure him.

Should I be worried? I slumped onto the sofa a bit too heavily, startling Merlin, who shot out of the room like I'd shoved a rocket up his bum. Looking smug, Arthur padded heavily over and settled in my lap, a lead-lined furry cushion.

221

"What do you think, Arthur?" I asked, knuckling him between the ears. His eyes slitted in bliss as he started to purr. "I've got to call him, haven't I? He'd be well pissed off if he found out I knew and didn't tell him."

I hit the dial button before I could talk myself out of it again.

Of course, after all that bloody angsting, it ended up going to voice mail. I wondered what he was up to, and why he wasn't answering his mobile—maybe he'd left it on silent by mistake? I'd done that often enough myself, before I'd worked out the connection between missed calls and lack of money to pay the bills.

Maybe Phil had heard about the Rev already and was snooping around Brock's Hollow? Why bother, though? What was left to investigate? I wondered if the Rev had left a confession, and if the police would still carry on looking for Melanie's murderer if he hadn't. Would Phil? Maybe he'd stopped already and was back home typing up his final bill for the Porters.

I couldn't help feeling a bit hurt he hadn't at least phoned to check if I'd heard the news, and if I was okay about it. He'd been keen enough to come round last night, after Merry's visit.

Perhaps he hadn't thought there'd be a shag in it this time.

Sod it. I sent Phil a brief text: *Rev is dead, suicide,* and then headed off to my customer in Harpenden.

Chapter Nineteen

The Harpenden job ended up taking longer than expected—twenty years of limescale needed to be chipped off before I could even get at the taps. The water round here's so bloody hard it practically comes out the taps in lumps. It wasn't so much plumbing as open-cast mining. By the time I'd finished, I was hungry enough to eat a pit pony, but I was running too late to stop for lunch, so I grabbed a cheese roll from the baker's in Vaughn Road and ate it on the way to the next job. Not great for the digestion, maybe, but at least keeping busy was keeping my mind off—well, off stuff I'd rather not be thinking about.

Later that afternoon, just as the sky was starting to get dark, I passed through Brock's Hollow. I'd been thinking about popping in on Pip—after all, if she'd been cut up about Robin getting taken in for questioning, how much more upset would she be about Merry's death? She was a churchwarden; she had to have known him pretty well.

This time, the lights were on in Village Properties, I noted as I parked the van in the lay-by next to the chippy. They were also on in the WI shop, and the old battle-axe in there glared through the window at me as I went into the estate agents. I made a mental note never to go in that shop in case she stabbed me with her knitting needles for fraternising with perjurers.

Robin gave a big, welcoming smile as I walked in the door—then he realised it was me and stopped bothering. "If you're here to ask more questions, I'm afraid I'm going to ask you to leave," he said, with a hint of steel in his tired eyes that didn't make him any less attractive.

"Nah—reckon you've had enough of that in the last few days, right? I'm just here to say hi to Pip," I assured him, turning to her corner. "Bloody hell!"

She had a bruise on her cheek. "Did that bastard hit you?" I demanded, striding over to her desk. "Pip, love, you've got to call the police. You can't let him treat you like this."

"It's all right," Robin said from right behind my left ear. "Persephone is with me now. He won't hurt her again."

Pip smiled shyly as I looked from one to the other of them, and she nodded.

"I've left Samantha. She can keep the house. I doubt she'll even notice I'm gone," Robin added with a touch of bitterness.

"Yeah, you've got that place down by the river," I said without thinking.

They both stared at me.

"Uh, sorry. Phil," I explained with a shrug. They seemed to get the drift. "So..." I pursed my lips. "That night Melanie died, when you were supposed to be working late—might I be right in thinking you were with Pip? Sorry, Persephone," I corrected myself.

She blushed. So did he. "You might," he conceded.

No wonder she'd been sure he hadn't done it. He'd been way too busy doing *her* at the time, 'scuse my French.

"So you've got a brand-new alibi, then?"

His turn to shrug. "If it's needed." He didn't sound all that bothered, but I wasn't sure why.

Then it hit me. "You think the Rev's suicide means he did it?"

He moved pointedly around me to put his arm round Pip, who wasn't smiling anymore. "It does seem fairly obvious," he said.

Poor Merry. Then again, if he'd really killed Melanie... Was that it? Had he killed himself out of guilt—nothing to do with his secret past? At least, not directly.

I didn't know what to think. I said my good-byes, and then, working on the basis that thinking's a lot easier on a full stomach, I nipped into the little Tesco's down the road for a Mars Bar. I got a bit distracted by the two-for-one offers and was just debating whether to get a pack of chocolate éclairs as well to see me through till teatime, when a hand touched my arm.

"Hello—it's Tom, isn't it?" It was the friendly old lady from the church. From the way she was smiling serenely, I guessed the news about the Rev hadn't reached her yet.

"Edie!" I said with a smile that probably wasn't nearly as serene as hers. "How are you?"

"Can't complain, dear, not at my age. One's glad to be still walking around after so many years! Have you met Judith?"

The woman next to Edie looked vaguely familiar. She had a worn-down, nervous face, and somehow managed to look ten years older than Edie while still being clearly thirty years younger.

I frowned at her, realised what I was doing, and tried to look a bit more pleasant. "I think I saw you at church, yesterday? Sitting next to Pip Cox?"

A spark of recognition flickered and died in her eyes. "Yes, that's right."

"Judith is our Parish Administrator, although she's taking a little break at the moment," Edie said.

The little wheels whirred and clicked, and I remembered. She must be Mrs. Reece, the one who'd been ill, and who Melanie had filled in for. I wondered what the illness had been. "Lovely to meet you," I said, offering her a hand.

She hesitated but grasped it briefly, her ice-cold fingers bony and dry.

"Must be a lot of work, that," I said, more to put her at her ease than anything else.

Judith jerked her head. It could have been a nod, but it also said loud and clear she didn't want to talk about it.

"Now, I shouldn't gossip," Edie put in, her head on one side. I felt like a bug under a microscope, the way she was watching me. "But I expect you'll hear soon enough about our poor vicar. Suicide, they're saying."

"I, um, yes. I heard." I must have sounded a bit off, because Edie patted my arm.

"Oh, dear. It is rather shocking, isn't it? Yes, poor man. He must have been deeply troubled about something." She leaned closer. "One can't help but think it must be connected to poor little Melanie's death. Remorse can be a terrible thing."

My chest felt tight. Was I the only one who still thought there was any doubt he'd done it? "That's...that's what the police told you, is it?"

"Oh, the police... They never tell you anything, do they? No, I heard it from Alison Mitchell. She goes to clean at the vicarage. She was the one who found him, poor thing. Hanging, he was. Such a terrible thing to find. Of course, we've had the police all over the village today." She leaned in closer and whispered, "That's why I'm keeping an eye on poor Judith today. I'm afraid she's—well, obviously she knew him rather well, you see."

I darted a glance over to Mrs. Reece, who was staring blankly out of the shop's glass front. Like you might do if, say, you heard someone talking about you and want to pretend you hadn't heard.

"You know what, I just remembered somewhere I need to be. Lovely meeting you, ladies." I left the cakes on the shelf and walked out of the shop, feeling sick. There was a railing just outside, so I leant on it, breathing in fresh, cold air mingled with exhaust fumes from the cars that ambled past, slowing for the speed bumps.

Was Merry the murderer? Had I been wrong about him, and about Melanie too? God, he'd been in my house.

I vaguely registered the automatic door opening behind me, and then Edie was at my side. "Are you feeling quite all right?" she asked. "Don't worry—I left Judith by the magazines. You can speak freely."

I wondered what on earth she was expecting me to say. I was still wondering when she spoke again. "You know, Judith had your young man round this morning."

"Phil?" I asked, startled. Although on second thoughts, it wasn't that surprising he'd wanted to talk to Mrs. Reece. I wondered why she was calling him my young man after the way he'd behaved last time she'd seen us together. In the end, I put it down to some kind of old-lady intuition.

"Yes. I'm happy to say he's *much* more polite when you get to know him. I'd gone round to break the news to her about poor Meredith. Judith doesn't get out a lot, not with her husband the way he is—I'm sure you understand."

I was sure I didn't, but I nodded anyway. Why hadn't Phil asked me to go with him?

227

"But he would go on asking her about Lionel, and well..." She shook her head. "Poor Judith isn't the strongest personality around, and Lionel can be terribly forceful when he puts his mind to it. He does so like to be in control of everything. That's why she had to take a little step back from it all. Just a little break, to recharge her batteries."

I nodded slowly. "Yeah, I can imagine she didn't find it easy working with old Lionel. Bit of a commanding figure, he is."

Edie nodded happily. "Judith and I always call him *The Boss.*"

A cold thrill ran through me. "Is that what Melanie used to call him too?"

"You know, now you ask, I think I did hear her call him that once. I imagine Judith must have mentioned it during the handover of responsibilities. You won't tell on us, will you?" Edie asked, wide-eyed, like a kid caught with her hand in the pick-and-mix.

"I—no, course not," I managed. "Look, thanks for coming out and looking out for me, but I'm fine. You go back to Judith. I'll be fine." I started to walk off, but then a thought struck me, and I turned. "Edie, did you tell Phil about Lionel's nickname?"

"Oh, yes," she said. "He seemed quite excited about it."

Phil still wasn't answering his phone, and now it was going straight to voice mail. I didn't like it. In the end I gritted my teeth and dialled Dave's number.

"Southgate," he answered curtly, putting me off a bit.

"It's me, Dave," I said awkwardly.

"I know it's you, Tom. But to coin a phrase, I'm kind of in the middle of something here. Is it about the case?"

"I—yeah. Kind of." I abandoned all ideas of asking Dave if he'd seen my boyfriend. "Is it official, now, that Merry killed Melanie? I mean, did he leave that signed confession you were after, or was there some evidence?" If they had proof Merry had done it, then Lionel's nickname couldn't mean anything. Plus, I was betting no one had bothered telling Graham, if so. At least I could go round and give him a scrap of comfort. It was even possible I might find Phil there.

Dave didn't say anything for a long time.

"Dave?"

"Look, Tom, you did *not* hear this from me, understand? And I'm only telling you now because you're a mate, and you were so bloody cut up about it all."

"Telling me what, Dave?"

Dave's voice went so low I could barely hear it. "The Reverend didn't kill himself. It was a setup."

"What? Merry was murdered?"

"You'd better not be in a public place spouting off like that, I'm warning you."

"I'm not—I'm in the van. Windows closed and all. But bloody hell!" That meant...that meant he *hadn't* killed Melanie, most likely. And his death definitely hadn't been my fault. Relief flooded through me, bringing guilt bobbing along in its wake. This really wasn't all about me.

"Exactly. Now, I'm not going to tell you not to mention it to the boyfriend—I'm not that bloody naïve—but you tell him from me, it stops with him, right? I don't want to find out he's tweeted it to all his bloody Facebook friends."

"Um. Have you seen Phil today?"

"Run out on you already, has he? He was around Brock's Hollow this morning, sticking his nose in where it didn't belong, but since then I haven't had the very dubious pleasure of his company. You want to get him tagged."

"Yeah, right. Listen, Dave—did you know Lionel Treadgood's nickname was The Boss? Edie Penrose told me that this afternoon."

"You're joking. Seriously? Bloody hell." Dave swore, this time with even more feeling. "I wonder what they're teaching them in Hendon these days, I really do. Couldn't find their own arses with a map and a sat-nav, some of 'em. Right. Cheers, Tom. Anything else?"

"Are you going to arrest Lionel now?"

"All in good time, all in good time. If I arrest him on hearsay, his lawyer'll have me for breakfast. We'll wait and see what forensics come up with. And no going round there to ask him if he did it, all right? I mean that, Tom. That's an order. You stay well away from Treadgood. Same goes for the boyfriend too. I'll see you around." Dave hung up.

I did the only thing I could think of—drove the van round to Phil's place. I had to park it illegally, which meant I had roughly thirty seconds before I'd be getting a ticket. I swear the population of St Albans halves when the traffic wardens go home for their tea.

Phil's car wasn't outside his flat, and when I rang his doorbell, following it up with the ones for all the other flats, no one answered. I swore, then ran back to the van. I hadn't got a ticket, but I'd have traded that for knowing Phil was safe any day. I couldn't help thinking he must have gone to confront Lionel. And he wouldn't know how dangerous the bloke was— wouldn't know about the second murder. He still thought Merry had killed himself.

Why the hell hadn't he called me to go with him?

Was it because he didn't think he needed me anymore? Dave's warning was eating away at me like caustic soda. I didn't want to believe Phil had just been using me—but I couldn't dismiss the possibility, either.

I didn't know what to do.

Chapter Twenty

Dark had fallen by the time I parked my Fiesta halfway down Pothole Parade, and went the rest of the way to Lionel's house on foot. One advantage of the rich liking their privacy was that the road was lined with high hedges, broken only by the entrances to long, twisting driveways, so I was reasonably certain no one saw me acting furtive. There wasn't even any street lighting, this being a private road. I felt my way along and tried not to curse too loudly when I stumbled.

The Treadgoods', with its wide, open-plan gravel driveway, had to be the bloody exception, of course. Even the crunching of the stones under my feet seemed louder than a pneumatic drill in the still, quiet evening. The security light came on just as I approached. I'd just have to hope Lionel and Patricia were having their tea, or maybe watching *EastEnders* to marvel at how the other half lived—at any rate, too busy to look out of the window and see me messing up their freshly raked gravel.

The water in the swimming pool was still messing with my spidey-senses—but there was nothing wrong with my eyes. And I reckoned the little summerhouse next to it would be pretty much perfect for stashing someone you'd, say, caught snooping around (on his own, the daft prick) and bashed over the head. If it came to a fight, Phil would beat Lionel easily, I was sure—but all Lionel would need to do would be to get behind him and catch him unawares—like he must have done to poor Melanie. He could have tied Phil up, gagged him so as not to annoy the neighbours, and left him there, ready to finish off later.

Or he could have finished him off already and stashed his body in there, of course. But I didn't want to think about that possibility. I wondered if I'd know—if it wasn't for the water in the swimming pool, would I know from the vibes whether the body I was searching for was living or dead? I hoped not. At a time like this, you want to keep hoping for the best as long as you can.

I'd expected the summerhouse to be locked, and it was. Good job I'd brought along a few tools. Dave could do me later for breaking and entering; right now I was all about getting in as fast as possible. I forced a flat-headed screwdriver into the lock. The surrounding wood started to give, and I tensed up, worried it would splinter with a crack and give me away, but in fact it more or less crumbled, damply and relatively quietly. The sickly sweet smell of decaying wood tickled my nose, overpowering the chlorine from the pool for a moment. Someone ought to tell Lionel to do something about the rot pronto, or he'd have the whole place tumbling down around his ears.

I was buggered if it was going to be me, though. Specially if it turned out he had my boyfriend hidden away in here. I smothered a nervous laugh, checked one last time there was no one sneaking up on me with a tyre iron, pushed the door open and stepped through, closing it behind me. My hands were shaking as I flicked on my torch. Moving its pathetically weak beam of light over the interior of the summer house, I listened out with my sixth sense for anything it could tell me.

Mostly, it told me there was a shed-load of water not six feet from my back. I wasn't having much more luck with senses one to five. The place seemed pretty bare, everything neatly packed away at the end of last summer, with just a few things, like a mop and bucket, showing signs of having been bunged in at the last minute. Where the hell was Phil? It was brass monkey weather, there in the damp chill of the summerhouse, and the sweat trickling down my back made me shiver. Was this all a bloody wild-goose chase? Wait—there. A chest. Big enough to fit even large, boneheaded private eyes. I scrambled over to kneel in front of it, got out my chisel to break it open— then realised it wasn't even locked. My heart pounding, I flipped up the lid.

Cushions. Sodding seat cushions. Damn it. Although it was better than finding a body.

Think, Paretski. If Phil wasn't in here—and I was getting more and more certain he wasn't—where else might he be? In the house? No. No way was I buying Patricia being involved in any of this. The car parked out in the drive? Plenty of room in the boot of Lionel's Range Rover to hide a body or two, but would he really have the nerve to keep something so incriminating out in front of the house like that?

Still, I'd have to look. I wouldn't be able to break in quietly, but I reckoned I shouldn't need to. Touching the car ought to do the trick. Using all of my senses, I took one last look around the summerhouse, then switched off my torch and headed outside.

Even the faint breeze that had blown as I'd got here had now dropped, and everything was eerily still. A tired moon lounged back in the sky, and a few stars twinkled blearily through the clouds. God, it was quiet out here. Round where I live, it's never quiet—even in the early hours, there's always neighbours having domestics, someone driving down a road nearby, or a bunch of lads laughing and joking on their way home from a drunken night out. But out here, the main roads were too far away for the traffic noise to carry, and all the houses had thick walls and double glazing. Not that their owners would likely dream of washing their dirty knickers in public or having the telly loud enough to disturb the neighbours.

Lionel's Range Rover stood sentry near the front door. I crouched down to cross the treacherous gravel as quietly as I could, muttered a brief prayer to anyone who might be listening that he wouldn't have a touch-sensitive car alarm, and put my hands on the boot to listen in.

Nothing. Nothing at all. So where the hell did that leave me? Bloody frustrated, that's where. Then it occurred to me—living out here, in a big posh house, just how likely was it Lionel and Patricia had only one car? Actually, come to think of it, where the hell was *Phil's* car? I had to assume he'd driven here.

Oh, God... My stomach churned as I realised there could be another reason for missing cars. Lionel could be out in one right now, about to get rid of Phil. Permanently. I crouched down behind the Range Rover and leaned against one thickly treaded tyre to take a couple of steadying breaths. I couldn't focus on all the what-ifs. I just had to carry on hoping.

There was a driveway running between the house and the swimming pool—more of that gravel. Lionel had to have bought up half a quarry's worth. There must be a garage down there—there certainly wasn't one up here, and this wasn't the sort of house that left your expensive cars to shiver outside in the cold and the weather. I peered cautiously around the side of the car, and when I saw the coast was clear, edged around the house.

Lionel and Patricia weren't big on closing their curtains after dusk, it seemed; light spilled from the large bay windows and onto the vast, sunken lawn at the back of the house. Flood-plaining, I guessed; the river ran along the bottom of the garden. I could feel it, a reassuring, constantly changing vibe, nothing like the flat, dead noise of the swimming pool.

A figure moved in front of the window, and I froze, but Patricia just reached up and drew the curtains, and I breathed again. It was darker than ever now as I crept through the shadows towards a low, white building that had clearly been built with more than one car in mind. It was on the same raised ground as the path, which made sense, obviously, cars and flooded rivers not tending to be a match made in heaven.

When I got to the garage, I felt horribly exposed against the bright white paint and slipped around to the side farthest from the house. It turned out to be a good move; I'd been wondering how the hell I'd get through the metal drive-through door at the front, but here at the back was a normal, people-sized door.

I reached for the handle, all my senses alert—and my knees buckled and nearly dropped me to the ground. Phil was here. Thank God. I could feel him, all tied up in tangles of fear and hate and anger. And a sense of something unfinished, which I clung to desperately.

I really didn't want Phil to be finished.

The door was locked, of course, but it was no match for my trusty screwdriver. Which was not to say it went down quietly. My heart racing, I winced at the loud cracking sound—why the hell couldn't this door have been rotten too?—and despite my desperation to get inside, I held my breath as long as I could, listening for any outcry from the house.

There was nothing, so I opened the door, flicked on my torch and stepped inside. "Phil," I whispered urgently, as loudly as I dared. "Phil, it's me. Tom." My torch lit on two cars parked side by side. I'd been right: one of them was Phil's Golf. I scrambled over to it, put my hands on the boot. Result. I barely managed to stop myself pounding on the hatch, desperate for some sign from Phil that he was still there, still alive. I hefted my chisel—then thought to try the lock. It opened, and I threw up the hatch.

He was there. Tied in some kind of tarpaulin. "Phil, it's me," I repeated, struggling with the knots in the thick cord that bound him. He wasn't moving. Christ, he wasn't moving. "Phil, it's Tom. I'm getting you out." I finally got the tarpaulin unwound. Shone my torch on his face. Phil's eyes were closed. Was that good? Dead people didn't close their own eyes, did they? I fumbled at his throat, my hand shaking. Where the *fuck* was his pulse? He was still warm, so that was good, wasn't it— except didn't they say you're not dead until you're warm and dead? "Don't you fucking dare be dead, you bastard," I muttered. He'd been gagged with a tea towel. I loosened the knot and yanked it off. There was blood on it—from a head wound?

Phil groaned.

"Oh, thank God," I breathed. "Phil, can you hear me? It's Tom." His eyelids fluttered open, then screwed shut against the light of my torch. He didn't look all that with it. "Phil, you've got to wake up. I'm going to get you out of here but you've got to bloody well wake up, all right? I'm going to untie you." My fingers were numb with cold and clumsy with nerves as I worked at the cord binding his hands behind his back. It was slippery and broad—a tie, I realised. It was like something out of *The Dangerous Book for Boys*—"How to incapacitate an enemy using stuff you find around the house". The tie was soaking wet—as were the rest of Phil's clothes—making the knot much harder to undo. God, it was a wonder Phil hadn't frozen to death out here. That tarpaulin had probably saved his life.

"Nearly there," I panted. Damn it, I had half a dozen blunt instruments on me—why the hell hadn't I thought to bring a knife? If I kept talking, maybe Phil would stay with me. "Just got to... There! Done it." I dropped the tie on the floor and moved to check Phil's ankles—

—and then light flooded the room, and a low, commanding voice said, "Stop right there."

I was paralysed for what felt like a hundred years, not even my heart beating. When I could, I turned slowly. Lionel was standing in the doorway.

With a shotgun.

He stared down the barrel of the gun at me, his face red with anger and twisted in disgust, as if he'd just found the place infested with cockroaches and I was the pile of shit they'd been rolling in. "How dare you trespass in my home?"

Too busy trying not to crap myself with fear, I didn't point out it was actually his garage. "You—you killed them, didn't you?" I stammered out. "Melanie. And Merry."

"Don't be ridiculous," he said, not lowering the gun one inch. "Meredith Lewis killed her, and himself."

"No," I said, before I had time to work out if it was a good idea or not. "It was a setup. You set him up. The police know it wasn't suicide."

Lionel's face paled, and the end of the gun trembled, just a little. "You're lying," he said. "Why would they tell you anything? You're nothing."

"Got a mate on the force, haven't I?" Inspiration struck. "He'll be here in a minute. DI Southgate. I called him, soon as I found Phil. He'd better be all right," I added darkly. God, I wished I wasn't bluffing. Why the bloody hell hadn't I called Dave the minute I'd found Phil?

"You're lying," he said again. "You came here on your own."

"Maybe I did, but I won't be leaving on my own." I hoped I sounded more confident than I felt.

Apparently I didn't. Colour seeped back into Lionel's face. I'd liked it better pale. "You won't be leaving at all," he said quietly. "I'm not letting you ruin everything. Not after all I've been through.

"Why did you do it?" I asked desperately. "Why Melanie? What did she do to you?"

"I didn't *want* to kill her," Lionel said, sounding put out. "She shouldn't have threatened me."

The barrel of the gun lowered by about an inch.

Hope searing my throat, I pressed on. "You didn't mean to kill her?"

"She—I—it's all that bloody Reece woman's fault. If she could only have pulled herself together and trusted me... I *told* her I'd pay the money back—it was a loan. I wouldn't steal anything," he finished in a tone of outrage.

"Course not," I said, trying to sound encouraging. I still had my chisel in the back pocket of my jeans—maybe I could throw it at him or something? I could feel Phil shifting behind me, but I didn't dare take my eyes off Lionel.

"If Meredith Lewis had had an ounce of backbone, he'd have convinced her. But no—he was useless. Completely useless, just like he always was. Maybe now we'll get a proper vicar," Lionel muttered.

"So...what did Judith Reece do?" I prompted, hoping it wouldn't make him even more pissed off.

"Judith?" Lionel seemed to have forgotten we'd been talking about her. "Oh, she worried herself into a bloody nervous breakdown about the whole thing. Said she couldn't carry on as parish administrator. Absolutely ridiculous. Then that wretched girl had to come poking her nose into everything."

"Must have been a right pain," I said, edging my hand around to my jeans pocket.

"Well, of course! A girl half my age, lecturing me on what I could and couldn't do with the funds entrusted to me—and then she threatened me. Me!" He wasn't even looking at me now, the shotgun pointing over to the side.

I closed my fingers around the head of my chisel, started to ease it out of my pocket…

"Get your hands where I can see them!" Lionel snapped. The shotgun swung back up, aiming directly at my heart.

Slowly, reluctantly, I moved my hand away from the chisel. Despair flooded through me. Maybe there had never been much chance I'd manage to take that gun off him, but it'd just gone down to zero. All I could do now was stall for time, desperately hoping for a rescue—but who the hell was going to rescue me now?

Then Patricia's musical voice rang through the garage like the bell at the gates to heaven. "Lionel? Darling, is everything all right in here?" The last word was cut off by a little gasp, and she stood just behind Lionel, one hand pressed to her mouth. "Lionel?" she asked uncertainly.

"Burglars," Lionel said wildly. "They've broken in. You go back to the house, darling. It isn't safe for you here."

"Call the police!" I begged her.

Troubled grey eyes looked from Lionel to me. Then Phil groaned and tried to sit up.

Patricia's eyes widened. "Is your friend hurt?" she asked me.

"Yes—he needs a doctor. Please, Patricia." I turned to Phil and helped him swing his legs out of the car boot.

"No!" Lionel shouted it, making us all jump. "Stay where you are! Common criminals—breaking into our property. They deserve all they get."

"Maybe we should let the police deal with it, Lionel," Patricia said.

"No…no police. I can't—darling, you don't understand. It's a…a business matter. You just go back in the house and let me sort all this out. It'll be fine."

"It's not going to be fine!" I was desperate to reach her with my words, my gaze. "Patricia, I'm sorry, love, but he's killed two people."

There was a bang that echoed through the garage. At the same time, someone grabbed me violently from behind and pulled me back, catching my head on the open hatch of the Golf. There was a stinging pain in my arm to match the one next to my ear, and I looked down to see my sleeve turning crimson.

"You bloody twat," Phil rasped in my ear. He was still holding me tightly by the waist, both of us half in the boot of his car. If he never let go, that'd be just fine with me.

Lionel stood there, his gun smoking. Patricia had both hands clutched to her mouth.

"You didn't have to tell her," he said brokenly. "Why did you have to tell her?"

I didn't answer. His aim might have been better next time. I felt Phil groping my arse and wondered wildly what the hell he was thinking of, getting frisky at a time like this—then I realised he must be looking for my phone. "Jacket," I whispered. "Inside."

The icy hand moved; extracted my phone; retreated.

"Darling, it's all right, but I think you'd better give me the gun now," Patricia said, almost carrying off a soothing tone. Only the wobble in her voice as she said the word *gun* gave her away.

Lionel turned towards her. Suddenly worried, I started in their direction, but Phil pulled me back. "Leave it," he growled. "Stop being a bloody hero. He won't hurt her."

He didn't. Looking like he was sleepwalking, Lionel reached out and handed the gun over to his wife. She smiled, unloaded it with surprising efficiency, then put it down on the workbench. She kept hold of the ammo. "Thank you, darling. Why don't we go and have a cup of tea?"

Lionel let her lead him away, her arm linked in his. Suddenly weak, I slumped back against Phil's chest. I could feel the damp chill of his clothes soaking into mine but somehow, I couldn't give a toss.

"Oi. Trying to dial, here," he muttered.

"Phone too complicated for you, is it?" I joked weakly. My arm was hurting like a bastard. And I'd *liked* this jacket. Not to mention the shirt underneath. "Or is it the number? Three nines. It's not rocket science."

"Tosser. I'm calling your mate Dave. You up to speaking to him?"

"I'm pretty sure he doesn't want to talk to you. Hand it over."

The phone rang several times before Dave picked up. He didn't sound very happy. "Tom, this bloody well better be good—"

"I've been shot," I told him.

"Fucking—*what*?" Sounded like I had his attention.

"Lionel Treadgood. I'm over at his place. He's your murderer."

"He's confessed?"

"Yeah. It was a bit rambling, but yeah. Sounds like he'd been dipping into church funds and Melanie found out." I paused for breath. "I'm okay, by the way. Got a shotgun pellet in the arm, but I think I'll live. Thanks for asking," I added pointedly.

"Tom, I've had calls from people who aren't all right. Generally speaking, they do a lot more screaming for an ambulance. Right, I'm on my way. What's the situation?"

"Er... Me and Phil are in the garage, and Lionel and Patricia are having a cup of tea."

"Might have known bloody Morrison would be involved. Is Treadgood still armed?" Dave's voice got a bit of an edge to it. "Is she in danger from him? Is anyone else?"

"No. At least I don't think so. On both counts. Or all three. Whatever. We've got the gun here."

"Good. Anything else I ought to hear about before I roll up there?"

"How about, *I told you to go and arrest Lionel*?"

"Don't push it, sunshine. I told *you* to stay away from the bloke, remember?" He hung up.

"He's on his way?" Phil asked.

"Yeah." I hesitated. "Um, you probably ought to let go of me before he arrives."

"No hurry. We'll hear the sirens." Phil's arms tightened around me, chilly but comforting. His breath warmed the back of my neck.

I shifted, and he took the hint and loosened his grip so I could turn round and face him. "Bloody hell, you look like shit,"

I blurted out. His skin was pale, and sweat glistened on his forehead. His hair was a mess, plastered to his head like straw left out in the rain.

"Thanks," he said drily.

"No, I mean it. You should sit down." The hatchback of Phil's Golf was still open, so we both perched on the edge of the boot, careful not to further damage our aching heads. "Are you feeling sick or anything? Faint? Can you feel your hands and feet?" That was about the limit of my improvised diagnostics.

"I'm fine." He laughed softly. "I'm not the one who got shot, here."

We looked at my arm. The tide of crimson seemed to have stopped, or at least slowed a lot. "Yeah... Thanks for that," I said, feeling awkward.

"What, thanks for getting you shot?"

"No, you muppet. You know what for." I don't know why it was so difficult to say it. Or to look him in the eye, right now.

Phil's hand came up and tilted my chin until I didn't have any choice but to meet his eye. He didn't say anything, just smiled and shook his head slowly.

"What?"

"You'll be the death of me one day, you know that?"

Actually, on current evidence, he was more likely to be the death of me. I didn't point that out, though. "Well, I'll miss you when you're gone," I said weakly. "It'll be dead boring, relatively speaking."

"Tom, I—" He broke off. "Did you hear something?"

"Like what?" I demanded, spooked—and then I heard it too.

Sirens.

Chapter Twenty-One

We decided to stay put, rather than go outside and risk getting caught up in any amateur dramatics Lionel might have decided to put on. Plus, I had a feeling my legs might be embarrassingly wobbly. When Dave turned up at the garage, looking weary but triumphant, he gave my arm a dirty look. "Didn't I tell you hanging around with Phil Morrison would be bad for your health?"

"Hey, if it wasn't for him, I'd probably be dead," I pointed out. "He pulled me out of the way of the blast—I hadn't even realised Lionel was about to shoot."

"Like you'd even have been here if it hadn't been for Morrison."

Okay, maybe he had a point. "You've got him, right?" I asked. "He's not still running around somewhere, pointing guns at people—"

"Pushing them into swimming pools," Phil put in.

"That's what happened to you?" I asked, twisting round to look at him. Now he mentioned it, I could smell the chlorine on him.

Phil nodded. "Caught me by surprise—pushed me in, then whacked me over the head when I was trying to climb out. Suppose I should be grateful he didn't leave me in there to drown."

"Too risky," Dave commented. "They'd have got chlorinated water out of your lungs. He was probably still hoping to pin it all on Graham Carter, and last time I looked, flats on the Hilldyke estate didn't come with their own swimming pools."

"Didn't think about the clothes, though, did he?" Phil said, sounding amused.

Dave shared a smile with him. "Amateurs, eh? But just as well your skull's a bit thicker than Melanie Porter's. Right, we've got an ambulance waiting for you, Tom—and you'd better get checked out too, Morrison. If you drop dead from hypothermia, it'll make a right mare's nest of my paperwork." He turned to grin at me. "Come on, Tom. You can't tell me you're not gagging to get him out of those wet clothes."

Bloody hell—Dave, joking about my poofy sex life? As I stared at his retreating back, Phil leaned closer to whisper in my ear. "Close your mouth, Tom. Much as I'd like to take advantage, I doubt I'll be up for any of that tonight."

He wasn't joking, I realised, as we staggered out to the waiting ambulance together. Phil leaned on me heavily, and his steps were stiff and jerky. The paramedics took one look at him and broke out the shock blankets. Then they whisked us off to hospital, and that was the last I saw of Phil for a while.

By the time I'd been through the system—getting shot tweezered out of me; stitches; police statement—it was beyond late and well into early. Dave came over personally to tell me they were letting me go, which I appreciated. "Want a lift home?" he offered.

I hesitated. "I might wait for Phil..." I stifled a yawn.

"You'll have to wait a long time. They're keeping him in overnight. Just for observation. Come on, you look dead on your feet. You'd be no use to him anyhow." He laughed.

"Are you always this cheerful when you catch a murderer?"

"Much as I'd like to think so, no, probably not." Dave paused for a moment, then burst out with, "Jen's back. Turned up this evening—last night, now. Said she realised she still loves me and asked if I'd take her back."

"Yeah? That's great! I mean, you do want her back, right?"

He nodded. "Yeah, in spite of everything—I do." There was a big grin on his face. "Now, let's get you home so you can get some sleep, because I'm bloody well not planning to." He winked, presumably in case I hadn't quite grasped what he was intending to do instead.

"Cheers, Dave," I muttered. "Give me nightmares, why don't you?"

Once we got in Dave's BMW and set off, I couldn't stop yawning. It would've been easy enough just to drop off in the passenger seat, lulled by the purr of a finely tuned engine, but something was still bugging me. "How...'scuse me... How did Lionel know Merry needed murdering? I mean, I get there was some kind of blackmail situation going on there, and that must have been one of the things Merry was going to sort out—but how did Lionel know?"

Dave's smile disappeared. "The stupid sod told him. Rang him up at six a.m. and asked him to come to the vicarage to discuss it. Lionel said he just flipped out, though not in so many words. Strangled the Reverend with the curtain tie, then strung him up so it'd look like suicide. Except he hadn't realised the bruising would be in the wrong place. See, when you strangle someone—"

"Leave out the details, all right?" I said, making a face. "That really is going to give me nightmares." I didn't want to think about poor old Merry with his face all red, his neck bruised—nope, didn't want to think about it. "Was it quick?" I couldn't help asking.

"There's worse ways to go, believe me." Dave's face was grim as he said it, and I decided I was bloody glad I didn't have his job.

"And it was all about him 'borrowing' church funds?"

Dave nodded. "Seems his construction company hasn't been doing too well lately. Treadgood started out just steering all the church work their way—breach of trust in itself—but it wasn't enough. Turns out that posh house of his is mortgaged up to the hilt, and the only way he could see to save it all was by taking a hammer to the church piggy bank."

"Was it worth it? I mean, how much money do churches have?" I was thinking of Merry's frayed cuffs.

"This one, apparently, had three quarters of a million quid. Emphasis on *had*."

"Bloody hell! What did they do—win the lottery?"

"In a manner of speaking. Get a lot of old people in churches, don't you? Round here, *rich* old people. You only need one or two of 'em to leave their money to the church when they pop their pious little clogs, and you're laughing."

"Lionel must have been," I muttered.

"Gift from the bloody gods, wasn't it? Of course, the way he tells it, he wasn't even doing anything wrong. Says he's authorised to make investments on the church's behalf. Trouble was, while he could bully the Reverend and the old Parish Administrator, Judith Reece, into going along with it, signing off on stuff, Melanie Porter was a whole different kettle of fish. She told him she'd report him if he didn't pay back the money—
248

which of course, he couldn't do, 'cause he'd already spent it on keeping the business afloat and the wife in foreign holidays."

"Do you think she knew about it?" I didn't like to think of Patricia going along with stealing from the church.

"No—at least, that's what old Lionel says, and I reckon he's telling the truth. If you ask me, that's the worst part of all this sodding mess, for him—having her find out what a god-awful pig's arse he'd made of it all. Bit of an old-fashioned marriage, that—*don't you worry your pretty little head about money*, that sort of thing."

I nodded. "That's what he said in the garage—*why did you have to tell her?*" God, I wondered how she was coping, now she knew the worst. Maybe I'd email her, tomorrow. Seeing as I was indirectly responsible for her husband ending up behind bars, I thought turning up in person might not be the best idea, at least until I'd tested the waters.

"Has he told you how he was planning to frame Graham for Phil's, you know, death?" I couldn't say the word without wincing. "I've been trying to think what motive Graham was supposed to have, but I'm coming up blank."

"Yeah, well, it looks like you're not the only one. Guess whose business card Lionel had on him?"

I yawned again. We were getting near Fleetville, and my bed was calling me. "Not a clue. Surprise me."

"Some Polish cowboy by the name of Paretski. Apparently, your boyfriend's untimely death was supposed to have been the result of a lovers' tiff, and the body was going to turn up in the close vicinity of your house."

Suddenly, I was a lot less sleepy. "What? He was going to frame me for it? Hang on a minute, how did he know me and Phil were seeing each other, anyway?"

Dave laughed. "Sunshine, *everyone* knows you and Morrison are seeing each other."

"Wish they'd bloody told me a bit sooner, then," I muttered, huddling down in the seat. We drove on in silence for a few minutes as I thought about it all—Phil, dead, and me arrested for it. I'd almost been feeling a bit sorry for Lionel until now. Then again, that wasn't exactly fair on Melanie and Merry either.

"How did Lionel dig up the dirt on Merry in the first place?" I asked as we drew into my road.

"He didn't. That's the sad part about it. I mean, yes, he was blackmailing the Reverend—but he didn't have a bloody thing on him." Dave shook his head. "Poor bastard—God knows what he thought Treadgood had found—apart from the gay thing, but let's face it, you could tell that just by looking at him. Seems all Lionel had to do was just *hint* about secrets Lewis might not want spread about, and the Reverend was bending over backwards to do anything Lionel wanted. Guess we'll never know what it was really all about, now."

I swallowed. "No. Guess not."

Oh, Merry, Merry, Merry. I didn't like to speak ill of the dead—or even think it—but Christ, what a fucking car crash of a life.

At least he'd seemed a bit happier after we'd spoken. Maybe now he'd finally found some peace.

I slept like the dead for what was left of the night and woke up late to the sound of someone banging on my front door. The cats were milling around in the hallway when I went downstairs, Merlin peeking nervously out from behind Arthur's solid form. From the general size and shape of the figure behind the frosted glass, I had a pretty good idea who was out there. My heart gave a little jump, like Merlin at his most skittish, as I went to open the door.

"About bloody time," Phil grumbled. He was still looking a bit pale, or maybe it was just the contrast with the dark circles under his eyes.

I couldn't seem to stop smiling at him. "Well? Are you coming in or what?"

"See you put on some trousers to come downstairs today," he said, stomping through the hallway. It sounded like he disapproved.

"You might have been the postman. Or the Jehovah's Witnesses. Course, that'd have been one way to scare them off," I added, thinking about it.

"Or get yourself into even more trouble than usual," Phil groused.

"Hey, it wasn't me who was tied up in the boot of his own car," I reminded him.

Without warning, he spun around and pulled me to him, crushing my bare chest against the soft warmth of yet another cashmere sweater. Maybe he had his own herd of goats. "Do you want to be?" he growled.

"Have you seen the boot space in a Fiesta? I might not be large, but even I wouldn't find that a lot of fun." I pretended to think. "The back of my van, on the other hand..."

"Kinky little sod."

"I do my best."

"That a promise?"

"Hey, are you really up for any of that sort of thing? When did they let you out of hospital?"

"I let myself out. Nothing wrong with me a bit of bed rest won't cure."

"I didn't think it was *rest* you had on your mind. Bed, yeah, but—" The end of my sentence was swallowed as he kissed me.

Soon things were getting nicely out of hand. Phil's sweater lay crumpled on the hall carpet, and my jeans were undone and with one of his hands shoved inside. But just about then, my brain finally woke up and reminded me I had a couple of unanswered questions. "Wait a minute," I said, pushing Phil off me—or trying to; it was like trying to move a mountain. A big, blond, horny mountain. "Oi, gerroff, will you?"

"What?" He backed off about a millimetre and stood there, face flushed, breathing hard.

Gazing into those darkened eyes, it was a bit of a struggle to remember what I'd wanted to ask him. "I just—what is all this, all right? You and me. Is it about me being able to find stuff for you, or you feeling guilty about my hip, or what?"

"Does it matter right now?"

I had to look away. "Yeah. Yeah, I think it does."

Strong fingers took hold of my chin and gently turned my face back towards him. "I'm not going to lie to you. The way I feel about you—it's complicated." His thumb stroked my cheek in a soothing rhythm, and he smiled suddenly. "Doesn't help when you go around saving my life either."

"Why didn't you call me before you went out there?" I asked, because that had been bugging me worst of all. "Decided you didn't need me anymore?"

"No, you twat. I was going to confront a bloody murderer, wasn't I? Why the hell would I want you putting yourself in danger?" Phil's gaze darted down to my bandaged arm. "Christ, when I saw he was about to shoot you, and you just bloody stood there..." He broke off and took a couple of deep breaths.

I slid my arms around his waist and pulled him close to me again. Someday soon, we were going to have to have words about this obsession of his with protecting me.

But for now, I reckoned I had all the answers I needed.

About the Author

JL Merrow is that rare beast, an English person who refuses to drink tea. She read Natural Sciences at Cambridge, where she learned many things, chief amongst which was that she never wanted to see the inside of a lab ever again. Her one regret is that she never mastered the ability of punting one-handed whilst holding a glass of champagne.

She writes across genres, with a preference for contemporary gay romance and the paranormal, and is frequently accused of humour.

Find JL Merrow online at: www.jlmerrow.com.

Finding love can be a bumpy ride...

Hard Tail
© *2012 JL Merrow*

His job: downsized out of existence. His marriage: on the rocks. It doesn't take a lot of arm twisting for Tim Knight to agree to get out of London and take over his injured brother's mountain bike shop for a while. A few weeks in Southampton is a welcome break from the wreck his life has become, even though he feels like a fish out of water in this brave new world of outdoor sports and unfamiliar technical jargon.

The young man who falls—literally—through the door of the shop brings everything into sharp, unexpected focus. Tim barely accepts he's even *in* the closet until his attraction to Matt Berridge pulls him close enough to touch the doorknob.

There's only one problem with the loveable klutz: his bullying boyfriend. Tim is convinced Steve is the cause of the bruises that Matt blows off as part of his risky sport. But rising to the defense of the man he's beginning to love, means coming to terms with who he is—in public—in a battle not even his black belt prepared him to fight. Until now.

Warning: Contains an out-and-proud klutz, a closeted, karate-loving accountant—and a cat who thinks it's all about him. Watch for a cameo appearance from the Pricks and Pragmatism *lovers. May inspire yearnings for fresh air, exercise, and a fit, tanned bike mechanic of your very own.*

Available now in ebook and print from Samhain Publishing.

PUBLISHING

It's all about the story...

Romance

HORROR

www.samhainpublishing.com

CPSIA information can be obtained at www.ICGtesting.com
Printed in the USA
BVOW07s1020010813

327582BV00002B/75/P